Ruth Less lives on the Wirral with her husband, Dave. They have two adult sons and Montgomery, their mischievous Jack Russell.

Ruth is a regular distance swimmer with a keen interest in yoga, enjoying the outdoor lifestyle. Before becoming an author she worked in Adult Social Care for twenty years. *Divine Timing* is the first book in a series of five volumes written in the UK and Australia. Although her writing is fictional with a supernatural twist, most of her inspiration was taken from the many paths she has crossed.

A natural storyteller with a determined spirit, tackling her own demon, which is dyslexia.

Divine Timing

Volume One

Ruth Less

Divine Timing

Vanguard Press

A CIP catalogue record for this title is
available from the British Library.

ISBN 978 178465 090 2

*Vanguard Press is an imprint of
Pegasus Elliot MacKenzie Publishers Ltd.*
www.pegasuspublishers.com

First Published in 2016

**Vanguard Press
Sheraton House Castle Park
Cambridge England**

Printed & Bound in Great Britain

I would like to dedicate this book to my good friends down under: the Lawsons in Perth W.A. and the Crabtrees in Melbourne, who supplied me with delightful retreats in the sun whilst penning this book.

Chapter 1

With Christmas rapidly approaching, shoppers battle against the acute weather conditions spreading over Britain. An unusually cold weather front grips the region with continuous drifts of snow and sheet rain, turning the already tenuous conditions outside into skating rinks, bringing the workforce to a relative standstill.

Father Jimmy peels off a few layers of clothing, to compensate for the overworked industrial heating system at his local hospital, chatting easily to the dedicated nursing staff who have managed to make it into work. Some are sleeping in the on-call doctors' rooms, at the end of a long hectic shift.

"Another homeless guy, Father Jimmy, frozen to death. That's the third causality this week. What a way to go: hypothermia," Sister Dodd says, with a quick shake of her head, her matter of fact easy tone, keeping a professional distance, as much as one can. A sturdy thirty-something lady with warm eyes and an infectious laugh, arms folded under her ample bosom. Caring is part of her nature.

The first frozen homeless casualty to arrive at the busy A&E department was a girl. Jayne Doe the staff called her. Young, with a fresh complexion, maybe fifteen, her face empty of all expression, not ravished by any substance yet, her body looks frail. Strawberry blonde tangled mess of hair, hanging limply, encases her pixie-like face. The multiple freckles on her nose and cheeks give the impression of someone much younger, those heart-shaped lips now tinged with blue. Didn't look like a Jayne at all, Father Jimmy thought to himself. No one was there to grieve for this half-starved creature, once somebody's precious daughter. A pair of tatty trainers thrown next to the bed, is an indication of the lifestyle she must has been leading. The priest wonders if anyone really cares, as he feels a crisis of faith, witnessing another life snuffed out as easily as breath on a candle.

Jayne Doe is making the national news, spreading shock and horror amongst the staff and local community. Victim number three is unlikely to generate as much sympathy: a middle-aged male, prolific drug user, a malevolent look immortalised forever on his face. It is surprising how quickly society resigns itself to these tragedies.

On returning to the relative comfort of his nearby parish, the biting cold not penetrating his clothing, as his temper boils, Father Jimmy fumes, "What a waste of another precious life, discarded without a thought. Frozen to death while the rest of society are in relative comfort."

His voice is thick with frustration, having observed heating systems spewing out steam as they work to their full capacity. Roaring fires cast warm orangey glows, cosy furnishings of the surrounding homes, all on show, are glimpsed through living room windows.

Kneeling heavily at the altar, with a sullen heart and anger in his voice, Father Jimmy asks for guidance. Slowly his brooding eyes rise, focusing on the ornate crucifix suspended above the altar, heart galloping in his chest.

"This can't be right, people freezing to death in the twenty-first century."

A thought booms around his head, loud and clear: "OPEN MY DOORS!"

Startled by the stern inner voice, Father Jimmy looks around him, his angry fog dispersing, eyes sweeping, searching his beloved church for an explanation. Caught by a blast of wind, the heavy wooden church door slams against the stone wall. His mind registers the shock as he glances over his shoulder, eyes greeted with silent empty pews. No one else is there in this normally peaceful, warm space.

Threadbare carpets run along the solid wooden floors and sturdy wooden benches; ornate stained glass windows depict biblical scenes. Adjoining the church is the parish centre, housing a large tea urn. An idea begins to develop in Father Jimmy's head.

"Is this what is meant by epiphany?"

His familiar grin decorates his fatigued face.

Wavering now, Father Jimmy decides to act before fear takes hold. Hastily leaving the warmth of the church, he grabs his hat and coat, guiltily wrapping up well before venturing onto the treacherous streets below, overriding the ancient heating system, leaving it on constant.

Father Jimmy enters the deserted silent streets as a fresh layer of powdery snow falls, heading straight for the town centre. Eerily quiet and echoing the brittle snow crunching underfoot, Father Jimmy strides forwards sinking into the soft white mass below, holding onto this sudden striking emotion. Gardens glisten with premature Christmas lights, snowmen standing proudly in their gardens decorated with last year's cast-offs, scarves and hats unaware of their fate. Unrelenting, the snow continues to fall, a beautiful visual element, hiding the relative poverty of the surrounding area, leaving the perfect picture postcard impression. Streets are now cleverly dressed in pure white splendour having carefully edited out the homeless community who normally adorn these spaces. Father Jimmy is aware the streets tonight do not truly reflect the everyday reality of men and women huddled in doorways wrapped in cardboard, some sleeping in large waste bins at the back of shops. He knows all the local haunts and rounds these poor unfortunates up with his charismatic character, taking every last drop of his courage, promising a hot drink and somewhere warm and dry to sleep.

Like the Pied Piper, Father Jimmy wanders amongst the abandoned streets, footsteps muffled in the fallen snow, dim streetlights casting shadows on the white carpet below, head down, hands deep in pockets, increasing his number of bedraggled followers as he goes. They trudge behind him, shaking and shivering with the Baltic conditions, leaving behind only their set of footprints.

Wearily Emma Lane leaves her deserted office building for the second time tonight, having left her tablet on her workstation. Tired and hungry, wrapped in a bubble coat stuffed with feather down, and large woollen hat, gloves and matching scarf, a gift from her mother-in-law. Wearing knee-length walking boots, she hugs her arms tightly around her torso to retain as much body heat as possible. Only her eyes are visible, greeted by a black and white image fighting against the constant flow of snow, delivering her straight into the path of Father Jimmy. He's a familiar figure amongst the local community, a bit of a maverick and known for taking an independent stand. Strange, she thinks, watching this procession of shabby followers shuffling along behind him. The journalist in her aroused, curious, she stops to enquire what he's doing. Emma shudders as the chill penetrates her clothing, promises of going straight home to her family, completely forgotten.

Tenderness in his half smile, Father Jimmy helps the homeless group settle in for the night at St Michaels, his friendly local parish church. Warm and comfortable, it is adequately furnished, with odd bits from other parishes and community centres. There is nothing of any great monetary value. Father Jimmy refused a refurb when the church's success was recognised, insisting any spare funding go to the needy.

Fascinated, Emma observes Father Jimmy with his smooth manner, having gained the trust of the forgotten community: not handsome in any conventional sense, his beauty comes from within. Filled with warmth and a genuine honesty about him, he's small in stature but huge in character. His mop of dark hair has stray silver strands that keep breaking through, and falls to one side. He has a well-appointed Roman nose and gentle greyish-blue eyes.

Father Jimmy sees past the human form, looking deep into the beauty of his companions' damaged souls. His eyes carry a hint of sorrow, although he conceals it well. Youthful looking for his forty-nine years on this planet, he is just starting to embrace the autumn of his life. Having heard stories of his unconventional way of guiding his flock, Emma feels humbled in his presence.

He moved around a bit before joining St Michaels five years ago, which is located on the outskirts of Liverpool. With the threat of closure, hanging over it. Within a short period of time, it was standing room only. Everyone welcome, with no strict opening times, it boasts an open-door policy. A large following from the gypsy and travelling community, it is rumoured that he visits the red light area, no soul too tarnished for Father Jimmy.

Pushing these thoughts to the back of her mind, Emma coaxes, "Just a couple of shots, guys. Then maybe I can muster up some interest from my readers."

Emma uses the carrot and stick technique. Standing poised and ready for action, she holds her camera in her hands. She is a self-assured and confident individual.

The band of homeless folk looks to Father Jimmy for guidance.

"It's up to you, guys. A few pics in the paper might encourage those with long pockets to release a bit of funding, then I could provide a hot meal." Grinning again, he adds, "Steaming hot soup and freshly baked bread dripping with butter!"

Father Jimmy teases, the group groaning now at the thought of hot food, making a pleasant change from rummaging in waste bins and eating other people's leftovers.

After a bit of mumbling and shuffling, most of the group gather together, desperate-looking characters feeling like an invisible part of the community, having walked a very different path to the rest of us. They all look older than their years, pain and desperation etched on their pinched faces, they grin uncomfortably into the camera lens, while catching the light, bringing these invisible individuals into focus, injecting real life into these images. They have rotting black teeth from years of substance abuse, causing severe tooth decay, fear rests in their dull eyes, a greyish tinge to their pale skin, dirty and dishevelled, wearing torn and soiled clothing. They carry a few prized possessions with them everywhere: a photograph from home, a reading book, a threadbare woollen mouse from childhood – items of no monetary value, precious only to their owner. With a click of the camera lens this moving image is immortalised forever.

"Come on, Father Jimmy, you're the ringleader," Emma encourages, a smile beaming across her cheeky face. Father Jimmy outstretches a coaxing hand to Peter, a sullen-looking young man in his mid-twenties, detached from the rest of the group. With a sharp dismissive shake of his head, Peter declines the photographic opportunity, slouching against the back wall, not open to Father

Jimmy's powers of persuasion, isolating himself from the rest of the group.

A large imposing figure silently watches, in tatty trainers and jeans so dirty it's hard to distinguish their original colour; good padded outer jacket. though, which someone must have given him recently. He has a dark beanie hat perched on his head that he is reluctant to remove indoors. Anger boils behind those dark dangerous brownie-black eyes, separating him from life, divided by an invisible barrier, warily talking only to Father Jimmy when necessary.

Peter is a well-spoken young man, bright and maybe educated, sparking the journalist's interest in Emma.

Anticipating that Father Jimmy, a well-known local figure, will pull at readers' heartstrings, Emma encourages him, using a bit of emotional blackmail. She knows that we have a tendency to ignore these desperate images depicting tragic lives, switching off and storing the pictures in the recesses of our minds.

"Not my idea," Father Jimmy says, pointing upwards. "It was the boss."

Emma is keen to run this story as Liverpool has welcomed this guy into their hearts, this city known for its community spirit. No one's sure of Father Jimmy's original roots, some thinking he was sent to the outskirts of a deprived area to keep his unconventional ways in check. Nobody predicted the roaring success of the small wiry figure moving amidst alcoholics and drug users with relative ease, surrounding himself with society's misfits. He watches mankind disabling themselves, through rash choices; haunted faces ravaged through drug and alcohol abuse, some functioning working addicts.

The heart of a lion, Father Jimmy joins his group of misfits, his charismatic character spreading warmth amongst life's dropouts.

Love binds this little group together. Another click and a second image has captured the essence of this man completely. Moodily Peter watches on from a distance, muffled with his coat pulled up to his ears. His dark eyes dictate a serious-looking young man, Emma thinks.

Chapter 2

Excitement spreads through the Buddhist community as their brother, Choden Lamas, returns. *Choden* means 'one who is devout' and *Lamas* means 'teacher' and this one has undertaken a long period of spiritually guided meditation in the hollow of a large ancient tree, bringing his life into balance, coming face to face with his own mind and learning how to discipline it. He is at one with nature, transforming his life in a positive and permanent way, cleansing and quietening his mind and soul, gained when at a higher level of meditation. His guide, the Supreme Being instructs him to travel to the West, to betoken one's simple philosophies to an angry hostile world, spreading reality, existence, knowledge, values, reason and mind power. Restoring life's balance in the West.

Choden Lamas starts every day with a positive thought, word or deed thanks to his slow methodical, disciplined practices. Encouraging others to follow, he passes on a positive chain reaction.

What we tend to hold on to in our mind will likely develop during the day. The monk concludes each evening with meditation that purges the mind of stress or negativity that one has encountered during the day, transferral of negativity is a big problem in the West. Encouraging positive change, to make ready to engage in restful rejuvenating sleep, he professes that to be the secret to longevity.

Having travelled extensively to the West previously, he observes negative chains of energy. People who have a great deal: modern technology, surroundings, money and food, wake up dissatisfied with their lives, spreading disharmony amongst society, greed and jealousy subtly attacking. They are like robots working long hours to provide the latest gadgets, without time to enjoy the fruits of their labours – family life ultimately suffering. Over-populated areas where people struggle with isolation and loneliness, an unpleasant emotional response, not knowing one's neighbours.

Choden Lamas is sixty-seven and remarkably agile for his age, embracing each day with his rituals of simple spiritual practices. Mantras followed by a variety of yoga, as a senior member of a monastic community, Choden Lamas gives his time freely to teaching others.

His Mantra:

"KEEP LIFE SIMPLE."

Using clear, easy to follow examples with his students, he recites, "It takes two to have an argument, if one walks away – no argument. Silence is sometimes the only answer. Listen to hear, not to answer.

Meditate to lose your anger, anxiety, depression, insecurities and fears."

Choden Lamas is repeatedly having a vision while meditating. A large rainbow is playing host to bright vibrant tones, each colour having different shades and tints, a breathtakingly beautiful image, surreal. One side of the rainbow is drenched in sunshine, electrifying energetic and dynamic, lush green fields and vegetation, the animals and plant life looking perfect. Happy contented healthy people are making him smile, bathing in the warmth of this wondrous image.

In complete contrast the other side is dark and grey spreading gloom, making survival a constant struggle. Plant life and vegetation shrivelled to nothing in a cold and damp atmosphere, the misery present making Choden Lamas' body shudder as he witnesses people being led into wretchedness, wandering aimlessly, no purpose or direction to their lives. Facial expressions melt away, disfigurement and disease visibly showing. People fighting, countries at war, ruining this precious planet, the sorrow and fear they carry as hostile forces walk amongst them, leading them blindfolded as they relinquish their free will. Hidden in full view, chameleons blending in amongst them.

Choden Lamas is unsure how to interpret this repetitive image, but he understandings its significance.

Father Jimmy is in hot water for opening the church doors to the undesirables earlier in the week. The Bishop has ordered a meeting, summoning Father Jimmy to attend the following day.

"I'm having to clear my busy diary," the Bishop fumes, reading the front page article produced by Emma Lane, gaining a lot of public interest and funding for these people existing on the edge of society.

"Media frenzy," he grumbles to himself. Titled *The Homeless Hero*, the article leads with a picture of Father Jimmy in the centre, surrounded by his group of shabby followers. A look of distaste crosses the Bishop's face, as he greedily shoves another piece of toast into his flabby mouth, butter melting down his double chin, slurping on his hot coffee, while eagerly absorbing the headlines with his beady little eyes, housed behind his spectacles.

News North West also ran the story giving these invisible people a voice. Investigating the lives of our homeless community, how they feel and what they go through on a daily basis. Drunks leaving nightclubs urinating on them as they try to get some sleep in shop doorways. These and cardboard packaging scrounged from nearby shops and skips are their only protection against the elements. Sometimes used as punch bags, but mostly ignored completely. Unseen by shoppers during the day, not bothering to make eye contact, as everyday life passes them by. Homeless for a whole host of reasons all eager to engage but one.

Wrapping up well, Father Jimmy ventures outside after clearing the church of any remnants of last night's pungent visitors. For five days now Father Jimmy has been opening the church doors at night with more visitors turning up daily. He had thought of opening the rectory but anticipation of his elderly housekeeper's reaction has dissuaded him. The majority of his guests helped him clean up in the mornings.

Father Jimmy inhales the sharp stale odour that hangs on, the scent of unwashed bodies and he makes a mental note to himself: *Must pick up a few cans of air freshener.* He chuckles as he thinks: *Good job the Bishop isn't visiting.* He walks briskly now, his cheeks ruddy against the icy wind, blood circulating around his body generating some heat, stinging as the snowflakes stick, melting instantly on his warm exposed skin. Puffing he pushes on, talking directly to God:

"I know sometimes you're testing me, but I could do with a hand tomorrow. The Bishop's really mad at me."

Breathing heavily now, his lungs fill with the sharp crisp air. Feeling a little unsure, doubt creeps in as Father Jimmy says:

"That inner voice, I know that was you."

After a pause, a thought pops into his mind:

"I'M BIGGER THAN ANY OBSTACLE."

Grinning with his familiar half smile, he says:

"Well, remind the Bishop of that tomorrow, will you?"

A pleasurable feeling of contentment comes over him. Father Jimmy feels sure he's on the right path.

Continuing a little further his eyes absorb the pure white backdrop, seeing the unmistakable outline of Peter, emerging from an entry, unsteady on his feet, built like a rock but looking the worse for wear. Sadness fills his heart as he approaches this giant of a man and he gestures for Peter to sit on the crumbling garden wall. The snow-covered ground camouflages the hopelessness of the area, disguising the deprivation and poverty. It presents a pleasant, peaceful, refreshing image, hiding the litter-strewn streets.

"Five minutes, Peter."

There is a kindness to Father Jimmy's tone, carrying no fear. Looking at this young man, the priest concludes he is self-medicating with heroin – a temporary distraction from the feelings of self-hate and loathing, experienced through pain, depression and anxiety. This temporary respite gives Peter a heightened sense of invincibility, before the all too familiar rebound, worsening his feelings of self-loathing and hatred which leave him feeling totally empty and inadequate.

Peter enjoyed a six-month honeymoon period with this substance. Euphoria flooded his mind as this powerful drug invaded his veins, spreading this potent intoxicant around his body, infiltrating his brain and obstructing his thought processes, providing an intense state of happiness and self-confidence at the start. This enables him to ignore his real problems, closing them down, removing them from his mind temporarily. Now, in order to perform a mundane task, his body craves this poison, to prevent the constant sickly feelings and the horrors of withdrawal. Never reaching that first high always just out of his grasp.

With a slow gentle voice, Father Jimmy says, "Anger is easy, Peter, forgiveness is the key belonging to the brave. It's the only genuine thing that will set you free."

Father Jimmy places his small, gloved hand onto Peter's large cold fingers with long blackened fingernails. Gripping with a strength reserved for a much larger person, his inner strength connects with Peter, who's looking lost. He is not used to attention, hiding behind that vacant mask. A handsome face just visible behind his grizzly beard, smudges of dirt on Peter's pale grey skin. No words are spoken by Peter who communicates through his dark serious eyes, his gratitude transmitted to Father Jimmy, a touching moment. Rising to leave, feet sinking into the freshly fallen snow, silencing his deep footsteps, Father Jimmy turns, calling out in one final attempt:

"You know where I am if you need me; any time, day or night."

It is said with real sentiment before he continues on his way. When he glances back briefly, Father Jimmy adds, "God gave us love, the Devil gave us hate."

Trembling, Father Jimmy sees the outlines of two angels behind Peter. Blinking rapidly, bringing his eyes into focus, he sees one white angel, gleaming brightly from the reflective light on the white surface, serenely calm and peaceful, patiently waiting, a delicate hand resting on Peter's right shoulder, radiating love. Peter's damaged mind struggles to accept this gift. The other angel is black and vile-looking, disfigured by life's vices. Its long extending tongue whispers in Peter's left ear. Both angels stand their ground. Reeling, Father Jimmy crashes into a garden wall, his hand gripping the cold surface to steady himself. Staring harder, he sees Peter's tortured soul torn in half and weeping his silent inward tears, endless images of an unhappy childhood bullied and berated while in care, believing life holds no purpose for him. Good on one side and evil the other, both watching this vicious internal battle.

Panic seizes Father Jimmy as he recalls this happening previously whilst conducting a healing service where both parties truly believed wonderful things could be achieved. Becoming more frequent now, he instinctively slides his right hand into his coat pocket to retrieve a small vial of holy water. Ripping his glove from his hand, he flips the lid before throwing its contents over Peter's left shoulder. Frantically reciting an impromptu prayer in Latin, while witnessing the dark angel as it shrivels in size, a sizzling sound and a putrid odour fill the air, making his stomach heave. It shrieks painfully. Before the calm as the charred remains blemish the snow-covered floor, an evil energy disperses into the vacuum that surrounds them.

The white angel grows in stature, serenely beautiful, bestowing calm and tranquillity on Peter as she wraps her wings around him, adorning him with profound love, like a mother enjoying her newly born child for the first time. She saturates his body with her devotion, his protector.

Looking scared, with slow, slurred speech, Peter asks, "What's happening?"

"You have free will, we all do, and you must use it wisely. Ask and it shall be given, to receive you must believe. Strength is knowing when to let go. Release your tears, Peter, they will cleanse you. Learn from your mistakes, we all make them. They are part of your spiritual growth, glory awaits you."

In this heightened spiritual state Peter weeps. Soft, quiet, gentle sobs at first, then the emotion builds, heaving his large frame and uncontrollable floods of tears roll down his face. Mixing in his dirty grizzly beard, they release years of anger and frustration. Father Jimmy watches with his mind detached, trying to rationalise these events, like viewing a television screen, as Peter's soul releases the pain and anguish of decades. His pure white angel, holding him upright, is circulating love, supporting every stage of this wondrous transformation. She whispers gentle encouragement into his ear as the angels of light surround him.

"The One needs you, Peter. You are his rock. Walk amongst his forgotten people, they trust you. Every single lost soul counts, regardless of how damaged. The keys to his kingdom are yours, all you need to do is ask."

Peter opens his eyes. The mist is lifting and the veil is removed as all becomes clear, like a blind man seeing for the first time.

"I don't need a second chance. I will take the first one," Peter mumbles. He is ready to follow his own dreams, excited to find out who he really is, acknowledging his unique gift. Standing his ground a little wobbly, it's time to rejoin his rightful path.

"Thy will be done," comes from Peter's lips, accompanied by involuntary shaking, his limp body supported by the most angelic surreal angel, witnessed by Father Jimmy. A magnificent sight to behold, having disorienting hallucinatory qualities that will stay with Father Jimmy for his whole lifetime.

"A thousand souls will be released from purgatory today, Peter."

Both of them look skyward as a mass of dull vapours are released from the dark earth, watching these earthbound souls soar upwards, gradually lightening in colour as they ascend and break through the heavy dense clouds to enter into the peace and light. Shards of brilliant sunlight pierce the heavy cloud cover, illuminating the greyness of the sky before enclosing around the damaged souls, creating a beautiful vibrant, hazy and miraculous sight.

With heavy footsteps silent and slow, the two leave. Creating a great unbreakable friendship that day that will last them a lifetime.

As a final preparation for his trip to the West, Choden Lamas engages in deep meditation and prayer. He is at his most vulnerable when in a deep meditative state. While he chants lightly, with the soft simple melody vibrating through his nose, a stillness fills the air as evil roams, desperately seeking to destroy this powerful alliance merging between the East and the West. Evil is participating in reckless actions as it plots its trap.

Much like a rainbow, distinctive superior colours emanating from his body surround Choden Lamas. Recharging his core, they fill him with strength and power ready to use his variety of spiritual techniques to guide others. Evil tries persistently to prevent him as the quest for good and evil continues.

Yet his faithful silent follower stands guard over Choden Lamas, draped in a saffron robe, symbolising simplicity and detachment from materialism. He is a rotund man with a shaven head and hazel-coloured eyes that are ever watchful, vigilant of dark auras that can be transferred from one person to another (if you know what you're doing). He is ever wakeful and alert.

Choden Lamas continues his simple life. His daily routine consists of exercise and a healthy diet, all contributing to his superior mental state and energy flow. He is a great believer in self-help, walking and absorbing the beauty of every season. He sits to eat slowly, enjoying every mouthful of food, chewing and swallowing. Savouring individual flavours, before putting more food into his mouth, he stops when his stomach is content and not when his plate is empty, thankful to the farmers who work hard to supply this wonderful energy source. Choden takes time to indulge in the wonders of his surroundings, knowing what a mammoth task lies ahead of him He is excited and a little apprehensive.

Emma listens to the bleep bleep bleep of the alarm clock, wrapped in her oversized pyjamas and woollen socks. She desperately tries to contain every molecule of body heat below the bed covers.

There is a warm dent in the bed where her husband has been lying, his familiar masculine odour evident. He is already up and in the shower. Not wanting to leave the warmth and comfort of her bed, Emma flops her hand from beneath the duvet, only to be bitten with the instant chill. She feels for the clock on the bedside table, before flicking the alarm off and irritably pulling the duvet back over her head.

"Just five more minutes," she hears herself say. Dave appears naked inside the bedroom doorway, his thick, dark hair slicked back. A glint of light filtering from the en suite emphasises his taut male physique, tiny droplets of water, resting on his firm body, highlight his masculine frame as he performs a muscleman pose. There is a naughty twinkle in his hypnotic eyes. He laughs as he drags back the bedding, diving under the covers, body still damp. Seeing that naughty grin, she knows that to refuse his advances is futile. Twenty years together and she still can't resist him. Laughing at how they met, on the other side of the world while travelling after university. Although originally they lived ten miles apart, having never met. Divine intervention, Emma called it. Two kindred spirits brought together, delivered on their paths at the right time, enjoying life's twists and turns, leaning on each other when needed. Treasuring all life's small precious moments, they make a masterpiece of their own.

"It's bloody freezing out there," Dave laughs, enjoying the heat from the bed, while his tacky body dries fully.

Chapter 3

Excitement surrounds the much-publicised Unity seminar, scheduled for the beginning of March, a state of oneness bringing many different religions and cultures together. There will be a chance to engage and encourage a better understanding of the philosophies behind different religions. Workshops and stalls promoting alternative therapies have been running for two years now. It is rumoured that Choden Lamas, the Buddhist monk, with a large following from the East, will be in attendance at the London the venue this year. The Bishop is worried about Father Jimmy attending in case he takes an independent stand to remove himself from his associates with his rebellious and disruptive behaviour. This latest development of opening the church to the homeless has caused much embarrassment. Handling Father Jimmy with kid gloves is needed as he has a large following of his own. The media show a keen interest in him. Moving him to one of the poorest areas to keep him out of mischief has backfired significantly.

With the imminent closure of St Michael's Church, due to the dwindling numbers of parishioners, the decision is reversed within six months because of the vast increase in Father Jimmy's flock. *All Are Welcome* is penned across a large banner hanging in the church. Going into the streets, mixing with drug addicts, prostitutes, alcoholics and any other minorities, he invites them into God's house. The last time the Bishop mentioned some of Father Jimmy's less than desirable members of the congregation, he was quick to defend them, passionately.

"Does God only want the good in his house, the tax payers, the respectable middle class? I thought it was my job to reach out to the sick and needy." Father Jimmy was always on the defensive, not afraid to challenge the Bishop, or the Church for that matter.

"How can we judge people, when we haven't spent a day in their shoes or travelled their paths?"

The Bishop is more apprehensive about this pending meeting than Father Jimmy. He will indulge in a long thought process before tomorrow.

Returning to the rectory, his homeless guest settled in the back bedroom, Father Jimmy hastily contacts an old friend, Paul Clarke, a drugs coordinator with thirty years' experience. Working within his own community, an ex-heroin addict himself, he understands addiction better than most. Yet he remains a hard-looking man with wild aggressive eyes, a bald head and a bent nose from years of brawling, with ugly, faded prison tattoos on his neck and knuckles. He has a clear insight into drug cartels, grooming the young, separating them from friends and family, before finally controlling them.

He started his own detox programme, enthusiastically explaining that the mind and body struggle to adapt to functioning without drugs after prolonged periods of use. Symptoms vary greatly depending on the drug in question, lethargy, irritability, increased pain, sensitivity and nausea are all common side-effects. Paul used natural herbs to reduce these side-effects.

Calming herbs to improve mood, pain-relieving herbs to ease the transition and energising herbs to regain strength and stamina. A follower of alternative therapies, values learnt while travelling, he combined the above with meditation, hypnotherapy and acupuncture, the mind healing itself to achieve empowerment.

Father Jimmy has brought Peter to the rectory, putting him in the back bedroom out of the way of Thursa, the housekeeper. A sharp, elderly lady, she sports a floral dress in the summer and a tweed wool skirt and two piece jumper and cardigan set in the winter, pale wrinkly tights that gathered around her ankles, frizzy grey bob sitting firmly on top of her head. Bushy grey eyebrows dominate her face. Painfully thin, she chain-smokes her way through box after box of cigarettes. Accompanied by a phlegmy cough, she carries a white cotton handkerchief. Tobacco feeds her body rather than food. Unsympathetic to drug or alcohol addiction, she refers to it as a weakness, oblivious to her own addiction. Cutting remarks continually trip from this elderly lady's tongue. Father Jimmy inherited her along with the rundown parish.

Anxiously, Father Jimmy joins Peter on his path for a while, declaring war against drug addiction, the battle commences, Peter is ready to swap the numbness and confusion of the drug world for realism. Each day is lived in a blur, watching the world go by from the side-lines. Shutting down his emotions, slowly allowing evil to grow inside him and not caring; replaced now with real feelings and emotions, he rejoins the human race. Sensations like raindrops on his skin, delicate and wet, wind in his hair bold and alive, refreshing as it massages his scalp. Learning to give and receive love, able to look in the mirror and see a handsome, intelligent young man instead of his usual self-repugnance. Peter is feared among the drug community – a character not to be messed with, an illusion he created for his own self-preservation. Emotion is buried so deep inside him, accepting rehab is a miracle in itself.

Paul starts Peter's programme straight away bringing along a sleeping bag, intending to camp out while getting Peter over the worst of withdrawal.

Paul, having tried conventional drug detox programmes in the UK to no avail, heard of a free treatment in Thailand run by monks. This is a simple programme of meditation and yoga, healing the mind to conquering the core of the addiction. Their mantra:

"The mind is the strongest tool we have."

The monks devised a herbal drink to be taken in the mornings that induced projectile vomiting, releasing the body of harmful toxins left behind from the drugs or alcohol. The patient had to endure the painful withdrawal symptoms – a permanent reminder used as a deterrent in order to resist temptation when back in familiar surroundings. With a ninety-five per cent success rate he tried it and the rest, as they say, is history.

Father Jimmy arrives early to see the Bishop, feeling dishevelled after being awake most of the night. He prays in the corner of Peter's bedroom as the demons circle above him, waiting for any sign of weakness. They want to re-enter Peter's feeble body as Paul guided him through the most painful part of withdrawal.

"Surrender to this pain, Peter. Feel it, embrace it, remind yourself, next time temptation comes calling. Think of this distress and torment, your body racked with pain, your brain screaming for mercy, unable to switch off. Never wanting to go through this again."

Paul administers the tonic, made purely of herbs, watching Peter's ailing body wince with pain, crying out loudly before retching and releasing the poisons

Peter shakes uncontrollably as gradually he grows stronger, repeating over and over, "Thy will be done. Thy will be done. Thy will be done."

Paul, this brute of a man, cradles Peter like a small child, Father Jimmy slumps in an easy chair by the smouldering fire. The crackling wood in the ornate grate, reassuring as it hisses and spits, heats this small space as he slowly drifts into a comfortable state of relaxation.

"I'm sorry, Father James Francis, am I keeping you up?" the Bishop booms with a sarcastic tone, slamming paperwork onto his polished mahogany desk. He plonks himself heavily in his superior-looking leather chair, which is stiff and erect, reflecting his personality. There is a look of disbelief on the Bishop's face.

Apologising, Father Jimmy explains that he has been up all night with a member of the community. He deliberately omits the details.

Dismissing his excuses with the wave of a flabby hand, there is clearly something more pressing on the Bishop's mind. "We can't have street people sleeping in the church; thieves and drug addicts, reeking of alcohol and urine. I have had numerous phone calls from members of the congregation." He screws up his face as he speaks.

"All of the congregation or just Mrs Hooton Smythe?" Father Jimmy says, looking disappointed. "We can't judge people unless we have walked their path, shared their pain and sorrow, experienced their doubts and fears. To move a mountain, we must move one stone at a time."

"I didn't ask you here for one of your sermons," the Bishop replies tartly, large creases forming in his forehead.

The droopy flesh hanging from his cheeks reminds Father Jimmy of a bloodhound. Needing to get back to the rectory to relieve Paul, he knows that winding the Bishop up won't do him any favours.

"The snow is due to thaw soon," he says. "I have been keeping an eye on the weather forecast. With the media coverage, we are hoping to have enough funding to open a homeless shelter before next winter. Money has been coming in from all over the world because of TV and social media interest."

The Bishop is surprised at Father Jimmy conceding so easily. Never one to look a gift horse in the mouth, he lays down a few ground rules, happy now that he feels in control.

"SILENCE IS SOMETIMES THE ONLY ANSWER." Pops into Father Jimmy's mind, grinning to himself he acknowledges the thought.

"Something amusing you, Father James Francis?" the Bishop asks, looking irritated.

"No no, I'm pleased we're on the same wavelength. I appreciate your input Bishop."

"I hope you're not playing with me, Father James Francis." The Bishop raises his droopy eyebrows, while his beady eyes narrow.

"Not at all."

"That will do for today." The Bishop dismisses him with a wave of his fleshy hand, letting him know who's in control. "And remember; any further decisions, run them past me first. Do I make myself clear?" he asks, peering over the top of his spectacles.

"Crystal," Father Jimmy replies, speedily exiting the Bishop's study. An uneasy feeling comes over the Bishop, sensing he's just been played.

Rushing to the train station, Father Jimmy is eager to catch the next available train. Proudly exhibiting his unconquerable soul, he moves amongst everyday people who profess to be masters of their fate. Listening to their conversations, menacing and untamed, blinkered by power and greed.

He thinks how simple life would be if we lived it backwards, knowing who and what we are. The old saying, youth is wasted on the young, springs to mind. Realising that the short time we are here is a learning process. Mistakes are necessary for our progress, not dwelling on past misfortunes but moving forward, dealing with the here and now.

The hustle and bustle of individuals gathering to wait for their incoming train, scurrying in the darkness of their circumstances, unable or unwilling to deal with life's complications, the smell of the underground station and the squeal of the brakes from the slowing train jolts him back from his thoughts. Sadly he observes many dark angels clutching unsuspecting souls, fewer light angels hover behind their charges, a real sign of the times.

"Hello again." A sweet voice greets him, Emma grinning from ear to ear. A content looking woman, happy with her lot, she is wise enough to enjoy her treasures. "Our paths cross again," she says.

Father Jimmy sees a golden angel behind Emma signifying a special gift or talent. "Nothing is by chance." Father Jimmy winks, at ease with this likeable woman.

"I would love to do a follow up story," enthuses Emma. "I have heard on the Grapevine that, Choden Lamas will be in London at the beginning of March at The Unity Seminar."

Father Jimmy waits.

"Will you be attending?"

"Not sure," he replies.

He would love to go and Paul has shown a keen interest, but he must think of Peter and not himself. "If I'm meant to go it will happen."

Pacing a little, Father Jimmy decides to share. "Emma, a thought popped into my head, hearing it loud and clear I acted on it, I went out bringing the homeless together as they wandered in the shadows of darkness. Inviting them into God's house to give them shelter. They in turn opened up to you, answering your questions candidly, images appeared in the newspaper and *News North West* ran the story. Generating interest amongst the whole community, eventually going global. People put their hands in their pockets and now we have enough funding to open a permanent shelter in time for next winter, some may call that an everyday miracle. A chain reaction if you like. If everyone helped one person and so on think how wonderful this world would be. That is the idea behind the Unity seminar, a powerful alliance between religions, spreading love not hate." A convincing tone to his voice.

"Why do bad thing happen?" Emma asks, unsure where that came from.

"We all have free will Emma; sometimes my free will may interfere with your free will, creating a hindrance or obstacle. We either all have it or we don't. If we have it sometimes bad things happen. Good people making bad choices."

"I'm a little confused," Emma confesses.

"Let's say a guy has been drinking, he chooses to drive his car home. He has cash on him, he could easily call a cab or even walk. By choosing to drive he uses his free will. Knocking over a schoolgirl on the way home, he kills her. The ripple effects of that accident are felt not only in her family but his too. That could have easily been prevented if he had used his free will wisely. We can't have it both ways.

"We have good and bad on this planet, leaders and followers. Listening to other people instead of listening to ourselves. That inner voice trying to get your attention that says don't turn left at the next junction, turn right, we need to learn to trust. Believe and anything is possible, little miracles happen daily. Unfortunately bad news sells, papers seldom report the good."

Raising her eyebrows in a thought provoking way, she acknowledges that he presents a good debate but doubt whispers in her ear, thinking that his explanation is too simple. Comfortably,

Emma and Father Jimmy settle into a busy compartment to enjoy the rest of the journey, relaxed enough to appreciate each other's silence as the train rocks them rhythmically back and forth, heading for home. Intrigued, Father Jimmy is sure this delightful lady has been put on his path for a reason.

Paul is relieved to see Father Jimmy return, pacing back and forth on the rectory landing, he needs a food break and some fresh air. Clearing his head of the horrors of his own detox, vivid memories flood his mind, still preventing him from returning to his old ways, a positive control mechanism.

Peter has been granted an iron will as he moves out of the darkness that surrounds him, enduring all that the sombre angels can throw at him. His body fights frantically against the toxins, as they are realised through the herbal cleansing tonic. Regurgitating any nourishment left in his barren body, dehydrated and physically weak, having reached an all-time low. His mind is blurred but his head unbowed, failure not an option.

Gradually Peter restores his strength again; unafraid, he moves away from the grey people living their lives at a different pace, a game of chance. Disconnected from the rest of society, they are lost to the blackness of immorality, albeit temporarily. As they are ravished from drugs, fog clouds their senses and their minds possess little or no control.

"That bloody woman has been hovering around me like an annoying wasp, the temptation to swat her has nearly got the better of me." Paul looks agitated as beads of sweat appear on his shiny forehead.

Father Jimmy laughs, hearing the phlegmy cough as Thursa heavily climbs the stairs. She is dragging her bony body with her, breathless from years of nicotine smothering her lungs. Father Jimmy swiftly intercepts her on the landing.

"I can't get into the back bedroom; that bruiser won't let me in."

She is still carrying a strong rhotic accent, a West Country dialect. Pointing with a bent arthritic finger, she indicates the closed door.

"Did you want something out of that room, Thursa?" the priest asks.

"Spring cleaning," she snaps, her suspicions aroused, with hands on her hips and an indignant look accompanying her challenging pose.

"We will leave it till spring thank you Thursa It's still winter and I'm sure there are other things you could be getting on with." Trying to be as polite as possible although all the hairs on the back of his neck are standing up.

Glaring at Father Jimmy she turns on her heels coughing and spluttering as she makes her way back downstairs. Her white handkerchief is gripped tightly in her right hand – defiantly, not a symbol of surrender.

Pondering a reoccurring thought Father Jimmy keeps visualising a wolf in sheep's clothing while in prayer and during sleep, constant mental images repeated over and over again. Evil has a way of getting inside your head during sleeping and waking hours. He has learnt over the years how to shut it down, a definite warning sign, the power of suggestion.

Reflecting while removing another bucket of vomit from Peter's tiny bedroom (which houses a single bed, a wardrobe and an easy chair), Father Jimmy knows his behaviour has upset the dark angels and he is aware that they wait to infiltrate Peter's mind.

Father Jimmy looks at this giant of a man who is slumped on the wooden bedroom floor and wearing a pair of pyjamas. Peter is sweating one minute teeth, chattering the next. Only his eyes hold the iron will whilst the drugs reduce him to this. Father Jimmy sits in thoughtful prayer after freshening Peter up, hoping to help this pathetic feeble individual.

"Lord bless the habitation of the just," the priest says with a sharp edge to his voice.

Not frightened to get his hands dirty, Father Jimmy throws the small window wide open, a cold blast of fresh air, fills the back bedroom, a welcome distraction from the pungent smell of fresh vomit and urine. He changes the bedding and supports Peter to bathe, as his body is weakened during the detox. Watching Peter restless during his bouts of fretful sleep. Sipping only water as his body is unable to digest solid food. Haunted by horrific nightmares moving and thrashing his limbs. Peter's facial expressions change as the detox progresses; he loses that angry dangerous look as it is replaced by a softer, kinder expression. Innocence slowly returns to Peter's ravaged face. Father Jimmy talks directly to God, the silent communication produces a feeling of complete detachment from the priest's body, he needs this reassurance.

"You want this young man as a prophet?"

Father Jimmy's a little puzzled.

"I NEED HIM."

Father Jimmy hears the inner voice loud and clear.

"What's his story?"

"Everyone has a story, his trust is fragile, do not break or lose his trust as you may not get it back"

"What do you want me to do?"

"Earn his trust, you have already changed his circumstances. Teach him in my ways. He will increase my flock tenfold. The poorest, hardest to engage members of society will follow him, the inaccessible, bringing with them the most satisfaction. Vulnerable individuals who are exposed to dark ways because they live on the edge of society.

"Be watchful for the wrath of the dark one as you arouse his belligerent nature."

Gazing now at Peter, a contentment fills the room as his guardian angel grows in stature, filling the small space with calm and tranquillity. Golden shards of sunlight fills the bedroom, blinding to the naked eye, accompanied by a feeling of warmth as a sweet fragrant odour descends. Hypnotic angelic music accompanied by an overall feeling of well-being. A gift bestowed upon them, honouring the occasion, from the Supreme One. His guardian angel morphing into a beautiful golden angel. Whispering encouragement, she unlocks Peter's heart to remove the confusion he carries and mark his vast achievement. Content, Father Jimmy sits and watches in amazement. The second golden angel in so many days, most people don't see angels in the physical form their whole lifetime. They dismiss their inner voice instantly, for acceptance requires patience and practice that our fast pace of life denies. Peter's blessed with divine inspiration a gift from God.

Paul marches through the freezing elements shivering, hatless, his bald head losing his body heat, trying to release his frustration and anger, that old galoot knows how to push his buttons. Head down, hands shoved deep into his pockets he continues on. A thaw is promised from the weathermen and he is daydreaming about spring, when plants burst into life. He admires the snowdrops, their heads popping through the snow, camouflaged amongst the white backdrop and only just visible in the winter gardens. He is looking forward to spring, a chance for new beginnings with the opportunity to attend The Unity seminar. He is desperate to meet Choden Lamas, the visiting Buddhist monk who is rumoured to be developing his drug rehabilitation programme further in the UK and preventing youngsters from stumbling onto the all too familiar path.

Paul recalls his tough upbringing his mother a single parent providing for her three sons, long before benefits were considered to be a comfortable option. A small amount of money was provided for their upkeep. Without a word, his father left home one night, watched by Paul from his small, front bedroom window, wiping a port hole in the condensation on the glass. Wearing his Sunday best suit, he carried a small overnight bag, with his few meagre belongings. Looking back at Paul's window, he gave a quick wave before disappearing out of his life for good. Paul, the eldest, bit his lip as tears rolled down his face, smudging his skin. He was unprepared to fill his father's shoes.

Molly, his mum, held down numerous cleaning jobs trying her best. Their clothes always second hand, laughed at and taunted in school. Paul took on the role of protector, thinking he was an entrepreneur. Organising his business venture, becoming a runner for a local drug dealer intending to help his mother out with a little extra cash, unbeknown to her. She thought that he was doing odd jobs at the local market, unaware evil was sucking him in. Paul was provided with details on a daily basis; he would go to a holder's address, often a respectable part of town. Pick up a package and deliver it to another address. The organiser never handled the merchandise, distancing himself from the illegal drugs, making prosecution all but impossible. Presenting a case against an individual breaking the law with no physical evidence was a non-starter. Paul intended drug running just long enough to get his brothers through school. His plans were shattered when he was arrested at fifteen, a shy inexperienced boy with a substantial amount of drugs on him. They were confiscated by the police and he was prosecuted for possession with the intent to supply. The fall-guy assuming all the risk. He spent three hard years in a young offender unit. Educating him on the wrong side of the path, the straight and narrow eluded him. On his release, he owed the dealer ten thousand pounds for the drugs that the police had confiscated during his arrest. He did think of absconding but the debt would be transferred to his younger brothers, if he left. He got himself into this mess it was up to him to get himself out. He spent years in and out of prison. Once on the police radar as a dealer, he was an easy target to apprehend. Paul started with the gateway drug, smoking pot in the beginning, to get him through the mundane lifestyle of confinement, gradually increasing with time until he needed to deal drugs to cover his fix. Watching the horror his lifestyle inflicted on his mother, ashamed at hearing her muffled sobs with her face buried deep in her pillow as she cried herself to sleep at night. A good role model, loving and caring, watching the disappointment in her tender eyes every time his good intentions failed.

He woke one morning, years later, confused and dazed in a large bin at the back of his local shops. Faeces in his jeans, limbs aching. He staggered out of the bin, freezing and hungry, and he caught his reflection in a shop window. Paul didn't recognise the bedraggled reflection. A sharp unexplainable pain in his chest spread to his throat, into his head, then behind his eyes, releasing floods of tears. As he looked at the worn out figure on the opposite side of the road, smartly dressed, clutching a leather handbag. Looking older than Paul remembered, through sheer hard work, she looks small and frail. His heart breaks as his mother passes by, not recognising her firstborn son, years of hardship etched on her oval face. It unlocks hidden feelings that break through his numb state, feelings that years of addiction (his life for the last decade) have subdued. After a couple of failed attempts at drug rehabilitation, he decides on a radical approach. Heading east, carrying a photograph of his mother standing proudly with her three sons before drugs devoured his life. The photograph is worth more to him than any precious jewel, regardless of its value.

Love was the only real thing in this life. He has damaged hers, if it's the last thing he does he will repair her heart and restore her respect.

Paul jogs back to the rectory, hoping to generate some body heat from exercising his muscles. On entering the kitchen, Paul shakes a layer of fresh snow from his shoulders, returning his memories to the vault in his mind, safely locking them away. Removing his gloves and scarf, he places them on the pulley above the open fire in the kitchen. Resting his coat over the back of a wooden chair watching the steam rise from the article. Inhaling the fresh air he has carried in with him, while visiting these painful memories. The phlegmy cough alerts him that he's not on his own. Glancing sideways he sees Thursa hovering in the kitchen doorway watching him, like a cat tormenting a mouse.

"You moved in as well?"

Shaking her head, Thursa tuts, Paul has learnt that silence is sometimes the only answer, a favourite saying of Father Jimmy.

Thursa looks straight through him, her act of defiance, this hard man is unnerved, sure she can see his secrets buried deep. Uncomfortably he stands, eager to leave the room and her prying eyes. Bolting upstairs, he re-joins Peter again.

Chapter 4

As winter firmly closes its doors, the illusion disperses as the streets melt into rivers of grey slush. Happiness fills the plight of the homeless community as spring bursts into life. Sunshine breaks through the heavy clouds, bringing with it renewed hope, nature carpets the earth with a beautiful display of fragrant hardy flowers.

Memories triggered by sense of smell enjoyed by Father Jimmy as he strolls through a bluebell wood, a pleasant recollection of his childhood visible in his mind's eye, accompanied by the silent Peter as he learns to collect these precious moments from life. Enjoying the simplicity and freedom of just being, Peter has hardly left Father Jimmy's side since his detox. Embracing the natural beauty all around them, something that we all take for granted. Three months now Peter has been drugs free, growing stronger with every day. Grateful to Father Jimmy and Paul for making this huge difference to his life, showered in their love and care. Their faith in him is unwavering.

Even Thursa has got used to him sitting in her kitchen devouring her baking, feeding this giant of a man. A pleasurable task, maybe even beginning to like him a bit, letting him get away with the odd joke. Father Jimmy feels a bit left out when those two are together and he knows Paul is extremely uncomfortable around Thursa if left on his own with her for any length of time.

Stopping now to sit at the foot of an oak tree, caressing the hard rugged bark, support for their backs, they talk openly and freely about life, anything bothering them, no subject is taboo. An important part of Peter's ongoing recovery is to talk through his troubles before they escalate, with honestly and trust. Peter enjoys studying nature up close, a window into life. He watches how different species treat their young, helping him to get a grip on his own life.

"What happened that day when I was sitting on the wall?" Peter asks having wanted to ask this question for some time, concerned about the authenticity of his recall, nervous and a little unsure.

"God put you on my path that day, every action I took before I left the rectory, delivered me with precision and accuracy, the key."

Nodding his head agreeing with himself, 'divine timing' pops into his head, grinning Father Jimmy says, "He's here with us now he called it, divine timing."

"But why me?" Peter asks, with a hint of scepticism.

"Why not?"

"I can think of a hundred reasons why not."

"Father Jimmy roots into his shoulder bag pulling out two apples, flipping one over to Peter watching him polish it on his clothing, before wolfing it down, loud crunching noises as his teeth sink into the piece of ripe fruit piercing its skin with ease.

"You have a hunger for life Peter for all things, doing everything to excess. God needs someone strong in mind and body, to reach his forgotten people, someone they will trust, his messenger."

The inner voice again, 'My Rock'.

"He calls you his Rock, I am to teach you his ways. I see the outline of a large golden angel not as clearly as the day she arrived because you have power within yourself now, not needing to draw from her all the time. She is always with you, entering your heart, guiding you, filling you with optimism. You have been given a special gift hence the golden angel."

"What is my gift?"

"You need to work that out for yourself."

Father Jimmy's attention is drawn to this young man, virtually unrecognisable from their first meeting. Trimming down his rich dark beard Shaped and defined, an anchor style framing his angular chin. Cropped, dark auburn-brown hair, deep dark eyes, more black than brown, carrying his secrets. This handsome young man is a bit of a dreamer, pleasant company, although his trust is a little bruised. Father Jimmy takes it slowly.

"That's enough for today."

Father Jimmy springs to his feet offering a hand to a slouched Peter, laughing he takes it nearly pulling Father Jimmy off his feet. The priest is as small as Peter is large. Walking back, comfortable with each other's silence, under the cherry blossom covered streets. At ease with the stillness between them, no need for constant chatter. A couple stroll ahead, hand in hand, their angels joined behind them showing a suitable match.

Unity springs into Father Jimmy's head, his inner voice again.

Underneath the trees, cherry blossom drops like confetti at a wedding, sprinkling their union with blessings. Inhaling deeply, Peter says, "It's great to feel alive."

There is a spring in the dreamer's step.

Finally the news that Father Jimmy has been granted permission to attend the Unity seminar, one whole week in London.

The Bishop could not really refuse as Father Jimmy hasn't taken much in the way of holidays over the years and as this is a spiritual opportunity, understanding other religions, building bridges, he would have been a fool to refuse. Father Jimmy does have some supporters higher up in the church, self-preservation always in the forefront of the Bishop's mind. Father Michael who has just returned from a month in America will be covering his own parish and Father Jimmy's for the week.

Always the professional Father Jimmy continues with his hospital visits even though he's officially started his leave.

Clare Martin has been struggling with anorexia for the last five of her sixteen years. A waif-like adolescent, she has lost her way in life after the sudden death of her beloved mother. The apple of her dad's eye, these two wounded souls cling desperately together.

Father Jimmy visits daily as she is failing fast. A talented swimmer spotted at an early age, she had high hopes for her swimming career, until a throwaway remark at the age of eleven started her eating disorder. Miss Burgess, her coach, was a bitter woman, a tyrant really. Using her power and position of trust oppressively, she let slip a harsh comment about Clare's swimming times and how they would improve significantly if she slimmed down. Already the fastest swimmer on the squad, her body changed through puberty, with a growing spurt and increased body fat, both perfectly normal with the release of the female hormone oestrogen and her moods going up and down. The thoughtless comment put her on a path of self-destruction. A classic example of one person's free will interfering with another's having disastrous consequences.

Intercepting Father Jimmy in the corridor – a cold, endless, impersonal white space, with harsh fluorescent lighting buzzing and flickering constantly – her father begs Father Jimmy, "Take me, not her."

Genuine sentiment and pleading to her father's voice.

"It's not up to me, Rob." The priest rests a reassuring hand on his arm.

"We have been praying for her."

"I have too," her father says, imploring eyes, sorrow etched on his handsome face. A biker wearing jeans and a leather jacket, enjoying the freedom and space of the open road, daring to be different. "I want to trade places it's not her time."

"It's not that simple Rob."

"Why do bad things happen? That bloody coach is to blame."

Thinking, Father Jimmy realises how that throwaway remark has impacted on this young lady's life. Reducing it significantly, keeping these thoughts to himself, he says, "Let's go and sit with her."

Guiding him slowly, they join Clare. Her complexion is pallid and she is painfully thin as she lies in the hospital bed. The light in her eyes fades as a veil draws over her face. Her angel cradling her, gently stroking her face, there is no fear in this courageous little one. The time is near, ready to leave one room and step into another. Hovering between the two worlds, her maiden voyage of trust awaits her as she enters the tunnel of brilliant light, both vibrant and inviting; bliss awaits her. Rob, her father, tells her how proud he is of her and her achievements. Laboriously pushing herself onto her bony elbow, a warm smile covers her innocent face. Temporarily, a little light returns to her young impressionable eyes.

"Don't be sad, Dad, I am only stepping outside I will wait for you, I will have no pain or fear, I will be able to enjoy food again. Time will pass quickly I will watch you every day. Before you know it, we will be together again."

Her voice becomes a whisper. "Do not be afraid, release is the kindest gift I could receive and forgiveness the key, I will send a message, let you know I'm alright."

In unison they both say, "I love you."

Slowly closing her young eyes, colour quickly drains from her peaceful face.

"Mother." The last word she utters before being released from this world. Swallowed up by a bright light and carried down a path of adornment, contentment is visible on her pinched face as she exits one world and is greeted into another.

A still silence fills the air as happy memories flood her father's mind; he is positive that she has been reunited with his caring wife. This parting gift from Clare helps him come to terms with his recent loss.

Choden Lamas and his trusted companion arrive; stepping off the plane, they are filled with excitement. Welcomed by a shy London sun and embracing a bold new world, they are greeted with a glimpse of western life. New places and cultures open their minds as they absorb their surroundings, different sounds and smells grabbing their imagination. Cooled by sheet-like rain as a greyness hangs over the city, large fluffy clouds fill the skyline. A smiling stewardess, with theatrical make-up, offers them an umbrella; Choden Lamas politely refuses with a bow of his head. He is enjoying the refreshing, invigorating rain pattering down on his head, a gift from nature. His eyes dart from one image to another, scrutinising the English people and their customs. Their clothing is very different and exciting, a flurry of colour greeting his tired eyes.

Choden Lamas, an ambassador for peace, is here to learn. Having mastered the English language, he is excited at the prospect of what he may ascertain. A large black limousine has been sent to pick him up from the airport; seeing other delegates representing their countries, he gestures that they share his vehicle. He wants to integrate from the beginning, bringing together religion as a whole, like meeting long lost cousins at a family wedding. He feels that we have tailored religion to suit our own culture over the years, following the bits we like and discarding the bits we don't.

He smells the leather of the seats, an organic product, having once been a living thing, carefully treated to leave a pleasant odour.

Thick and comfortable, they sink into them, bemused by an array of refreshments inside this large vehicle. Passing through the busy streets of London, he admires the architecture of the buildings. Large grey clouds hang menacingly in the sky, threatening heavier rain, then he sees them.

The grey people living on the streets of London, discarded like bags of rubbish as they huddle in corners and doorways, sitting on cardboard, some wrapped in sleeping bags surrounded by a handful of meagre possessions. Begging on the cold, concrete pavements, these tortured souls with well-worn dishevelled characters, male and female, young and old. Homelessness makes no distinction, pain visible to see if anyone bothers to look. Yellowing ashen faces, rotten missing teeth, the monk sees their grey and black auras feeding on their damaged souls. Controlling them with addiction, relinquishing their free will, a great sadness about the street people, existing rather than living, the plight of the invisible community. Society too busy to stop or notice dashing about in suits and clothing that looks expensive. Red auras surround the people in suits, representing sex, money and power. Choden thinks that's what they must mean by power dressing. Infrequently the monk notices a dash of blue and green auras, representing people with strong personalities and green, expressing nurture and healing.

He watches these people rushing aimlessly in their pursuit of paper money, reminding him of a hamster on its wheel.

Father Jimmy, Peter and Paul arrive in London. To them, this is a familiar city, boasting an array of bars and restaurants, awash with expressionless faces scurrying from one place to another.

They have travelled down on the National Express, for Father Jimmy is not one to waste money. He yawns and stretches as he exits the cramped coach, resembling Thursa's stray cat. A gang of rowdy young women on a hen night exit the vehicle at the same time. They are dressed as nuns, but not in the conventional sense.

"Are you the stag lad?" a brassy blonde, with orange tinted skin and eyelashes like spider's legs, enquires. Two of the other women are wearing rollers in their hair, faces fully made up.

Before Father Jimmy can answer one of the other women enquires, "How many times you been down the aisle then?"

Laughing as she gyrates her hips, Paul looks away horrified.

"Now that would be telling. I've lost count," Father Jimmy says, winking with those grey-blue eyes.

They scream with laughter as they wobble off in their ridiculously high heels, a disapproving look covers Paul's face. "Why do you encourage them?"

"They're young, they should be having the time of their lives," Father Jimmy says, showing his humorous side. "You're only young once," he adds.

The three musketeers finally arrive at a cheap B&B excitedly unpacking before a quick freshen up. Father Jimmy has a front room overlooking the busy main street below, Paul is complaining about a musty smell in his room, wrinkling his nose.

"Come on, Paul, people will be sleeping on the streets tonight, you of all people should appreciate that."

"It's not that bad," Peter interjects, hand on his rumbling stomach, always thinking about food.

Father Jimmy rubs his hands together hearing a growling noise from his own stomach, louder than he would have liked, getting the right reaction from Peter.

"Time to eat."

Roaming the busy streets, they navigate their way embracing London and its culture, so much to see and do.

A large crowd is gathering on the opposite side of the road, rooted to the spot Father Jimmy sees a magnificent white and gold angel the most powerful sight he has ever experienced. Colours of the rainbow radiate from this serene celestial being, far superior to anything he has ever witnessed before, taking his breath away. These angelic visions are becoming more frequent, scaring him a little as he is carried into the unknown.

Central to the gathering he sees a darker, robed figure, majestic in manner, amongst the unmistakable saffron robes, a statement of simplicity and detachment from materialism. Choden Lamas the teacher, enlisted as a messenger, sent to walk amidst the common people who flock to him. A little envy creeps into Father Jimmy's heart, as the dark angels plot to keep these two powerful teachers apart.

For the first time since landing in London, Choden Lamas has seen the unmistakable image of a violet, purple aura. Violet auras are reserved for powerful, intuitive people, whose potent abilities enable their owner to bring healing, comfort and peace to any situation, good mediators. Each messenger mirrors the other's thoughts. Glancing across the busy main road, their eyes lock for a fleeting moment acknowledging the other's presence. A telepathic message from Choden Lamas transmits his greeting to a comparable messenger, without any sensory channel or physical interaction, Father Jimmy interprets the address.

"Peace be with you."

He bows his head gracefully and joins his hands in the prayer position, in respect of another messenger. Traffic has slowed to observe the commotion on the pavement, a feeling of uncertainty comes over Father Jimmy. Hearing the crunching noise at the same time as seeing it, a white van hits a cyclist, catapulting him into mid-air. Observed in slow motion, the cyclist rotates freely in space amidst a strong white glow as the angel of light carries his body through the air before he finally comes to rest heavily, his head hitting the windscreen of the vehicle. A sickening thud as his skull cracks and his lifeless body slides down the front of the vehicle, landing awkwardly on the Tarmac flooring – time regains its normal tempo, noise and people buzz around. The young man, not wearing a helmet, leaves a trail of blood spattered on the windscreen and down the front of the van. The driver shakes uncontrollably, distressed, in a state of shock, as the mind slows the thought process down, giving him time to register what has happened. The cyclist resembles a rag doll, deposited motionless on the cold road surface.

Puzzled, the cyclist is standing over his own body, observing his lifeless carcass, bent and twisted, unmoving on the floor, detached from his physical being. Confused as no one can hear or see him, he feels no pain, separated between the two realms. A strong smell of lavender perfume surrounds him, a favourite of his grandmother, she appears with her radiant smile, he recalls her home, always a happy place when he was a child. A smallholding with a few chucks, two pigs, Gert and Daisy, surrounded by open fields, space to run wild and play, his grandmother having passed over five years ago. Her warmth of character embraces him, no worries or fear, wrapping her loving, protective arms around him, filled with peace and love.

"It's not your time," she says gently, fading in front of his eyes. "You must go back, you're needed."

Before he can argue, he's back inside his body writhing in pain, drowning in the noise, filled with mortal fear. An off duty doctor sitting in a local restaurant rushes to attend to him while waiting for the ambulance to arrive. The casualty is sure the priest perceived what had just happened.

Looking up again to see that Choden Lamas has disappeared in the commotion, Father Jimmy feels a sense of loss.

The accident outside is quickly attended to as the emergency services swiftly arrive, with lights flashing, sirens blaring and the professionals taking control. Moving the traffic on, swilling the blood stains from the road surface as the young man is rushed to hospital, the faster pace of life in the capital returns to normal as the debris is removed.

Finally the three sit in a Chinese restaurant waiting for their food to arrive, Chinese being one of Peter's favourite. Father Jimmy sits in silence as he tries to make sense of what has just happened. Peter and Paul chat, unaware of their friend's dilemma. Father Jimmy stares at his rice dish, steam rising from the food, aromatic herbs and spices visit his nostrils. A vegetarian, refusing through choice to eat other living things, is not popular at Thursa's table. Enjoying the taste and texture of this delicious dish, he is lost in his own private thoughts.

Two loud suits sit in the opposite corner chatting, the larger of the two guys is sure his interview went better than his colleague. Clicking his fingers for attention, he is full of arrogance and self-importance. One of his nostrils continually drips with a clear mucus. A functioning drug user Paul thinks, while Father Jimmy focuses on the black angel, larger than the white, gaining control whispering in the large guy's ear, encouraging his pompous and ostentatious behaviour. Surprisingly, the companion has a white angel with bits of grey bleeding into her wings. This guy isn't a good influence on his younger associate. The guy with the nasal drip has a loud, raucous, attention-seeking laugh, he probably succumbed to his addiction, within the last half hour. Hence the overbearing personality.

"Hey, Chinaman, I want serving."

One hand in the air clicking his fingers, the other texting on his phone, while dipping in and out of a conversation with his companion, wanting to only talk but not to listen. Paul leans over and says quietly to Father Jimmy and Peter, "His dilated pupils and runny nose are a dead giveaway."

Red faced, the guy storms over to their table. Ignoring the protests of his companion, he slurs, "What did you say?"

Defensively Peter makes to rise but Father Jimmy puts a protective hand on Peter's arm and says, "Karma."

Just that one word.

Peter remains seated, ignoring the suit, and the three continue their conversation.

Angrily he shoves their table, wanting a reaction. Father Jimmy's mouth opens and the words fly out, "This time tomorrow your companion over there," pointing to his seated friend, "will be your boss, cocaine is interfering with your ability to do your job. You have taken one too many risks. Sleeping with your boss's wife was the straw that broke the camel's back."

This guy is speechless, shock visible on his ruddy face.

"This time next year you will be unemployed, the reason your manager will give is restructuring the workforce. The real reason – his wife. We are all here to learn. For an intelligent man you keep missing the point, repeating the same mistakes, sex, drugs and power ruining your life. You will hit rock bottom before you regain your self-respect." Closing his mouth, Father Jimmy finishes his impromptu speech.

The suit quickly returns to his table, filling his seat, unable to speak, fearing the priest's intuitive predictions.

Paul and Peter look as confused as Father Jimmy.

"Where did that come from?" Paul asks.

Father Jimmy shakes his head. "I have no idea."

Choden Lamas sits on his bedroom floor, deep plush carpets of the boutique style hotel, totally unaware of what that means. He misses the freshness of the outdoors, so he opens his window slightly, sending the blinds rattling. Nature comes calling as a small brown bird sits on the window sill foraging for food. Admiring the splendour of this tiny creature, he rips the crust from a sandwich, breaking it into tiny pieces, placing them on the exterior sill. Familiar with city life the bird retrieves the food before moving some distance away to eat it uninterrupted.

Lost in his meditation, he works through the events of the day. Floating in pleasure, he sees the persistent rainbow again, unsure of its significance. The priest in the street, he is sure, was put on his path, the reason yet to become clear. Telepathic, able to communicate without words, a special gift, he must be close to his God to be trusted.

These two modern day prophets united on a path of learning and enlightenment, chosen to speak out for the Supreme Being. Guiding his people, who walk alone, lost souls on the brink of destruction, back onto their rightful paths, enabling them to retake control. Yet danger is near as dark forces roam, waiting to discredit these two pioneering messengers.

Chapter 5

Father Jimmy is aware that his insight has increased significantly since his arrival in London, his arrival somehow harmonising and purifying his thought process. The incident yesterday an indication that a much bigger force is at play. He has been seeing angels for a few years now, intermittently at first. It started with signs – white feathers, coins, scents and sometimes flashing coloured lights, subtle touches grabbing his attention, signs and symbols appearing before some sort of transmission. Then the inner voice, loud and clear, letting him know he wasn't alone. When his path was hindered or when times were tough, he was guided. Then he witnessed a spirit leave a child's body, released from the pain of anorexia, floating freely, a gaiety about it.

Eventually he embraced his intuition, let it in, he seized the moments, interpreting their meanings. He saw things he couldn't explain driven by a powerful inner force. He had been frightened a little by this direct perception and feeling humbled, for he was a simple, unassuming man, not wanting or needing much. Helping the hardest to engage members of society his forgotten people, whom have lost their voices and their way.

Busying himself, Father Jimmy waits in anticipation of the start of the seminar.

But later that day, the priest watches the hands of time pass ever so slowly, aware our lives are governed by time. Peter and Paul have gone out for a brisk walk, pleased with this developing friendship. Part of Peter's ongoing recovery programme for his addiction is that a healthy body equals a healthy mind.

With the mind guarding his emotions, counselling and meditation help Peter to move forward with his life, leaving guilt behind with his addiction.

Paul stops by the riverbank, his physical exercise done. This encourages a domino effect, with the release of chemicals and oxygen that promote increased blood flow, causing the brain to perform more efficiently. Now for a bit of mental training.

"What would you do with £86,400?"

Peter looks perplexed, "Another of your games?"

Paul stands still, hands shoved in his jeans' pockets, his familiar hard-man stance as he takes in the view of the Thames, watching the army of ant-like people moving aimlessly about their daily life. Not stopping to acknowledge one another or the gifts they have been given. Too busy rushing from A to B.

Enthusiastically Peter answers, "I would use it to open another shelter for the homeless."

A simple, truthful answer from Peter.

"What would you do if I gave you £86,400 every day, on the proviso that you spent it within the twenty-four hour period?"

"That's easy, charities would be rich."

Peter's smile holds an innocence about it as he concentrates on the conversation.

"Think what a difference that would make. I have read about people that have so much money they will never spend it in their lifetime."

Life is time borrowed from God, each day bestowed upon us is a gift, that's why we should make every day count, when tragedy strikes we find ourselves begging for the return of a mundane life.

"God deposits 86,400 seconds into our life account everyday a gift to each and every one of us. All he asks in return is that we use it wisely."

Peter looks deflated, adding, "I have wasted years."

That look of self-hate and loathing returns to his handsome young face. Paul turns to face him, placing a reassuring hand on his shoulder and looks deep into his transparent eyes.

"Life is about balance, you get out what you put in, mistakes happen in our lives, we learn from them and move on. People are quick to judge other's mistakes, being a passenger and watching evil is as bad as taking part. Positive actions speak louder than words. You have been given a special gift Peter, trusted amongst your peers. Like a shepherd you will lead your flock back into the light. Not one or two but hundreds, time is never wasted if you extract knowledge."

Peter looks unsure,

"You're a work in progress, perfection doesn't exist"

Both are laughing now.

"To become a teacher, we must first learn."

"Where did you learn all that?" Peter asks, mystified.

"A monk in Thailand; same message, different god."

Reassured, Peter feels a weight lifted.

Paul continues, "A rich man gives away a thousand pounds from a relatively large fortune, will he not be treated better than the poor man who donates his last note to charity. For the poor man has given everything he owns and left himself with nothing. While the rich man has calculated a small percentage of his wealth. The amount means nothing it's the sacrifice made by the poor man. You Peter give the most precious thing we have, TIME."

Big Ben interrupts, chiming ten o'clock, a musical masculine tone startling both men. They both jump slightly and are amused at the other's reaction. They make their way through the busy crowded streets as people dash about their daily life, laughter visible on their faces. They move amongst different races and nationalities, all coming together in this large city which hosts an immense choice of eateries to cater for its diverse population; flavours and smells from all corners of the earth fill the air. Metal tables and chairs on the pavements where the proprietors sit, eagerly awaiting the lunch time rush. Coffee houses in competition with one another and even a Chinese tea room, a delight to the nostrils. They salivate as the odours tease their taste buds but Peter is secretly missing Thursa's traditional home cooked food. A difficult woman who is a growing on him, looking around himself to make sure no one has heard his revelation. Able to wrap Thursa around his little finger, she is the grandmother figure he never had.

Father Jimmy awaits their return, having indulged in some privacy during his prayers. Time to quieten his mind, engage his thoughts and purify his mind.

The pleasure Father Jimmy feels upon seeing this young man returned from his drug fuelled life-style – a miracle in itself –as well as both Peter and Paul carefree and laughing as they return from their morning meditation, fills him with contentment. Confirming that with belief anything is possible, both men proceed on life's journey. Crashing through the door with his normal finesse, Peter enters first. Talking ten to the dozen, a far cry from the early days when all his emotions where on lock-down. Peter was a large-framed and menacing individual, filled with gloom and reluctant to speak.

Living under the radar having moved from Frankby on the Wirral years ago. Living on his wits, an outsider at first. Immersing himself amongst the homeless community of Liverpool, doing whatever he could to get by. His life before Liverpool was taboo. Respecting his privacy, Father Jimmy has taken his first meeting with Peter as day one, a fresh start.

Eager to attend the seminar the three men leave, walking the twenty minute journey to the venue. Wanting their minds to be as alert as possible, the exercise boosts the blood supply pumping around their bodies as they briskly walk, encouraging mind activity.

An extremely large lady manoeuvres her mobility scooter along the busy pavement, going a little quicker than she should. Pedestrians politely move out of her way, grumbling once she is out of earshot. Looking closely, Father Jimmy sees only sadness draped around this ladies shoulders like a shawl. Addicted to junk food filled with additives, a vicious circle as she gorges herself on saturated fats to quell her cravings. Disabling herself in the process, a modern-day tragedy. She wakes every morning, looks in the mirror and is disgusted at what she sees. Then the cycle of self-destruction begins, Father Jimmy is amazed at how many unhappy people he passes. Individuals in high-powered jobs using drugs and alcohol as performance enhancers. Functioning addicts, clean shaven, wearing expensive suits, leather brogues on their feet, Rolexes decorating their wrists. Outwardly an indication of their success, inwardly looking miserable as sin. Father Jimmy sees large, swollen organs overheated and overworked, struggling to maintain the pressure of daily life. Success an addiction in itself, while concentrating on other's goals and not their own. A spiritually starved population. Father Jimmy feels their pain, using his real and powerful form of telepathy, uninvited, that started again yesterday after his encounter with the monk.

Glancing up, Father Jimmy sees a large community hall. A simple billboard outside advertises the Unity seminar. Still chatting, Peter and Paul impatiently cross the busy road. Spiritually sensing danger, the temperature drops as an uneasy, sickly feeling sends shivers down Father Jimmy's spine. He sees a large black feather float to the ground, finally resting by his feet. It is a warning. A ghostly, dense cloud temporarily blocks out the sunlight casting dark grey colours across the sky. Father Jimmy becomes aware that Peter is in danger. A speeding BMW X6 is heading straight towards him and he is too far away to intervene. Father Jimmy's stomach turns as adrenalin pumps through his body and he is consumed with real fear. Coming out of nowhere, he watches time dilate, slowing events. The monk floats, linking arms with Peter and swiftly ushering him out of the path of danger. Losing control, the vehicle comes to a sudden stop, wrapping itself around a lamp post. People scream as the bloodied figure sits slumped over the steering wheel. There's something familiar about this man. Upon closer inspection, Father Jimmy sees the rude guy from the Chinese restaurant yesterday. Frantically looking for the monk to thank him, but he's nowhere to be seen. He rushes to attend to Peter.

"Are you alright?" the priest asks.

"Bloody fool came out of nowhere."

"It's a good job the monk saw what was happening."

Looking confused, Peter asks, "What monk?"

Laughing, Father Jimmy says, "Very funny, Peter."

Bewildered and a little shaken, Peter doesn't reply.

Making their way into the hall, stepping through a hefty wooden door frame, high ceilings and large ornate windows, bouncing sound off the walls, everything echoes in this vast open space. They feel the divine power circulating among the messengers and prophets, a sacred life force that exists in all beings.

Choden Lamas is hosting a meditation session in one of the workshops. Father Jimmy asks one of the organisers if he can join the workshop.

"I'm only a couple of minutes late."

"That session has been running for fifteen minutes, there's another one tomorrow."

"I have just seen the monk outside. You must have heard all the commotion, a car accident."

Father Jimmy points in the direction of the street.

"I think you must be mistaken sir, Choden Lamas has been in the building for the last half hour."

"Be On Your Guard."

This isn't his inner voice, this is something different, mind to mind direct communication between two people. Telepathy transmits information from one person to another forming images and emotions. When we know a friend is sad, we read their emotions by facial expressions or body language, telepathy is the next step.

Father Jimmy trawls through the stalls of different religions, their message always the same, glimpsing a divine portal on this planet, spreading peace and harmony, explaining their sacred teachings. His eyes scan the information but nothing sinks in. The priest's mind is firmly set on Choden Lamas. Unable to concentrate on anything else, his mind is abuzz with questions, excited and scared. Wondering what just happened outside, doubting himself now, was that all in his head. No. No, he did see the monk levitating slightly, guiding Peter away from the danger. Why didn't Peter sense him too?

Wafting past Father Jimmy, a tall, dark, beautiful woman catches his eye. Drenched in expensive perfume, too pungent for his liking. A willowy figure, wearing leather trousers and a cobalt-blue chiffon blouse, with long straight flaxen hair. Everything about her screams money. Interested in religion or just a curious observer? She turns slowly, tottering on her absurdly high heels, hair moving sensuously. Father Jimmy is surprised as the face of a much older woman greets him, painstakingly concealed. On closer inspection, the signs of the ageing process are all there, skilfully camouflaged with beautifully manicured eyebrows, long, thick false eyelashes, maybe a lower face lift which looks a tad too taut, and pouting lips. Botox, he presumes. Flashing back and forth in his mind are two conflicting images. The one standing in front of him, smiling sweetly. Then the same image minus the heavy make-up, concealment against her predators. A much older, wizened looking woman, missing the heady indulgence of youth, trying to defeat the ageing process. He blinks rapidly, unsure of what's going on.

Adrianna enjoys the attention, flattered. She realises that Father Jimmy is studying her, flashing him a pre-rehearsed smile with her whitened straight teeth. Her image alters again. Through his sense of perception, he sees vapours appearing tangled in Adriana's hair. Father Jimmy sees the haunted face of a young woman, beautiful and innocent, taken before her time. Stuck between the Earth and Astral planes as body snatchers savagely remove her hair to sell to this rich, spoilt, arrogant woman. Uncaring, no feelings, selfish, constantly looking at her own reflection; a conceited, phoney individual. Demanding real hair extensions, refusing the best synthetic product on the market that money can buy, Adrianna knows the cost of everything and the value of nothing. Haunted by the hair's original owner screaming at the injustice of it. Repulsed by her vain appearance, Father Jimmy turns away. Catching a horrifying glimpse of another plane where evil reigns.

He wanders over to the refreshment area, needing time to absorb what he has just seen. The familiar odour of coffee draws Father Jimmy nearer. The distinctive coffee bean floods the hall, arousing memories long forgotten. Scents can transport us back, triggering powerful emotions and flashbacks from our past. He finds himself sitting at his grandmother's table, with a black cat meowing outside the back door. Freshly cut daffodils dominate the centre of the table; they are plonked carelessly in a jam jar but their scent lingers in the kitchen. There is a roaring fire in the hearth and the smell of fresh baking. Love and kindness were always on his grandparent's lips, encouraging, happy in his safe haven, grandma's hands wrapped tightly around her coffee cup. He always returns to this precious memory when he is troubled.

Feeling a presence behind him, he turns hastily. Choden Lamas, with his hands in the prayer position and fingertips resting between nose and eyebrows, tilts his head slightly and bows a greeting. In a state of intense elation, Father Jimmy feels intoxicated in this dream mode. These two figures, the monk and the priest, communicate without words, closing their eyes, cocooned in a bubble-like state, being carried away on the flowing current of love. With heightened senses and perception, visiting each other's lives. Like twins that have been separated at birth, re-joined for the first time. In the knowledge that they are on the same path. The rest of the world melts away as they sense each other's strengths. A very special and powerful bond forms, an alliance between east and west. Anything is possible when these two commanding forces come together.

"At last we meet."

Choden Lamas' greetings are drowned out by the sound of a storm directly overhead. The roar of thunder, followed by forked lightning, spreads across the darkening sky, then the clattering of rain on the tin roof of the centre. This heavy intense downpour is an indication that evil is aroused. Looking through the window, the pair witness people darting about the street, trying to escape the heavy rain wherever they can. For the first time since arriving in London the two messengers witness people communicating with one another. Laughing at each other during the downpour. Helping one another as phones and tablets are shoved away in pocket or bags. Adversity brings them together, acknowledging Mother Nature, a powerful unrelenting force. Pedestrians squeal with delight, gawking at a vibrant double rainbow as it appears above the city. Breathtakingly beautiful in appearance as vibrant colours bleed into one another making further shades and tones. A symbol, two messengers brought together as one. Genesis' account of a rainbow appears right after the great worldwide flood brought in order to remove sinful and evil-minded people from the earth. It symbolised God's mercy and the covenant he made with Noah not to destroy the world. Choden Lamas is beginning to realise the colossal task that lies ahead of them. Bringing unity back into this broken world, the bigger the risk the bigger the gain. Looking skywards at the clouds, Father Jimmy sees two white horses each with very different riders not unlike himself and Choden Lamas. One from the east one from the west. Their task is to disengage society from modern day distractions, since technology replaces conversations and companionship. People aimlessly communicate through computers and phones, hiding in a virtual world which leads to the death of conversation, replacing it with messages that lack feelings and emotions.

Discreetly the dark lady studies the two figures, while adversity watches on.

Till now, Thursa's life has been one long continuous lonely pathway, choosing to travel it alone, her fate sealed a very long time ago when misfortune came calling, burying herself in her work, ignoring emotions and feelings. Then an unlikely character walked into her life, completely unexpected, a tiny chink of light slipped into Thursa's weathered heart, a very special and precious moment. Gradually awakening a fountain of maternal feelings in the confirmed spinster. She misses Peter terribly, this flawed young man filled with stubbornness, awkward and clumsy, his powerful presence fills the house with his appealing character, larger than life, clattering around her home, leaving a trail of mess and destruction in his wake. She loves every one of his faults with real and unconditional love. Talking candidly to her about the evil growing inside, his weakness, feeding on it, increasing in size until it was so large he was unable to control it, not knowing how to cope. That was before he was put on Father Jimmy's path. Thursa has the desire to protect him, cradle Peter in her arms, stroke his unruly mop of hair in an all-consuming love.

Motherhood.

A wonderful precious gift, bestowed on the few, trusted to guide another that, up until now, Thursa had been denied. Guiltily now she remembers complaining about Peter when he first arrived. Making extra work for the elderly housekeeper, even Father Jimmy has grown on her, but more than that, he has gained her respect. Making her feel included, more like a family member than an employee. The rectory feels so quiet and empty now, neat, unloved rooms, hollow empty spaces, a shell. Thursa admits to herself she feels lost without them both. Sitting chatting to her in the kitchen, carrying the laundry basket down the stairs to the wash room. Helping her with the shopping, she realises that if evil can slip into this caring young man's soul, it can get into anyone's. Now with faith and conviction Peter walks tall, ignoring chants from former associates. He finds the courage of his convictions as he is led onto his rightful path. A fixed, firm belief that he is now their rock.

Chapter 6

Emma Lane sits in the corner of the refreshment area, sipping a cup of black tea. Her vacant eyes stare as steam rises from her cup, making shapes, before they disperse into the atmosphere. She talks quietly into her Dictaphone as her mind recalls the day's events. A refreshing looking woman, sparse use of make-up, imparting vitality and energy. Her genes have been good to her, healthy looking fresh skin, bright intelligent eyes, shoulder length, sleek blonde hair lightened slightly. A firm body structure that looks as if fitness is part of her daily routine. With a good diet complimenting her inherited genes, giving an overall glow about her. A bit of a sceptic due to her line of work. Glancing back, Choden Lamas indicates for Father Jimmy to join him. Drifting gracefully, the monk proceeds, relaxing into his seat opposite. A fluidity about his movements, these two messengers perceive the other, aware of each other's spiritual gifts. Encased in light, surrounded by wisdom and knowledge. Wise men seeking each other's teachings. Guided together for the first time, they share a connection far outreaching this world. Emma's eyes are now in focus, intrigued. She watches silently from the corner, trying to interpret their intense body language.

"I see you bring the Prophet." Softly spoken, with the ease of a life-long companion, Choden Lamas enquircs.

Father Jimmy looks confused.

"He will guide many people wielding a powerful weapon – no enemy can prevail. Removing doubt from the mind-set of the lost, engaging their hearts filling them with trust. A powerful mind is one of the strongest tools we have. He has been put on a path very different from the one that he knows and is adjusting well. The way has been prepared for him. He surrendered to his lord when he came calling, relinquishing his old ways, totally and unreservedly. If he stumbles we will pick him up, when he sheds a tear we will wipe it away. If weakness takes over we will make him strong, when evil comes calling we must be ready."

Father Jimmy asks the question but he already knows the answer.

"Who is the Prophet?"

Smiling, an infectious smile, Choden Lamas says, "He is your Rock."

Instantly a feeling of unease comes over Choden Lamas, a sickly feeling in the pit of his stomach accompanied by a bitter chill which encases the two men. He senses harmful forces.

"It isn't safe here, evil is very close disguised as another. It will try desperately to keep us apart, blocking our paths."

Father Jimmy can't see an angel by the dark lady.

"She is powerful and is hindering your perception. I am struggling to see her aura, but I can just make out a grey black colour."

Father Jimmy is a pure soul wanting to help the poorest of society, whether they are financially or emotionally poor. However, he realises that the path of learning and enlightenment is quickly turning into a battleground between the two forces.

"I will find you tomorrow," the monk mumbles in his low voice.

Before Father Jimmy can protest, Choden Lamas swiftly departs, leaving the priest feeling the pain of separation.

Ever vigilant Emma Lane sees Choden Lamas exit the building accompanied by a bald, burly monk. Keen to speak to him hurriedly she approaches, catching up with him on the street. His robe sweeps the damp concrete floor, his feet invisible. An elegant flowing movement, floating rather than walking, she is observed by his companion who has not left his side.

"Excuse me," she says, reaching out and touching his arm; a friendly gesture, trying to grab his attention with the hustle and bustle of city life drowning out her small voice.

He quickly turns to face her and she experiences a surreal feeling of love and well-being. His face is beaming, eyes genuine and bright, reflecting his personality. Their eyes engage briefly, blocking out all the sound and noise of the capital. Focusing deep inside her, Choden Lamas examines her soul – real love resides there. The core of her whole being, love for her husband, powerful and strong. Unconditional love for her daughter, unbreakable. She is aware of a strange inexplicable occurrence happening at that moment. But, so typical of the west, she doubts herself and these feelings, letting them disperse and disappear. When she releases her arm quickly, the sensation ceases.

"Can I help you?"

The monk's words sing out of his mouth, reminding Emma of the nightingale, open and responsive.

"I would like to do a feature on you, I am a journalist."

Her voice shakes, doubtful of herself now.

"You have questions to ask me?"

Choden Lamas is direct. He takes Emma's hands firmly in his own, which are delicate and soft. Unexpectedly, she travels fast down a tunnel bright in colour shade and depth, sensing another dimension. She has never experienced anything like this before.

Similar to a blind man opening his eyes to see for the first time, experiencing the wonders of life in disbelief as he brings everything into focus, devouring all that he can see.

A large portal appears, it mesmerises Emma; peering into it, she sees her daughter come into focus, standing in her wedding dress seven years from now and beaming with delight. An innocence about her beauty blinded by the first flush of love. Standing at the altar gazing at her husband to be, giving love, watching it return. Tugging her hands away from the monk Emma is physically shaking. It feels like hours have passed when only seconds have.

"She's too young to marry, she has her whole career ahead of her," Emma challenges, "Performing arts. Top of her class in dance"

"You don't want to see?" the monk enquires.

Choden Lamas, undeterred, takes her hands again, travelling through the tunnel again she sees her daughter performing, achieving worldwide coverage, enjoying different countries, exciting and new. Emma is confident that she is right to push her in the career she has trained for. Trying to release her hand, the monks grip tightens. They continue on the journey, five years on, her beautiful daughter struggling to keep up with expectations. Using cocaine to help with her gruelling schedules, as well as appetite suppressants. Emma tries again to release herself from the firm grip. Another five years on, dancing in an adult only club, too heavily made up for her dainty fine features. Fat old men ogle her

The monk releases his grip.

Shocked, she asks, "Why did you show me that?"

Calmly the monk tries to explain. "We all have free will and we must choose our own path. Ava wants to marry. Love is covert, you don't see it coming, but once snared, it is all consuming, a special bond between two souls that will last the test of time. She is fifteen now, too young for such a connection. They will split for a few years and it will be painful as their love is deep; when they reunite, it will be more powerful. They will travel the world, see the sights; discover new cultures together, waking in each other's arms. When she stumbles, he will be there to catch her; when she is ill, he will attend to her. They will laugh and cry together, building precious memories to last them a lifetime. Broadening their minds, his love goes deeper than the way she looks. They are old souls who belong together, she will build a career, a lasting one, not being led off her path, if she is; you have seen the consequences. The ripple effect will be far-reaching. We are all here to learn you cannot buffer your children's path. Sometimes the most obvious path isn't the right one. Learn to trust your instincts, then interpret them, Emma."

Physically shaking she makes to leave, two minutes have passed in which her life has been turned upside down. Rushing now Emma makes for the train, legs feeling wobbly. Inhaling deeply as she extracts the last of her energy stores, running the last few yards, sprinting up a flight of stairs to safety. Not sure what has just happened as her brain struggles to process the images she has been shown.

Emma sits quietly in the warm train compartment, lost in her thoughts and wanting to get home after an eventful day. Hissing, the train door shuts as Emma escapes into her own little oasis, watching the world pass her by. Outside, blurred images flash past at speed, seen through the large windowpane, obscured rather than clear, vague and uncertain, like her meeting with the monk. The train and her mind are moving too fast. Reassured by the rhythmical movement as the train takes her in the direction and safety of home, she is eager to switch her mind off. Puzzled by what has just happened with the monk, masses of information crammed into a few seconds. Like watching a film on fast forward. Seeing and experiencing every emotion and detail, now able to recall it at a regular pace, her heart is still pounding in her chest.

The dark lady sits opposite her, observing her emotional state. Bewilderment covers Emma's pretty face as the dark lady politely enquires, "Did I just see you with the monk?"

Smiling sweetly, Emma is struggling to put an age to her face. First rule of journalism: know your subject. "I'm sorry; do I know you?" This gives Emma time to think.

"We were both at the Unity seminar, I thought you looked uncomfortable when talking to the monk."

Sensing something unsavoury, trusting her instincts for once, Emma replies, "Oh, I was asking him if I could run a story. I'm a journalist."

"Nothing else?"

Persistence to the dark lady's dulcet tones, as she tries to extract information from Emma. Her large eyes are hypnotic, drawing Emma in like pools of water swishing and swirling on a hot summer's day. They captivate her mind, making weighty eyelids heavy with uninvited sleep, rocking her back and forth with the rhythm of the train. Relaxed drowsiness seduces her, closing her eyes briefly. Emma blinks rapidly to regain control and stop from falling under this feline spell. A feeling of contentment, losing her conscious awareness of the outside world in which her ability to function is voluntarily suspended and the desire to do whatever her companion wants. Mesmerised by the dark lady, freedom in this delightful state as the train continues to gently rock. Hearing a purring noise like her childhood cat, pleasant and rhythmic. Her eyes remind Emma of a feline, large for her face with tints of amber; finally, she slips into a trance-induced sleep.

A buzz buzz buzz noise comes quickly as her mobile rings, vibrating forcefully in her pocket, wanting to be heard. A shard of light briefly reflects from street lighting outside, intense, hurting her eyes and bringing her bleary vision back into focus. Dazed in a half-conscious state, between sleep and waking, yawning she sees the dark lady's pupils constricted showing specks of anger.

"Excuse me, I need to get this."

Emma grabs her belongings and is relieved to see her daughter's name flash up on the phone screen. She exits the compartment, clumsily moving her limbs as blood-flow returns and she opens a window to get a cold blast of air.

"Hello, darling, I wasn't expecting…"

The conversation is left unfinished.

"I have…" Ava struggles to speak. "…split up with Charlie."

Emma reassures her beautiful, caring daughter, reflective as she listens to her suffering. Pushing the events that have just happened to the back of her pensive mind, she focuses on what's important.

"I'll be home in fifty minutes. Love you."

She is glad now that she had decided to commute to London and not sleep over, as was first planned.

The monk's words ring in her ears. Although she is chasing a good story, she is not so sure about it, as it seems to be dragging her family life into it.

On arrival, Ava anxiously greets her mother at the front door, falling tearfully into her arms. Her confident, witty daughter is wrapped in a blanket of sorrow, wandering aimlessly around the house. Wearing her pyjamas not bothering to dress, glossy hair tied on top of her head in an untidy knot, not a trace of her usually well-groomed exterior.

Crazed with anger and grief, new to love, immersed in hate, sinking fast, her emotions are a jumbled mess, Emma finds this revelation scary.

Choden Lamas has retreated to the hotel garden, empty this early in March. It's been a memorable day. He sinks into the soft green carpet below his feet, abloom with yellow and blue flowers. Heads start to close as the sun retires for the day. Tickling his feet as he proceeds through this magnificent walled garden there are fantastic shows of daffodils and bluebells at this time of year. Looking deeper, the colours have many different shades and tones, bluebells display violet, blue and indigo. A wise oak tree sits at the far end of the garden retaining many secrets, masculine and strong in stature. Surrounded at the base by tiny snowdrops. This cold-loving plant enjoys the nip returning to the air. Appreciating this seclusion, the monk detaches himself from the here and now. Choden Lomas' tiny piece of heaven, in this over populated city, is to block out the traffic noise and watch the last of day's sun low in the sky as it bids goodnight. Practical as ever, Choden Lamas is tightly wrapped in a fleecy blanket, around his slender body. The cold, damp weather is no deterrent. His silent follower is a permanent fixture by his side, large in stature, stout rotund middle, feet planted firmly on the ground, reminding Choden Lamas of his beloved tree. Finding an overgrown spot at the very back of the garden, he enjoys the seclusion. He rests his exhausted body against the familiar oak tree, pure pleasure in the sensation as he sits cross-legged, absorbed in nature. A rich earthy smell fills his nostrils, seasonal fragrant blooms a feast to his grateful eyes. Filling his lungs to capacity, ready to burst with delicious fresh air in its purest state, revitalising his mind and body. During separation of his mind and body, he chants softly, relishing the freedom of detachment. His aura is vivacious, lively, spirited and drenched in colour, changing as his meditative state reaches a crucial point between two planes. Filled with a feeling of calmness and total joy, surreal. An intense bright light radiates through his aura and his physical body. Electrifying, painful to the human eye. Disassociating his mind from his body, he feels the conversation, rather than hearing it, between himself and the Supreme Being.

"WE have a mountain to climb."

"I'm not sure about the priest."

"Move one stone at a time until you have moved the mountain. You will teach him, he will learn."

"I will try."

"You will succeed, you are all parts of the Supreme Being each and every one of you, Touch his soul, enrich it. Many followers are relinquishing their free will to the evil one, with catastrophic effects, displacing them from their rightful paths."

Feeling a tugging sensation surrounded as he is by love and adornment. Choden Lamas observes his physical form as he renters it, always a strange sensation. Time has distorted as only seconds have passed.

Separated by half a mile, the monk and the priest ponder their new alliance both experience the same feelings and doubts, aware it is better to have tried and failed than to not have tried at all. A bond is forming, binding these two men together. Father Jimmy is now aware that a celestial force has woven their paths together, uniting their powers and making them so much stronger combined, using both belief systems, blending races and cultures together. But fear is an old adversary of Father Jimmy's, buried deep inside his head. He seeks reassurance during prayers to avoid his courage from unravelling.

"I shall perform miracles in proportion to your surrender,
Bring me to your belief,
Then I shall grant the requests of the faithful,

Sowing treasure troves of graces,
When you are in your deepest poverty."

He's not sure why this came to mind. Frantically feeding his familiar wooden rosary beads through his fingers, he finds this connection comforting. It brings to mind miracles that happen every day.

The sun rises on the horizon, rain falls from the sky, crops grow producing food, animals feed from the crops, we feed on the animals, all cogs in the bigger wheel.

Mind power, belief in oneself, we all have the power within, insight into our inner characters revealing the truth. Once you truly believe in yourself anything is possible, then you will have the strength to believe in others. Replacing his worn rosary back in his pocket, a greater understanding rests within Father Jimmy, a familiar half grin returning to his face.

Paul is feeling out of his depth while Peter is shining like a star, enjoying the here and now, leaving the past behind. The broken, flawed, incomplete Peter is not hiding anymore; his faults are there for all to see. Once he accepts himself, then so will others. Greeting each new day, as it arrives, like a new friend. Brimming with excitement and anticipation at what it may bring, reborn is the word that springs to mind. Meditation washes away anger, anxiety and any other insecurities, especially fear. Paul has heard Father Jimmy talk about Peter, referring to him as his rock. But what about Paul? *Let another man praise thee and not thine own mouth*, springs to mind. Jealousy, a subtle beast, visits us all.

Does he fit into the equation? Self-doubt and fear, old enemies of Paul's, worming their way back into his thoughts. Finally he realises that our biggest hurdle is often oneself. Paul needs to take control of the direction in his life; understanding, he must take the first steps to redress the balance with his mother. Desperate to mend that severed bond, he feels the pull of the umbilical cord running between mother and child, giving him life, Joining these two souls together forever, the most precious gift we have. No physical pain is as severe as a broken heart. Finally grasping that for his own personal development, he must control his actions and muster up the courage to visit his past demons. Until then, Paul can't move forward –he is stuck in the dark dim past, like many buried in self-doubt. Grasping uncertainty he is ready to lay the past to rest. An understanding comes over him; now, this time, he accepts what he must do.

Father Jimmy waits patiently, conscious of Paul's plight, seeing his angel supporting him and of late, sometimes carrying him, whilst he is buried in his work. Sorrow, which has been concealed, reflects on his angel's face, an indication that an inner battle is being fought. No hiding places for your emotions with these celestial beings.

Paul assembles his thoughts and summons his mind and spirit, enabling him to face his inner dilemma, choosing how he will handle the beast that resides within him.

Calmly Father Jimmy waits, anticipating Paul's difficulties, trusting his own intuition. Knowing he needs to re-join his path previously travelled, visit his old life build a few bridges, learn to forgive himself, the way he readily forgives others. Paul is one of life's fixers, a practical, caring man whose intentions are genuine, giving his time freely to help others but not himself.

He is held in high esteem, admired for his qualities, especially of the instinctive nature. Beloved friend to Father Jimmy, an essential cog in life's big wheel, like many of them.

Moll exits the little shrine in the heart of Liverpool city centre. A friendly community finishing lunch time prayers. Predominantly older members of the congregation, rushing against the harsh rain.

Ladies wearing their best coats, a flurry of colour on this otherwise grey day. A petite lady battles with her umbrella, a duel against the wind, drenched, she tries to regain control, stopping her umbrella from turning inside out. Mumbling from passers-by complaining about the heavy persistent rain, long mournful expressions on their faces. Moll's heart is singing, she feels like dancing in the rain, filled with delight as raindrops refresh her face. Trickling through her hair, tasting the droplets running across her lips. Brimming with life, full of vitality, she feels complete.

While praying at the lunch time service for her prodigal son's return, she felt a real connection to him. Like he was sitting next to her, that unique bond between mother and son. His wayward life behind him, having sunk as low as he can go. The sensation of rebirth and new beginnings, convinced her prayers have been answered. Travelling every day to the shrine is her pact to God. Not missing one single day her promise fulfilled. Even when she was ill, dragging herself to the shrine, truly believing, lost now in pleasant thought.

Moll jumps as a car horn honks loudly, admiring the black sports car, her youngest son, Daniel, sits in his suit visible behind the wheel, a good lad. A feeling of warmth fills her body; he always brings a smile to her face when she sees him. He is wise beyond his years.

"Mum, get in; it's pouring down."

Laughing, a gaiety about her he hasn't seen in decades, she looks younger than her years. Throwing his car door wide open, she clambers to get into the low seat.

"What you doing over here?" she asks.

"They haven't blocked up the tunnel yet Mum."

A joke shared between the Liverpudlians and the Wirral, Separated by water, accessible through the, Mersey Tunnel.

"Thought I would catch you here. Fancy some lunch?"

"What about work?" Moll frets.

"Even surveyors get a lunch hour," Daniel jokes.

Her youngest son, the apple of her eye, is educating himself. Working two part-time jobs and studying at the same time, he has built a new life for himself. Wanting to move away from the poverty and deprivation of the inner city life, he lives on the Wirral. Separated only by the River Mersey, leaving behind the trauma of his adolescence, brought on by his eldest brother and his life choices. Even now, Daniel struggles to use Pauls name. Living in Caldy, a moneyed area on the Wirral, surrounded by greenery and wonderful open space, Daniel and his partner share a pleasant life. They are two male professionals, accepted by their community.

Famished, mother and son enter the fish and chip bar with tables. The pungent smell of vinegar soaking the chips, and cod wrapped in golden batter, sends his salivary glands into overdrive. This is her favourite place. Just through the tunnel in New Brighton, perched in the window seats, mesmerised by the courageous sea, not unlike her life, lapping and crashing against the sea wall. Escapism for a limited amount of time, from the routine of daily life. Cod, chips and a splodge of mushy peas, the fish that big its tails hangs off her plate. Memories of a birthday celebration when Daniel was younger, she always found the money to treat them. Travelling on the train, jumping out at New Brighton station, three excitable boys filled with mischief playing on the dips, a local beauty spot in New Brighton, running wild and free, collecting shells on the beach, visiting *The Black Pearl*, a shipwreck made from driftwood, treasured by the locals, giving children's imagination the opportunity to run wild. By the time they reached the cafe, they were ravenous. They ate out; it was the cheaper option. Fish and chips wrapped in newspaper. Sharing the food, huddled together on a park bench, life was simple then. An ache in his throat as he pushes these memories aside. The smell of the fish and chips too much for their tummies to bear, waiting impatiently for their arrival, as their mouths water.

Daniel, the quiet one of the three, always sat in the middle of his brothers, persistent memories of Paul, the eldest, his childhood hero, stepping up when his father vanished one night, walking him to school, his protector against the street bullies who sensed something different about Daniel and were always waiting to pounce. A sudden emotional pain rears its ugly head again. He swallows hard to quell his tears, having buried these feelings in the past.

"How's James?" Molly enquires, her son's happiness more important than narrow-minded homophobic individuals. Flashbacks taunt Moll: one son is a drug dealer whilst the other is a nancy-boy. She quickly erases these thoughts and wipes the pain from her face.

"We're fine, Mum, it's you I'm worried about. I've talked to James about building a separate annex for you."

Molly tries to protest. Daniel raises his hand to silence her, continuing, "I know you like your privacy and we're out till late with work. You would have the run of the whole place through the day and when you've had enough, the annex is there. James adores you, thinks the world of you, we both want to look after you."

"You know I can't leave, he won't know where to find me."

Anger crosses Daniel's face briefly. He tries to cover it –too late, she has seen it.

"After everything he put us through, the sacrifices you made, drug dealers knocking on the door. Threatening to stamp on your head if you didn't pay his debt, the terror of travelling home on the bus from school, easy prey." Daniel recalls his adolescence vividly.

"Don't let anger in, darling. It's like a poison travelling round your bloodstream. Forgiveness is where the power lies and we didn't pay up, thus removing their control."

Moll takes her son's hand in hers, gentle to her touch; small dainty hands. A hardness to her skin from years of doing other peoples' cleaning. That smile of hers melts his heart he's so proud of this woman. Courageous is too small a word. Kindness is always visible on her face. He hates dropping her off in the street he spent his childhood in. Rows of tall imposing terraced houses crammed together. Next door's argument is filtering through the paper-thin walls. Square backyard with an entry running along the back, dogs barking in the street, drunks staggering home.

Her house the most posh on the row now, having updated it for her, giving Moll some comfort in her later life. Daniel has an ominous feeling as he witnesses a new generation of dealers, exchanging packages on their pushbikes, hard looking youngsters. Bringing back that unmistakeable feeling of foreboding and dread. Closing his car window, he screeches away shutting out the distinct odour of his childhood days. His shiny new car driven by the same shy, damaged little boy.

Inside number thirteen St Anne's Square, Molly sits, sinking into her soft, comfy armchair. Another gift from Daniel, it hugs her tiny body. Enjoying a full stomach and a feeling of contentment, she admires her crystal vase sitting proudly in the bay window. The crystal reflects light; perched on a nest of tables filled with freesias, her favourites, it fills the room with a fragrant bouquet. They arrive every week from a stall on the market; they are a gift from Matthew, her middle son. Knowing that the stallholder has them imported out of season, Moll worries about the cost. Using flowers rather than words to show his mother how much he loves her. Matthew the comedian, always making them laugh, his chosen career the police force. A talented sportsman at school but Paul's life choices affected Matthew greatly, changing his direction, wanting to make a difference. With his good, first-hand knowledge on how drug dealers operate, he rises quickly in the police force, the drugs squad his chosen career path. Trying to stop some of the misery and pain that drugs bring. Good local intelligence and informants help to bring down the big guys, the Porter brothers, his nemesis. They have eluded him so far; he has a score to settle with them. Inviting his big brother in when he was a youngster. Offering him friendship then crucifying him when he lost the drug package to the police during his first arrest. Encouraging him to use the gateway drug to draw him in, before long he was totally drugs dependent. Their greed meant more to them than peoples' lives. Powerless watching silently from the side-lines, Matthew knew what he must do. Moll is filled with pride when she thinks about her middle son, happily married, first a grandson, followed a couple of years later with a beautiful granddaughter, Moll counts her blessings. Matthew surprising them all, her courageous comedian.

Snuggling in front of the open fire tucking her feet under her, in the over-sized armchair, smiling to herself. Molly takes a piece of paper and rests it on a magazine upon her knee. She begins to write, with soft flowing movement to her pen. Having put this off for too long, the words gush:

Dear Paul,

I feel like chunks have been ripped from my heart, pain so severe, crushing me. You are oblivious to the impact your actions have had on me and your brothers. We felt battered and bruised emotionally as we tried to understand your behaviour. My tears flow freely in private, hiding my pain and anguish as I watch this terrible drug eat you up. Stealing your beautiful personality and smile, leaving you filled with anger and rage, no thought for yourself or your family.

In public I try to hide my emotions, laughing at jokes that I haven't listened to. Taking my cue from others' behaviour, I feel totally drained. My firstborn child, whom I truly love, you are part of me; I hated seeing you act this way. Seeing my heritage disappear as evil grabs hold of you. Replaced with an unknown individual who is selfish and uncaring. I have battle scars from life that I can deal with, but nothing and no one can hurt me like you. My precious son.

Not wishing you any harm, I break this destructive cycle, empowered in prayer, belief in my miracle and today it was answered. I felt a burden lifted from my shoulders, my agonising constant pain replaced by an inner peace, that I haven't felt for decades. Sensing you today, for the first time in years, by my side as I prayed. Forgiveness is our key, easy to say, harder to do. Releasing us both from this evil trap.

I forgive you son, as I know great things can be achieved when you truly forgive.

Sending you blessings.

Love you always.

Mum x

Discarding all these painful memories, Moll screws up the letter in her tiny little overworked hand before she tosses it onto the fire, symbolising letting go. She watches as the flame quickly devours the paper. Changing from reds and oranges, to a black, charred mess, before disintegrating. Removing every last trace of hatred and pain from her heart. Replacing it with a feeling of release and victory. She has healed her own heart; now she must heal Paul's to set them all free. Filled with renewed strength, Moll ponders on her eventful day.

It was a pleasant surprise, seeing Daniel; what started off as a cold, wet miserable day has turned out to be delightful. She looks at the mantelpiece, the battery operated candle flickers in front of the boys' picture. Changing the candle for a real one. Not liking to burn real candles when she's out, for safety reasons. Striking the match, she watches the flame dance. Transferring the flame to the candle, watching it flicker amber and gold aglow. A flame permanently burns next to her treasured photograph, a message to Paul. His light to guide him home, to let him know he has never been forgotten. She keeps it burning in anticipation of his safe return.

Chapter 7

There are tantrums in the Lane household as Ava stomps from room to room, doors slamming in her wake. Like an injured animal unable to communicate its feelings, she lashes out at her nearest and dearest, pure rage on that china doll-like face. Ava not grasping that things happen in their own time for a reason. She feels powerless to control this potent love that arrived too early. No one understands her; every minute of every day is flooded with desperate emotions. Emma is glad another female's not involved, this girl's like a volcano ready to erupt at any moment. Two days ago, Emma would have weathered the storm, been over the moon. Now replaying the images in her mind that the monk displayed, finding them terrifying. She gazes at her husband packing Ava's lunch box. He still makes her heart skip a beat, a physical education teacher specialising in diet and nutrition. Firm muscular body, turning round, he catches her staring at him.

"What?" he enquires, dimples showing through his angular, bearded face with those seductively mischievous hazel brown eyes. A grin emerges; he's still able to wrap her round his little finger. Both encouraging each other on their chosen paths, never suffocating, respecting the other's choices, mistakes are rectified before moving on. Life is good with love in it. Does she have the right to interfere with Ava's chosen path?

"Problem?" Dave says. He can read her like a book.

"We'll talk this evening I'm running late."

"The Unity seminar?" he asks.

"Yes."

She plants a kiss on his lips, tasting sweetness; strawberry jam, from the half-eaten piece of toast on the counter top beside him. She enjoys the ticklish experience of his facial hair, touching the smoothness of her own skin, before she dashes out the door.

Sitting on the train, the rhythmic motion helps Emma's thought process flow. An escape from the drama at home. A two hour commute gives her time to write up her notes. She will need to be on the 18:40 train home to get her into Liverpool just after nine pm. It's peak time so she has booked her return seat. Hoping not to bump into that woman from yesterday. She ponders the most important things in her life: her love for her husband and daughter. Her career is important to her, but she could live without it. Could she live without her daughter or husband? The answer to that question is no. Love is the only real thing in her life. Everything else is replaceable. Why then is she so convinced that Ava is too young for this relationship?

"Hello again!"

The dark lady slips herself into the seat next to Emma with feline mannerisms.

"Going to the seminar?"

Her heavy pungent perfume makes Emma sick and she notices a few imperfections to this woman's upon closer inspection. Older than Emma first thought, modelling expensive clothing, designer handbag and killer heels.

"I'm Adrianna."

She extends a well-manicured hand with pointy finger nails, painted red on the tips giving the illusion of being longer than they actually are, defiantly designer.

Limply Emma takes her hand, out of politeness It's very smooth to the touch, probably never done a day's work in her life. Instantly Emma feels naked, revealing all her inner thoughts; this woman is reading her. Remembering the monk yesterday, she removed her hand quickly, shoving it deep inside her coat pocket.

"That's an unusual name; it means dark one, doesn't it?"

"Touché." Adrianna replies, grinning to reveal brilliant white teeth. Emma wonders if any of this woman is the original article. Thankfully their station is in sight, springing to her feet Emma excuses herself, after hours of self-centred conversation. Hovering inside the train door, Emma hears it hiss as the pressure releases the door; she feels relief as she vacates the train, straight into the biting spring air, and disappears amongst the vast gathering of commuters. Unsure of this woman's intentions, Emma struggles to distinguish an accent. Pinpointing where Adrianna's s from is difficult. Twice now Adrianna has been on the London to Liverpool train. Coincidence or something sinister?

Taking five, Father Jimmy removes himself from the others. Seeking guidance before another puzzling day at the seminar. Sitting alone in his bedroom, absorbing the quiet as he lights a unity candle; a symbol of two becoming one, empowering and energising both religions as they merge. Letting go of worry and holding tightly onto their faith, shutting out the constant noise of the city traffic rattling by. He watches a small bird land on a tree, the branch bending under its weight. Descending gracefully, expanding its wingspan, floating to a halt, ruffling its feathers. He admires the beauty and simplicity of this cheeky little creature of God's design. Small and compact with a brave character shining through. Survival part of its everyday life just as he is part of something else's food chain.

Father Jimmy decides on direct prayer, a form of meditation, closing his eyes, he is carried away as blackness fills his space, alone with the one. Life melts away during this technique, temporarily he enjoys this heightened state of relaxation, breathing deeply, oxygenating every cell in his body. Calm comes over him as he seeks out his God. Father Jimmy visualises a steep incline, covered in grass. The country smells entice him, drawing him in, exerting himself he marches up the hill. Filling his lungs with cool, fresh air, he is greeted at the top by a rickety wooden bench that invites him to sit. Resting his body on the wooden structure, he looks out over a silent sea with wonder, while fresh salt air invades his nostrils. The sun is rising, setting the sky ablaze with colour, like an artist, frantically lashing colours randomly onto a bare canvas. Incredible untamed beauty unfolds. Contentment comes over him, He feels free. Sensing his presence, a vast powerful energy, he has the Lord's full attention. Talking to him, he explains that he's scared. The task ahead is immense. Frightened and alarmed, suddenly self-doubt rears its ugly head.

"I will only ask you to carry the load that you can manage."

A concise transmission.

"I don't want to let you down."

"James Francis, you are a work in progress. Do not confuse yourself with worry."

Father Jimmy feels reassured as if someone is hugging him. A child running into its mother's arms, when they have fallen and hurt themselves, receiving unconditional love.

"Surrender to my work, I have put the messengers on your path, you three are wise, help each other. Remember I am always here, No obstacle is bigger or stronger than I."

Opening his eyes, light floods back into his familiar surroundings just as the remarkable image disperses. Thankful for his cheap and cheerful abode, grateful he has a roof over his head. His feathered companion has flown, foraging for breakfast elsewhere. With renewed confidence, he is ready to tackle another eventful day and so he rejoins the others.

No incidents this morning, Father Jimmy and his two companions arrive safely at the seminar. On day two, a tatty board, advertising workshops with times and locations, is standing in the reception area. A willowy woman with fierce red hair briefly tamed in a neat bun on top of her head, is on hand to guide all to their relevant workshops. Father Jimmy's restless; having lost interest in the alternative therapies, he seeks out Choden Lamas.

This is the second day running he senses that he is being watched; not easy in body or mind, he uncomfortably feels that someone trying to penetrate his being and access his inner thoughts.

The dark lady stands behind him. She swiftly intercepts him.

"Adrianna, pleased to meet you."

She extends her slender hand. Politely, Father Jimmy accepts it, shaking it feebly. The positivity he felt this morning while in direct prayer is slipping away from him; defensively removing his hand quickly, he senses something evil hidden beneath this female illusion.

"Which workshop are you attending?" she enquires. Her pushy nature and large fake smile distract him from her deceptive eyes.

"I'm not sure yet."

Rather abrupt for Father Jimmy, but he's got other things on his mind and the female charm offensive isn't working on him. His vow of chastity is still very much intact. Excusing himself he makes to leave, proceeding briskly down the whitewashed corridor. Adrianna sticks close to him like glue; she is chatting nonsense, not one to be dismissed. Father Jimmy swerves into the gents' toilets, his legs shaking as he grips the hand basin tightly and stares at his reflection in the mirror over the washroom sink. Worry lines are now visible on his forehead.

He slips into a daydream, releasing him briefly from this madness, recalling his first encounter with his parish in Liverpool. Having moved from a parish on the Wirral. He arrives early for his first service, an introduction from the retiring Father Luke was planned. An elderly priest in his late seventies clinging onto the remainder of his dwindling flock. Easter Sunday has a particularly good turnout. Early bird, Father Jimmy perches himself on the church wall. Having taken a week off, to take stock of the direction his life was going. Looking a bit dishevelled, travelling up from Cornwall after a week camping. Embracing nature, time to declutter his mind before engaging on a new challenge, this failing church. He had meant to go to the rectory for a bath, quick shave and a change of clothes. Unfortunately Father Luke had been called to the bedside of a dying elderly parishioner. With no firm arrangements in place, he decides to help out at the Easter Sunday service. Get a real feel for the place and its people. One of the first parishioners to arrive is an elderly lady, bent double with arthritis, leaning heavenly on her wooden stick. Neat bun in her grey thinning hair. Knitted woollen cardigan, heavily pleated skirt covered in cat hairs, a slight odour of tom cat about her. She ignores the strange looks from the other parishioners. She greets him with a warm genuine smile, while carefully slipping a pound into the palm of his hand, gnarled painful fingers encasing his hand, showing real empathy.

"For a cup of tea, love," she whispers, depth in her faded blue eyes, no judgement, mistaking him as homeless. Another parishioner marches past them. A male about fifty, bald head, wearing his Sunday best suit, shoes squeak as he strides by. Hands shoved deep in his trouser pockets, an arrogant swagger about him, flicking a cigarette butt in their direction. He throws a look of distaste at Father Jimmy as he mutters, "Parasite," before continuing into the church, with his head held high.

Thought provoking Father Jimmy realises that the little old lady in homemade knitwear probably gave him her last pound. That's how the idea developed in his head, perched on the church wall, hand extended.

"Spare any change, guys?"

Only one other person donated, a young boy about nine retrieving a half-eaten Easter egg from his coat pocket, chocolate moustache a giveaway that he'd had a go at it earlier, his prized possession.

Slipping in the back way, Father Jimmy had a quick wash in the sink at the back of the parish centre. Appearing in the church as the collection plate was passed amongst the parishioners. Watching as the notes flowed, each trying to outdo the other. Father Jimmy walked over to the plate to add the old lady's pound. A look of amusement crosses her face, having worked out who he is. The guy in the suit almost wrestling the collection plate from him, decided to judge a book by its cover. Later, Father Jimmy discovered the guy in the suit was a local councillor. His first sermon was performed to a few red faces, with the exception of Miss Davies and Stevie Curtains. The only two parishioners prepared not to judge.

"I would like to introduce your new parish priest, Father James Francis."

Silence filled the space for what seemed like a life time, until the elderly lady pushed herself awkwardly to her feet. Standing, she began clapping until everyone joined in. This showed Father Jimmy the true Christians amongst his decreasing flock.

The restroom door slams against the insipid pinkish toilet wall, bringing Father Jimmy back from his thoughts. Hesitantly exiting the bathroom with a searching glance, he is greeted with an empty whitewashed corridor. Realising the closer he gets to God the more obstacles are put in his way. He is aware that evil discreetly watches as individuals are pushed to the edge of their comfort zone. Personal battles causing hope to wither. The evil strikes, feeding on the weakness of society. Latching on, spreading like an untamed ivy Eating away at the people who are killing themselves with substances or else with working long hours – two or three jobs – just to earn enough money to buy the latest gadget, only to be too exhausted to enjoy it. Family life suffering, no time to sit around the dinner table and chat, enjoying the little things in life, not understanding they are the foundations of family life. The art of conversation is disappearing rapidly. Direct communication is becoming a thing of the past as families sit, glued to the TV, IPad or mobile phone, together but sitting in silence. The only form of communication is technology and so the death of conversation begins. Convinced that their time here is endless, they ignore the unfound beauty of the outside world waiting to be explored in all its rugged charm. Walking and cycling are things of the past. Destroying forests that provide shelter and food for many different types of species, causing havoc for humanity. Father Jimmy fears that his role is going to require a mammoth task.

Peace descends, an uplifting rush overwhelms Father Jimmy, as he lingers in the corridor deep in private thought, background noise trails off before evaporating. Encased in a dreamy state, he slips between the realms of wakefulness and dreams. The hush between thoughts, his mind takes an extended pause. Accompanied by rhythmic essential breathing, his whole body enjoys the oxygen fix. Pacifying his physical body and slowing his racing mind, which are so closely linked. Background noise is stifled, then fades away. A choir of Angels is humming in their refreshing gentle angelic tone, the reassurance that he needs, and then fades out. A dim light appears out of the darkness, beckoning him in. Increasing in size and luminosity as his concentration heightens, breaking through the void, achieving oneness.

Choden Lamas senses his frustration; he uses guided spiritual techniques, meditating a mantra in his mind's eye before transporting it directly into Father Jimmy's receptive, open mind as he drifts back out of the gap.

"Leave your worries to me, complete surrender, produces your desires, resolving all difficulties, accept my care."

Receiving Choden Lamas' direction with eyelids firmly shut, Father Jimmy senses an eye in the centre of his forehead, perceiving what is really going on in front of him without using vision, an experience unlike anything he has known before, hypnotic and pleasant.

"Believe," the monk transmits.

Doubts persist, telepathically he intercepts these complex images, palms touching Choden Lamas' palms, fused together in that moment, partaking in each other's treasured gifts. An explosion of colour surrounds them, marking this magnificent event. People of all races and religions coming together to help one another.

"Release your worries, watch them flow away, trickling at first, then faster like the stream. Grab hold of your faith, grasp it tightly. Watch as we start a positive ripple effect, no kind gesture is too small, or goes unnoticed."

But like everything it must start somewhere. He, Choden Lamas and Peter are the keys.

"We must change the way people think; remove the negative and replace it with positive.

"Those who walk in the footsteps of the wise men, will themselves become wise.

Those who persist in following the footsteps of fools, will continue in foolish ways."

Enlightenment fills him during this astral projection. He is fully aware and reassured.

Interrupting, Peter approaches. Gently tapping Father Jimmy's arm, he gets a blast of the images. Parachuted in during this deep state of telepathy, he staggers backwards, concentration broken now. Disentangling the three, Father Jimmy sees Choden Lamas retreat to the back of the room. Less than a second has passed. Time distortion again. Peter's unexplainable behaviour has caught Adriana's watchful eye.

The meditation workshop clashes with Father Jimmy's, Spiritual Growth class. He has been working on this presentation for some time, trying to interest the majority. Delivering it to a society that is used to computer consoles, films with special effects, the twenty-first century a hard act to follow. Deciding to keep it simple, he reiterates two real events. His arrival at his parish, throwing a few jokes in while keeping his audiences attention.

A young man of about twenty-three has been pointed out to him, a bit of a heckler from the previous day. He is dishevelled-looking in his dirty wax jacket and crumpled clothing that has seen better days. Trainers the colour of which is hard to distinguish, with tatty ungroomed hair. Sitting opposite him in the semi-circle, breaking Father Jimmy in mid flow.

"You can't prove that God exists."

The mischievous look on his face reminding Father Jimmy of a school bully, petty and annoying. Disruptive in class with a disposition to tease or vex, craving any attention.

"You can't prove he doesn't."

Not quite sure where that came from, Father Jimmy hadn't intended on engaging with him, as it only adds fuel to the fire.

"What about all the bad in the world?" the young man adds, irritated by the way Father Jimmy is closing him down.

"What about all the good?" the priest replies.

The group begins sniggering, Peter sits to the side of Father Jimmy, like a guard dog protecting its master, clouded with anger. A disapproving look from Father Jimmy tells Peter to leave it.

"I have been homeless for two years now, no one offered to help me." Trying for the sympathy vote.

"Which parish are you from?"

Before the man can answer, Peter interrupts, "You're the only homeless guy I've seen with clean fingernails and those reading glasses poking out of your pocket look designer, you wouldn't last five minutes on the street."

Angrily the young man makes his exit, pushing his chair with such force it wobbles before falling over, ignoring the outburst Father Jimmy continues.

Hesitantly a woman in her thirties, raises her hand. "Why don't we come with a rewind button?"

The rest of the group are laughing.

"You make a very good point. Life's a journey, sometimes it's beautiful, and sometimes it's painful, but always worth the effort. Every single person has been put on their path for a reason, maybe to teach us something about ourselves. Unfortunately we have no control over someone else's free will.

"Even the bad people?" she asks.

"Especially the bad people; they too deliver lessons. Frequently, they put us onto the best part of our paths. Do not be afraid to walk alone sometimes, trust your instincts. When things become dark, choose to move into the light, remember what's really important. If you were in a house fire what would you save first. The new TV or the children. Cherish the things that are irreplaceable, tell your family you love them, enjoy the good times. Hold dear those special unique moments, build a reserve of positivity for when you need it. Close down the negative.

Negative people, talk negative conversations, producing a negative energy and mood. If things don't work out, don't be afraid to have another go."

"Do bad people treat everyone badly?" She's growing in confidence now,

"No, why? Because they know they won't get away with it," Father Jimmy replies.

A woman who suffers domestic violence at home behind closed doors, her shameful secret, hiding her inward tears, pushing the pain down, blaming herself. A productive member of her community, holding down a demanding job respected in the workplace. She has freedom of choice, to stay or go. Does her husband hit other women? His uncontrollable temper that he blames the violence on. Manageable it in his own workplace, controlled in most social settings, even on the street. Sometimes it is exasperated by drugs or alcohol. But mostly it is a form of control, exercising restraint over another person. Only abusing the people who let him. Never attacking strangers for fear of the consequences. Eventually, when the woman learns to love herself, she will look at her reflection, oozing with confidence, her curvy figure, a woman's gift, facial lines, portraying life's adventures, respect for herself and her achievements; then she will leave him. People only treat us as badly as we let them. Mistakes are a valuable lesson learnt. Let go and move forward, forgiveness is the key. Then you will find your freedom and regain your control; the power rests within your hands.

By keeping hold of your mistakes, subconsciously you are allowing someone else to influence you. Hatred is a heavy beast to carry."

Defensively the young woman comes back, "I would never forgive someone who beat me. I would take my revenge."

Too much emotion to her statement.

"Revenge only shows you still care."

She breaks eye contact not sure what to do. Innocent looking, wounded blue eyes, cast downwards, staring at the floor. Her clenched hands rest in her lap.

"Forgiveness helps people move forward, breaking the negative cycle that is so easy to pass on."

Slowly her telling eyes rise to meet his gaze.

Father Jimmy continues: "Not straight away, but over time, the wife grew in confidence, saw through the lies. She rebuilt her life from within. Reaching a point where she didn't care enough to hate him, released from her matrimonial chains, blossoming like a beautiful flower. Here only for a short bloom not prepared to waste it."

"And the husband?"

"Silence was more painful than any injury he had inflicted. Refusal to communicate or speak. A state of being forgotten, left behind, eating away at him, removing his mental power as she retook control. An impressive individual with a lot to give. Moving away from the negative influence leaving the past in the past. Concentrating on the here and now."

Peter is only half listening as he watches the young heckler talking to Adrianna at the back of the room.

Emma has been moving between the workshops, watching Father Jimmy with his two companions. Paul, a familiar face, known locally as an uncontroversial drugs worker. Having been clean from drugs for several years now. A hard looking man, shaven head, small piercing blue eyes, a bent nose, possibly broken over the years during street fights, wearing battle scars on his muscular body, he looks like he knows how to take care of himself. Producing a wonder drug containing herbs grown in Thailand. Some species unknown to the testing labs, ahead of his time. Not apologising for being right, ignoring his critics. It's the other companion that has taken Emma's breath away. She had heard on the grapevine that Paul had been working with the sullen homeless guy, Peter, if her memory serves her right. The dangerous looking guy, his transformation is radical. Physically he looks different. Clean, tidy, even healthy springs to mind, good looking chap now that dirty beanie hat has been removed. He has trimmed down his bushy beard, his complexion is bright and clear. But it's the emotional side that has surprised her the most. The anger has disintegrated, replaced with a warmth. A couple of the homeless community had told her he was ex forces. His mind struggling to come to terms with the horrors of war. Re living the terror in his comrades eyes. Unimaginable pain sustained from horrific injuries with minimal medical supplies screaming with agony as the pain overwhelmed their feeble bodies. While the nerve endings transmitted pain to the brain. The lucky ones, released from this life into another leaving behind their damaged bodies. The not so fortunate, maimed for life, trying to come to terms with their disfigurement. Peter joined the army to keep himself out of trouble, having been in care for most of his childhood, before that no one knows, Emma has a friend in the Children and Young People's department, of social services, she will try her later. Possibly get some background information.

Approaching Father Jimmy at the end of his workshop, she requests ten minutes of his time.

"I can give you five, Emma."

Having an agenda of his own, he wants to arrange a private meeting with Choden Lamas.

"I have a few questions about Peter," Emma asks while loitering in the corner.

"Direct them to him." He is short with his answer and brusque in his tone as he packs his things away haphazardly, throwing them into his bag. His back is to Emma and he is not giving her his full attention. "He's still in the recovery programme and I don't want him upset."

"I thought that was finished," Emma pries.

"Every day throws up new challenges, I expect Peter to continue to do well, but until he deals with the root cause…"Cross with himself, Father Jimmy says, "I've said too much."

"When will he be ready to deal with that?" Emma fishes.

"Only he knows the answer to that question." A hint of sarcasm to his tone.

"If there's nothing else… there's someone I need to see… Good."

Closing his briefcase and the conversation, before marching off, he leaves Emma still rooted to the spot.

Surrounded by old relics, Thursa sits in the rectory, feeling like one herself, surplus to requirement. Superking ciggy stuck to her bottom lip, with an ash long enough to fool a magician, curling up at one end as she inhales deeply, coughing and spluttering continually into a brilliant white hankie. Pondering on Father Mike, with his new ways of increasing productivity. Running the church like a business, not a vocation. Church full up, with his flash friends offering them cheap rates to use the parish centre for training and business. Cancelling the midday services to save on the fuel costs, his excuse, other commitments, locking the church doors through the day, cancelling church quiet time for parishioner's contemplation He is also worried about theft, not that there is anything of any monetary value to steal. Thursa fears he's trying to dissuade the undesirables in favour of his business contacts. Father Jimmy's congregation is built on trust and an open door policy. Numbers are already dwindling in this short period of time.

Father Jimmy and Peter have only been gone a few days and she misses them terribly. Like a griffin guarding the church gates, a mythical animal mixture of lion and eagle. The lion is considered king of the beasts, the eagle king of the birds, a powerful majestic creature. Its duty to protect treasures and priceless possessions. Thursa, self-appointed guardian to protect the church and its followers in Father Jimmy's absence. She was not keen on him in the early days, the little man with the big heart. Taking risks, thinking of others, never taking the bait when she deliberately wound him up. A patient, placid man, now part of her adoptive family.

His absence gives her the opportunity to do a bit of digging. She checks through the parish records. Finding two males born on Peter's birthday. Having spent most of his childhood in a Catholic children's' home. Deducing he must have been christened into the faith. The first child is William Gibson, the family known to her, Billy to his friends, lives with his older brother and mother. His father died when he was seven. Then she sees the name, Peter Walsh. The name is familiar but she can't recall why. Mother: Juliet Walsh, unmarried. Father: the space is blank. Searching in the recesses of her mind trying to withdraw the information, niggling as she knows it's buried in there somewhere. Finally, after much searching of the internet, she finds what she is looking for, in the archives of the *Liverpool Echo*.

Baby abandoned on church steps, wrapped in a blue blanket. Only possession, a knitted woollen mouse, discarded in a cardboard box. She had seen that bedraggled mouse in Peter's coat pocket when he first arrived. It caused quite a commotion when she tried to wash his coat. A self-fulfilling prophecy, left on the busy streets of Liverpool in a cardboard box. Lived as an adult on the streets of Liverpool often using a cardboard box for shelter. Scrolling further back, searching old news she finds an article titled, 'Woman raped after attending bogus job interview'. A young woman appeared in court today having been lured to a false job interview, Thursa continues scrolling down the article, retaining all the information, before finally reading, 'Respondent, Juliet Walsh was present as the defendant was sentenced'.

Thursa has a vague recollection of this. It shocked the tight-knit community, realising that Peter has been born out of such violence, a beautiful, perfect child, undamaged coming into the world. His courageous mother, facing her fears, not able to remove her anger. Doing the only thing she could. Gave him life, not terminating the foetus, as was suggested by her closest friend. Her shattered heart was incapable of loving him. Leaving her baby in a place of safety, the church, after skilfully hiding her pregnancy. she was shamed a second time when her parentage was uncovered.

Peter in turn, wanting to make something of himself. Joined the army, a fresh faced kid with no idea of what lay ahead of him. Desperately wanting to make his mother proud of him. Not expecting to see love in her eyes, but he would settle for not seeing hate. Having finished his stint in the army, the terrifying memories firmly lodged in his mind. Vile, painful flashbacks, humans killing each other. He decided to track down his mother, more shame for this woman with her identity being discovered after abandoning her child. Accessing his care records, discovering the full horror of his conception. The straw that broke the camel's back, he drifted into homelessness and drugs. Unable to contact this woman who gave him life. Thursa understands him better now, with an overwhelming desire to bring these two broken souls back together. Forgiveness from both sides, essential to set them free.

Chapter 8

Jubilantly Father Jimmy has a private meeting with Choden Lamas. Packing Paul off to Kirkdale, a working class district of Liverpool, boasting mainly Victorian housing, having undergone a great deal of regeneration since his childhood, with good rail and bus routes into the city centre. Time to make peace with his past and his mother. To heal old wounds and restore the balance of his life. Time to live in the present, spiritually Paul has grown. But to those who really know him privately, his pain is obvious, scars visible to see. The timing is right for him, his path awaits his arrival, delivering him to the doorstep of that cramped, overcrowded house he once called home, where love and affection overpowered hardship and poverty.

Arriving separately from Choden Lamas at his hotel, a necessary precaution, Peter accompanies Father Jimmy watchful for any danger, unaccustomed to the experience he encountered earlier at the seminar, leaving him confused and curious.

A strange-looking pair of companions, Peter is as big as Father Jimmy is small. Subconsciously both are guided into the hotel gardens. Still blue sky as the sun blinks behind the cirrus clouds, like curls of hair, suspended in the paleness of the blue wash. They shut out the twin tower blocks looming straight up, breaking the skyline like neglected concrete prisons. An oasis of tranquillity in the confines of the hotel, the walled garden shuts out the hustle and bustle of city life. Cleverly planted to drown out the mayhem outside, they watch nature come alive through its smells and sounds. His feet feel the grass, soft and springy, so pleasant to walk on. This spring garden giving his mind time to register this joyous everyday event that we all take for granted. Tree branches move back and forth whispering their arrival. The fragrance of spring flowers lingers in his nostrils, tickling his nose. Colourful flower heads, more vibrant than he has ever noticed before. His mind is open to engage with new dimensions. His body absorbs this inner peace and tranquillity which surrounds them. Restful pleasures encase his mortal body. Choden Lamas appears with an expression of delight upon his face, his faithful, silent follower by his side, using his mind's eye to transport his inner being around the garden for protection. Seeking out any dark entities that might be lurking. Disruptive to their personal growth. Flabbergasted, stopping him in his tracks, Father Jimmy admires Choden Lamas, dazzled by the brightness surrounding him, an eloquent superior figure encased in a simple saffron robe. Behind him a spirit that takes the form of an angel, a testimony to Father Jimmy and his religious beliefs, exquisite in every way. Far more powerful than anything Father Jimmy has ever encountered. All the excitement that he has felt through his lifetime there in an instant.

Beckoning the priest to sit under the large groaning oak tree which moves freely in the pleasant breeze, keeper of many secrets They shelter under its outstretched arms, smaller branches like knobbly fingers producing its flowers in spring (catkins).

The monk offers a silk cushion displaying the intense colours of a peacock for him to use, while Choden Lamas sits on the hardness of the cold spring ground. Peter and the faithful follower stand at some distance, keeping watch in their own individual ways. Father

Jimmy declines the cushion, handing it to his host in a genuine gesture.

"I serve as you serve; you are my guest," the monk says.

He displays great dignity, majestic in manner, advocate to the supreme being, telepathy again, softly delivered, sitting cross legged in the lotus position, Choden Lamas reaches out, entwining his little finger around Father Jimmy's. Gently introducing the priest to the supreme powers entrusted to him.

"Do not confuse yourself with worry, I am here to guide you."

It is a humbling experience, sitting opposite this unassuming man, meek in nature. This sacred place generates a positive energy flow from the monk.

Now his palm rests against Choden Lamas' palm. Still, clear silence fills the space as the birds quieten, trees cease to whisper as they enter another realm. Father Jimmy feels like a bird; elevated, soaring the vast open sky with its wing span fully expanded, gliding, viewing the world from a very different perspective. Freedom and weightlessness from his head to his toes as life's pressures disintegrate. Slow fluid movement in this serene state, complete abandonment as he ascends. Other birds join him on his maiden flight, big and small, all different. Some birds fly higher than others, but all are content, embracing their freedom. A magnificent rainbow has appeared; the temptation to fly through it is overwhelming. Recklessly skimming through the mass of vibrant colour, he sees an idealistic view of the world with lush green fields, a productive human race, helping one another with laughter and joy. He wants to stay in the moment. A breeze carries him through to the other side, to be met by a dark, grey, dismal world. People fighting and battling with one another's families, neighbours, communities and finally countries. Anger and resentment weigh heavily. There are odd specks of vibrant colour; a graceful flower pokes its head through the dark earth as it bathes in a speck of sunlight, only to be crushed carelessly under foot. Society listlessly going about their daily lives. Forgetting what is important as hostility replaces love, with money and possessions replacing families and community spirit. Using substances to get them through their gruelling days. Hatred and contempt as evil spreads like a virus, attacking the weak and lonely. Presenting himself as a friend but staying as an enemy, gradually attacking the brave with greed, jealousy, lust and our old favourite, revenge. Free will and desire used for all the wrong reasons. Desperation fills Father Jimmy, wanting to remove himself from these images. Then he see a chink of light, bright and strong, minor miracles performed when needed. Looking closer he sees more and more chinks of light appearing.

"Hope… We still have hope."

His familiar inner voice blinks and he's back in his body, exhausted. Mere seconds have passed.

With a delicate, smooth, clear voice Choden Lamas interprets what Father Jimmy has just experienced.

"We have each been given the most precious gift of all –life. Every one of us is different, special and unique in our own way, like the stars in the galaxy. We have a path to follow, finding our gifts, individual to each of us, our participation in the human race. We must learn to face our fears and ignore doubt as it blocks our dreams. Enjoy every aspect of life, fulfilling our potential, building a library of memories, surrender to real love, take a chance on life. Most importantly remove anger and replace it with forgiveness. Then we are free.

The two sides of the rainbow show firstly how the Supreme Being wants us to live. The dark side is how humanity is actually living. The shards of light are his foot soldiers helping people back onto their rightful paths. Technology can be a blessing and a curse;

people become engrossed in communicating from behind a screen as they live in their virtual world. They miss out on emotions, an important part of our lives. The art of conversation is slipping away, slowly. Darkness knows that the Supreme Being, promised us free will and is using that to distract us. Each religion needs to come together, to share lessons learnt. To encourage every visitor who crosses our path that they are significant in some way. We are here to learn from each other. Whether visitors join us for a lifetime, a day or just a moment. The beggar on the street, we see for a moment. Most people don't even make eye contact with him. Could we spare a smile, an acknowledgment of his existence as he carries on his life story which is unique to him? The Supreme Being comes amongst us, the poor man, the bullied child, the old lady wanting a few minutes of our time. Providing graces for those who help, repeating the lesson for those who don't. Suppressing darkness in its wake, you and I must proceed with caution."

Father Jimmy is unsure he is the right person for the job.

"Together we are extremely powerful, we have been brought together, our paths cross. I will walk alongside you until you are ready to walk it alone. Darkness will do all it can to break us. I am here to teach you and you in turn will teach others," Choden Lamas continues.

Paul, wandering down the familiar, cramped street, feels a suffocating sense of desolation. Not much has changed in decades for this rapidly built Victorian terraced housing, on a narrow cobbled street, with uniformed frontage hiding the squalid living conditions of the working classes in their small crowded narrow dwellings, fitting into the meagre space available. Every arrival noted by one of the neighbours from behind the curtains. Groups of young lads on expensive push bikes gather on the street corners, greeting customers with a handshake and a handoff. A brazen attitude as they deal drugs in broad daylight, in full view of the residents who are too scared to grass on them. Now a part of everyday life on this street. One of the pushers has a crowbar strapped to the frame of his bike. Two younger lads, about ten, are used as lookouts on opposite ends of the street, serving their apprenticeship as they begin their descent into drugs. Paul marches up the street, head held high with a confidence about him. A muscular figure with a shaven head, a snappy dresser who is watched by the pack on the corner. Maybe a new dealer on their patch, eager to control their territory? Eagle-eyed, they watch the intruder. Saddened by what he sees, now a normality on this street whilst nothing else has changed in decades. Paul stops outside number thirteen seeing the familiar wooden door, feeling apprehensive as his heart quickens and his palms sweat. There is a sickly feeling in the pit of his six-pack stomach, causing him to inhale deeply.

A new brass door knocker greets him as a grin rises on his face. Admiring the lion's head, he gently lets it drop and the noise rebounds inside the house to bounce off the interior walls. Reminiscing back to his childhood of a sparsely furnished dingy house. His mother stood there, admiring a lion's head door knocker in the second hand shop, on the corner of the Main Street. Wistfully smiling every time she passes, with her face pressed against the dirty shop window; she was a woman of few possessions. Something about the lion amused her but her finances prevented her from purchasing it; she never had any spare money. Desperately wanting to get it for her, one Mother's Day they set about achieving it. Making a lion's head knocker out of cardboard, cutting it out carefully, painstakingly colouring it in. Using sticky tape, they had stuck it to the front door, there was sheer delight in her loving eyes when she saw it. He is filled with warmth recalling these memories. Softly pushing the door as he enters, his feet sink into the plush deep carpet. He shakes his head at the door being unlocked. Walking directly into the sitting room, nicely furnished these days, a far cry from his childhood, cornflower blue, hois mum's favourite colour. Calling out to her, eyes drawn to the mantelpiece dominating the centre of the room, he sees the photograph, himself and two brothers as youngsters; next to it, a candle flickers. He's drowning in shame, a burning sensation in his eyes and throat, reflecting on the misery he caused her. This woman immersed in poverty, and he went and made it worse. Emotions locked away for decades in a vault and buried so deep inside him. Now released, they flood his being; staggering slightly, he grips the mantelpiece as raw unforgiving emotions attack. The front door flies open with a bang hitting a small nest of tables just inside, making him jump, a scruffy ten-year-old stands brandishing a crowbar.

"What yer doin' in Molly's?"

Real fury on his face, the scrawny looking street kid from the corner, short and puny with dark cropped hair, something in his dark eyes, mocking him, dirt smudged across his urchin face but wearing all the latest gear.

A noise from the back kitchen grabs their attention.

"What's all the commotion?"

Molly appears from the back yard, wet washing slung over her shoulder. Wearing a spotty pinny, its front pocket bulging with clothes pegs. Silence fills the void, instantly recognising her first born son. Her body shakes, legs tremble, as a smile as big as the Mersey Tunnel crosses her face, to be soaked in a downpour of happy tears.

"He's tryin' to rob yer, Molly."

Rushing forward, she embraces Paul, an invisible navel cord unbroken between mother and son, love all consuming, desperate for this moment, filling her entirety. She would happily leave the planet at this moment. Catching Daz's eye, the latch-key kid realising that her work here isn't done.

Finally, she gasps, "He's my son, Daz."

Contentment fills her.

"He ain't the poof or the copper?"

"I have three sons and I've told you about calling Daniel a poof."

Before she said Daniel's name, Paul knew who Daz was talking about. The signs where all there, a quiet sensitive lad, hiding something very personal, unsure of how his family would react. No need to worry on that score.

"Soz, Moll!" Daz shouts.

Before Paul can introduce himself the little guy and his crowbar disappears through the battered wooden door, crashing it as he exits. Paul gets it totally, this little guy could be him, thirty-odd years ago, never one to judge his mother. That's what makes this such a tragedy, he chose the wrong path, doubting that young Daz has a choice.

"What's his story?" he asks his mother, looking into her caring wet eyes. She still carries beauty, inside and out.

"You know, the usual, his mother's addicted to pills, speed mostly, just about able to still pull the wool over Social Service's eyes. Never any food in the house, practically feral he was. Thank God she only had the one. Anyway, enough about him; I want to hear all about you."

No blame or repercussions, no recompense expected.

"I knew you were coming." Moll says, excitement beaming, mixing with her infectious smile.

"Dare I ask, how did you know?"

"I have been praying for you, every day since you left, never giving up, then the other day in mass, I felt your presence alongside me, so strong. I knew you would be heading home."

"Why have you never moved? It's not safe here." There is pleading in Paul's voice.

"I had to make sure you would know where to find me, when you came looking."

"What if I never came?"

"You were always coming back, I just didn't know when."

"Mum."

This is the first time he has used that word in decades; it grips his heart like a vice and uncontrolled sobbing takes hold of him, the convulsive spasms making him catch his breath. Tiny little Moll reaches up, pushing herself onto her toes, and cradles her first born, wrapping her delicate arms tightly around his heaving body. Transferring years of love, he rests his head on her dainty shoulder, still a little damp from the washing. Her eyes are raised skyward as she silently mouths the words,

"Praise the Lord."

Thursa's set on her decision to track down Juliet Walsh, the biological mother of Peter, although she is not confident that it's such a good idea, revisiting a desperate depressing error of the woman's life, wrestling with self-doubt.

Getting her to agree to a reunion with her son will be difficult. Jools Brown, as she is now known, recently widowed, no trace of Juliet Walsh in her title anymore and maybe that's how she wants it. Having married when she was thirty something, to an older man, for security rather than love. Disposing of Juliet Walsh, the way she did her illegitimate son. That part of her life is too painful to deal with; she deletes that emotion, burying it so deep, never wanting to revisit those terrible events.

"Little miracles happen every day," Thursa mutters, reassuring herself.

The Catholic community in Liverpool is close-knit, ascertaining the facts about Jools should be relatively straightforward. Tracing Jools through the voluntary work she does at the local hospice, having worked there five years now since her late husband passed away. It would be easy to bring Jools and Peter together through volunteer work, let them get to know each other, see if they get on, even bond. When the time is right, reveal who they are. It's a gamble and could affect Thursa's relationship with Peter, but she must put him first. Confident now that this is the right path.

Returning to his small hotel as greyness fills the sky and the clouds struggle with droplets which are waiting to fall and replenish the dry yearning earth. A feeling of impending doom hangs over them.

Father Jimmy talks candidly to Peter, with complete openness. Explaining the path that they are on, warning him of the dangers that lies in wait, lurking under the shadows of darkness.

Each one of us made in God's own likeness, traits of the Supreme Being, male, female, black and white. Colour is a protection against the sun, never meant to be a barrier between societies. No distinction between religion, race, colour or gender. Finding our individual gifts, caring, giving, belief, healing, tuned in to our inner voice, listening and learning from one another, sharing gifts and ultimately blending.

"The choice is yours Peter, will you continue with me down this dangerous and difficult path?"

"I'm surprised you need to ask, faint of heart never won the day."

Enthusiasm fills his youthful tone as he enjoys feeling needed.

"Think long and hard Peter, this path will be treacherous, evil will not fold easily."

Sitting on the floor, cross-legged, his eyes meet Father Jimmy's gaze, this giant of a man gradually opens his heart, taking a gamble on trust.

"We don't get to choose how or when we come into this world, or leave it. Understanding why I was born, out of lust and hatred, a man raping a woman my parentage. Joining the army, to make something of myself, to no avail. I had one trusted friend on the streets, older than me. I looked up to him, hung on his every word. Believing him when he said crack was not addictive, media hype, foolish misguided trust. The first time I smoked the pipe with him, all my worries dispersed and in that moment I felt truly alive. No fear or self-doubt, I was invincible. Watching the rest of society scurrying around to exercise, work, shop and home, I felt superior for the first time in my life. It was a week before I smoked it again. Convinced he was right, by the fifth time I smoked the pipe; as soon as I had finished, I wanted it again. He had me hooked and I belonged to him. Quickly becoming one of the grey people, gaunt, with an ashen tinge to my complexion, dark sunken eyes, body not craving food, my mind living for my next high, but spending most of my day on a very low, low. No in betweens, doing whatever it took to get my next fix. A slave to the drug, scrabbling around on the carpet of his bedsit, trying to retrieve any crumbs of this powerful unforgiving drug. I got to the stage where I no longer cared. A night person venturing out after dark reverting to a wild state. Creeping amongst the streets, avoided by society, darkness was the best time to locate money.

Then you came into my life a bright shining light, hope entered my head, emotion stirred. Like coming out of a coma, I really saw things for the first time. I was drunk on life.

Then the detox, feeling this vile poison leaving my body, retching as I suffocating from this intoxicant. As each drop of poison left my body, enabling life to flow freely within me again, shaking, burning up, able just to bear my load. I was guided, I felt my angel support me.

In the short period we have known each other I have learnt more from you than anyone I have ever met. Unable to change my past, I have decided, it's more important what I do with my life from now on. It's my turn to give back."

Father Jimmy feels overwhelmed by this young man's progress. Looking at his angel, no longer supporting him. Evolving into a strong, independent brave warrior, indicating he is nearly ready. Squeezing his shoulder, affection in his warm smile, there is no need for words.

"When you were with the monk and I touched you, I saw deep colours surrounding both of you. Yet when I was detoxing I heard an angel's wings fluttering, why was that?"

"We see what we need to see at difficult times in our lives. Guides come in many different shapes and forms, relating to our belief systems, helping us through. It's like language, different countries speak different languages, even though they are saying the same thing."

Laughing Father Jimmy says, "I'm still learning myself, but what I do know is you have been chosen. I was told you are my Rock. Many will follow you, because you have walked in their shoes, experienced the drugs culture that clings onto the weak, devouring their free will, removing them from their rightful paths. Rippling into family lives, following many generations, infecting their blood lines.

Each one of us has a purpose. Losing sight of our individual gift can alter our chosen path, a working clock needs all its parts, from the smallest cog to the biggest. "

"And evil?" Peter asks.

"It's always with us, lurking in the shadows, a thick dense inky aura, sucking the breath away, until your lungs feel ready to burst. It latches onto human positive energy, needing a host body to seize, to devour free will. Present long after the original source has dissipated. Animals sense evil with their heightened senses. Interpreting our intentions long before we act on them. They smell our fear, with an ability to detect the presence of evil that can find our weaknesses, slipping through the cracks, fooling us that we still have control. A gentle courtship with evil, money, power, control and substances, infects and spreads through the feeble minded, only too ready to ingest. Subtle in its attack as we are distracted by the fast pace of life and the pressure to keep up, family time forgotten as the decay gradually sets in. Isolating the needy and the rebellious young, separating them from their pack whilst grooming their trusting souls. Complicating the simplest of tasks to remove enjoyment and pleasure."

This is all too familiar to Peter as he listens to Father Jimmy's poignant words, describing the decay of vulnerable members of society.

"I heard a story about a man whose wife had become very ill. He was devout and prayed every day, for her recovery. Evil sensed his weakness, slipping negative thoughts into his open, receptive mind. He stopped attending daily mass, angered by the injustice of her illness as his faith took a battering. Separated from his pack, he felt vulnerable and alone, having become an easy target.

The priest visited him at home. Reluctantly the man invited him in, clouded with anger as evil anticipating defeat. Both men sat either side of the open fire, no words were spoken. Belief struggled to make itself heard. Finally the priest leaned forward, picking up a pair of tongs, taking a piece of orangey-red coal from the centre of the roaring fire and carefully, placing the hot coal on the hearth. Quickly when separated from the fire, the reddy orange coal lost its colour, going out rapidly. The priest got up and left. He was showing the man the power of friendship. Without the fire, the coal went out quickly – with the fire, it burned brightly. The following day, the man returned to church. Evil has a way of separating us from those who care for us the most, leaving us feeling lost and alone. Without guides our inner fire goes out and we lose our way."

Peter and Father Jimmy sit quietly, recharging their energy as they release the stress and tension that has built up during the day.

Praying out loud, stronger in unity, their minds slowly fill with love and spontaneous inner joy. Their bodies become lighter as they visit a higher plane. Peter rests his eyes while visualising his angel guide, lifting him as he floats. Clearing his head of any worries lurking in the recesses of his mind, he believes that all is possible. A self-fulfilling prophecy as he accomplishes total relaxation.

"Ah, bliss," Peter sighs.

Father Jimmy continues with direct prayer, recalling a sacred image, sitting on his rickety wooden bench at the top of a grassy knoll, looking out over the expanse that is the sea, sensing the Supreme Being beside him, clearing his mind of fear and self-doubt. Unloading his worries, on his most trusted friend, without fear of repercussions, putting them into clear thoughts, no secrets in direct prayer, revealing himself totally, his soul bare. Feeling the sea breeze tickling his face, smelling the salt water, hearing the waves toss against the sea wall, careless and totally free. His thought process vivid, mind images are lively and animated. Absolving him of his responsibilities, albeit temporarily, relishing pleasure in the state of total enchantment.

Chapter 9

Returning home on the busy northbound train, Emma collapses in her seat, shaking her shoes from her painful feet and wriggling her toes, enjoying the freedom, as her shoes are rubbing slightly on her little toe. She feels the cool floor of the train beneath her feet. Slouching, alone at the back of the carriage, Emma flicks through her notes from the Unity Seminar, scribbling intensely in a small pad. Passionate about her work, she recalls the events of the day in minute detail. The faint cry of a child further forward on the train breaks through her isolated thoughts, making her think of her own daughter and concentration slips from her face. Unusually tired, this commute is taking it out of Emma. Stretching her limbs fully she is thinking of a hot bubble bath, her tired body submerged in the soapy hot water, candles dotted around the bath, lighting setting the mood, before slipping into comfy warm pyjamas and soft fluffy slippers. Going home is always a pleasant experience. Dave will be waiting up for her, she's got enough information on the seminar now and some great photographs, enabling her to complete her piece of work from home tomorrow, no need to travel back to London again. The commute adds an extra five hours onto her working day. She must be getting to old for this, her energy levels are zapped and thinking about Ava's tantrums aren't helping her stress levels.

Peter, now he's another story arousing her curiosity. A hardened drug user, filled with stubbornness and rebellion, living on the streets, feral like, reverting to a wild state, disrespecting all who come into contact with him. Sitting in the shadows, bound with his ongoing afflictions, mocking and scorning whoever crossed his path, he was a frightening figure. Turning his life around with the desire to follow, taking religious instruction, willing and obedient in a matter of months, removing him from the hands of his old enemies, with no known relapses, and his life prior to now witnessing untold horrors during his period in the army. Now that's a story she would rather write, getting her investigative juices flowing.

Chugging along through the countryside, the train heads for home, pitch blackness through the window as they fly through open countryside. Occasionally farmhouses with lights in windows dotted around the vast open spaces, twinkle like stars in the night sky. Then continuing through a small village, street lights visible, like fairy lights on a tree. Thankfully familiar surroundings appear, home is near. Rumbling along the track steadily, the brakes hiss as the train slows down to stop. Wearily Emma exits the train, greeted by a welcomed intake of fresh familiar northern air.

Nervously, his voice quivering, Father Jimmy relays the news to Thursa that Choden Lamas will be returning to Liverpool with them as their guest. As private time together has been limited with the seminar and avoiding dark forces. A humble man, Father Jimmy wants to keep a low profile, only to find himself hurled into the spotlight and onto a path of teaching and enlightenment. Conscious of the wrath of his housekeeper and her sharpened tongue, there are surprisingly no grumbles from Thursa. Having endured isolation and loneliness in their absence, she secretly missed them all.

"One more mouth to feed, won't stretch me," she informs him.

The Spirit Of Truth, is a specialist centre that Choden Lamas and Father Jimmy hold close to their hearts, promoting health and well-being to the hardest to engage members of society. Tackling addictions head on, with people of all generations, with diverse faiths and cultural backgrounds, including those with no faith at all, advocating positivity and guidance. Combining leadership and counselling, they encourage community spirit, with an army of volunteers. Protecting the vulnerable in their daily battle against the greed of the drugs cartels draining every last ounce of respect, from these misguided individuals. Teaching them to make their own informed choices, not being led with the promise of a quick fix. An ambitious dream but definitely a do-able one.

The secret of an area like Liverpool is, although poverty is rife in some of the surrounding areas the community spirit is huge. Encouraging residents of drug flooded areas to speak out against, local dealers, pushers, drop houses thus protect their young that work for these individuals, from a very young age. Preventing the descent into the drugs world, because of no alternative means of supporting themselves and family members. Kids who should be in school the most likely targets of the drug lords, ripe for the picking. A huge task for Father Jimmy but a rewarding one, stamping out rebellion and defiance of the young, untamed spirit.

Thursa has missed their companionship while these men have been in London, Choden Lamas is only one more moth to feed and she'll be glad to see the back of Father Mike and his skulduggery. With his secret meetings with the Bishop, suddenly stopping their conversation when Thursae enters the room, which makes her feel uncomfortable in her own home.

"Cheek of the man," she mutters to herself,

Only just into his thirties, grin and dazzling white teeth on show all the time. Being a tall gangly figure, over six foot. Nodding her head in agreement at her recall, slim build, with suntanned skin all year round, not sure if he's mixed race or conceited enough to use some sort of tanning product, always grinning at his own reflection as he passes a mirror, vain and arrogant, what a combination, she shakes her head now. With a faint odour of liquor, permanently carrying a packet of strong mints in his pocket. Nothing gets past this elderly housekeeper. Thursa is relieved to be getting back to normal, meeting the monk, having read up on his lifestyle and beliefs. She likes the simplicity of his chosen path, nature and natural remedies, mind power and self-belief. Intrigued, Thursa is interested in life again, slowly mellowing, embracing the seasons of life in all their glory. The precious, priceless gifts given to us all. Soft spring breeze waft past as plant life awakens, bouncing back after hibernating over winter, forcing new growth through the dark hardened earth. A spring surge, a sign of new beginnings, bringing with it renewed hope, reminding her of the carefree ways of children. Warm enchanting sunshine of high summer penetrating her face, feeding her bones with vitamin D, lifting everyone's mood, like the carelessness of youth. Then autumnal tint, colours that follow, a natural phenomenon decorating the leaves shades of russet red, yellow, purple and brown. A season in our lives when everything is starting to fall into place, truly understanding. Finally the sharpness of winter, the stage of her life she is now entering, as snowflakes magically fall, with its brilliant white dazzling blanket of snow. Brightening the darkest of corners. Bringing a pure radiant light and renewed hope, resembling wisdom of the older population, with life's experiences stored in their memories, patient enough to have worked out what life is all about. Seasons similar to the cycle of life.

The pressures of daily living, all of our own making, needing, wanting, putting that pressure on ourselves, when what we really need is all there, free and waiting to be explored.

Adrianna returns to her cult, The Fountain of Youth, re-joining her group of social deviants, departing from the norm. So desperate to be different, engaging in unorthodox beliefs and practices, with restrictions far greater than any mainstream organisation. This band of nonconformists, slowly and gradually release their free will.

A plain child, Adrianna, aware of the sniggers from her peers, stick thin with lank colourless hair, a distinct kink residing in it, with small eyes, the right having a slight turn, encased behind thick glasses, hoping to repair a lazy muscle behind her eye. A prominent nose with a slight bump in the middle and large protruding front teeth.

The youngest member of the family, surrounded by women growing up, she watches the art of seduction and lies, as her siblings transformed themselves. Observing her female relatives painstakingly applying cosmetics to make the best of a bad job. Manipulating and moulding their male companions with contrived emotions, using a calm and rational manner, working on their charismatic nature, the end result an elaborate plot. Relinquishing the unsuspecting males of their hard-earned cash. Men like nothing more than a confident, powerful woman.

Adrianna was always a skinny child, fading into the background, ignored and overlooked. Developing her own skills of deceit over the years, lying becoming a natural flair, a master at misleading. A natural born leader with an aptitude for human nature, well versed in the power of suggestion to the lost, gullible souls looking for direction. Starting a social group, with appealing beliefs, Adrianna surrounded herself with male companions. Bamboozling the vulnerable into devotees, using auto-suggestion, with threats of curses, manipulating situations, from anyone foolhardy enough to leave. Hers was a narcissistic personality in the pursuit of her personal gain and fulfilment.

Adrianna introduces nightmares, filtering the subconscious of the weak, experiencing horrific images, thoughts and feelings. Introducing the power of suggestion, another form of control to keep her sect intact. The entrepreneur in her starts a new religion; The Fountain of Youth. Extracting money from her followers as they hand over their tithe. Working hard on her charismatic characteristics, transforming the once plain exterior into someone unrecognisable, landing a tenth of each individual's income. Set apart as an offering to the gods for work or his mercy. Putting the finances into property yielding a substantial turnover. Brainwashing the men while playing on the women's vanity.

With money comes power and ultimately control. In her search for eternal youth, she lets evil cross her path. In exchange for her constant bloom she, in turn must bring innocent souls to the evil one. Addicted to money and power Adrianna continues to push the boundaries. Having benefited from the short term gains from evil, still true happiness eludes her, always just out of her reach, she is never satisfied. Looking in her large oval mirror at her purchased beauty, the cracks have started to reappear. Envious of the reporter on the train with her natural soft beauty, inside radiating out, with her luminous smile oozing happiness and contentment.

Real beauty, being what others perceive, starts on the inside, transmitting out. Realising that money can't buy that, or true love, happiness, health or inner peace. Something that always eluded her. Feeling her powers weaken as the monk and the priest joined forces. Experiencing desperation for the first time in her life, penetrating her defences unable to infiltrate enemy lines. Smiling sweetly at her reflection, a confident manipulator, she chooses a face to suit her mood. Stifling her inner anger as she prepares her attack starting with the monk, while he is most vulnerable during deep meditation and then his followers. A wicked grin crosses her face.

Arriving home discretely enjoying the place he now calls home, strolling past St Michaels parish church, named after the archangel of battle and defender of heaven, the first thing Father Jimmy notices is that the church doors are firmly closed. He feels this as a very personal attack. Stamping up the familiar rugged path, the large wooden doors are uninviting and can be interpreted as 'Keep Out, Not Welcome'. As he gets nearer frustration covers his face, a dryness in his mouth, he swallows deeply as anger floods his body. Hush fills the surrounding area, he hears his fierce heart pounding. The sun is in hiding again as a light spring breeze drifts from the north, wrapping itself around him. The large oak trees groan an unsure greeting, while the external branches wave a welcome gesture. A yellow rose just starting to bud, its colour only partially visible; an early bloom for this time of year, a sign of friendship. Incensed by the work that went into building this dwindling flock, riled, he reaches deep into his cassock pocket to snatch the church keys and thrust them into the worn lock, the temporary custodian of this sacred building. Throwing the doors wide open and hearing them crash against the sandstone walls, he is greeted by that familiar smell of candle wax and furniture polish. Stepping onto a simple coconut mat reading the word 'Welcome', his temper gently subsides as he enters this peaceful, calming place. The last of the evening sunlight peeps past the dense cloud, breaking through the ornate stained glass windows, shards of sunlight bounce around the altar, inviting him in, as harmony slowly returns between him and his maker.

Standing at the altar, he asks, "Why?"

Anger still audible in his voice but gradually decreasing, he is hurt at this very personal attack on his precious work. Feeling another presence he turns swiftly to see Choden Lamas moving majestically towards him, smiling as he feels the richness that permeates these surroundings, an oasis amongst these claustrophobic streets.

"We are all going to be tested in the future, we must take control. Small actions can have profound consequences on our lives and the lives of others. "

The monk gestures with his hands, throwing them wide open, with a sweeping motion.

"This is a beautiful tranquil place, I can see why you like to pray here, it feels good."

Smiling, that infectious smile, Father Jimmy joins him.

"Your flock will be back, before nightfall."

Confident about his statement, entering this environment, embracing change, here to learn from one another. Growing spiritually with the other's experience, appeasing the mood.

"You have brought education, with that comes knowledge and opportunity, to deal with whatever life throws at your flock. Empowering the disadvantaged."

Standing in the doorway, Choden Lamas' faithful follower calmly waits, statue-like, having taken a vow of silence so as not to get distracted while guarding his spiritual teacher. An imposing figure, he fills the church doorway, blocking out some of the fading evening light.

Rob Martin, one of Father Jimmy's flock returns as he is leaving the church, falling in step alongside him.

Talking so quickly he can't get out the words. "Clare sends me a little robin every morning since she passed over. The first morning I was buried in my grief, suffocating in it, I felt I was going mad, I couldn't eat or sleep, roaming around the house. The cheeky little bugger tapped on the window with its beak. At first I ignored it but the persistent little thing did it again. Then I remembered Clare saying she would send me a message. Remember when we were in the hospital?" Looking at Father Jimmy for confirmation, enthusiasm in his eyes, he continues, "It was a crisp day, I walked in the garden wearing only my pyjamas and found it sitting there, waiting for me. I felt no cold, only surrounded by love, real paternal love." His eyes are gleaming as he recalls every minor detail of the event. "Happiness filled me. It comes every morning, greedy little thing eats everything I put out."

Full of hope, Rob is encased in his orange aura, the colour associated with good-hearted, kind and honest individuals, who are very in tune to the emotions of others and can sense and feel their pain and joy. Orange aura people can be very charming, but part of their charm is in their sensitivity to others. Having the ability to make everyone feel at ease in their company.

Choden Lamas discreetly observes that Father Jimmy really is a shepherd to his flock.

Turning quickly to see Rob Martin pacing along, looking fit to burst, excitement covering his tired face.

"Happiness filled me. It comes every morning, greedy little thing eating everything I give it."

Amused, Choden Lamas, wanders outside to give them some privacy, watching as the curtain twitchers have observed Father Jimmy's arrival, presumably picking up their telephones to contact one another. They spread the news of his arrival, quicker than a set of talking drums used by some cultures who reside deep in the forests, as a form of long distance communications. As this grieving father brings his tale to an end, the flock are flooding through the church gates, his army of parishioners, abuzz with questions, marching up the winding path, having eagerly awaited Father Jimmy's return. What a wonderful gesture as his community acknowledges this quiet man's achievements. Understanding totally now why this man has been chosen.

Thursa has been cooking up a storm, a large pan of scouse gently simmers on the stove. Carrots, onions, potatoes chopped or cubed, neck end of lamb, black pepper and couple of Oxos for good measure, covered with water and left to simmer. The secret to the success of the recipe, cook long and slow, nodding to herself with agreement. Next to it on the cooker, a pan of homemade vegetable soup bubbles along, all the ingredients finely chopped, a few garden herbs covered with water, seasoned to taste steadily cooks, a treat for the conquering priest. The smell fills the whole house, making mouths water, awakening their taste buds. She's even made some homemade bread, a welcome home treat, for her adopted family. The old oak table, central to the kitchen, with five seated around it, is groaning under the weight of the feast. Paul is away, visiting with his mother. A crackling fire fills the hearth, with steam rising from half dry clothing on the pulley. Father Jimmy and Peter sit one side of the table, Choden Lamas and his silent companion the other, Thursa dominates at the head, serving ladle in one hand. Joining hands, Father Jimmy says grace.

Thursa eagerly heaps the appetising food onto their plates, steam rising from the multi-coloured stew. Peter has already started his and is in the process of tearing a chunk of the freshly baked bread to dip it into the gravy, an eating machine in motion. Father Jimmy enjoys his soup chopped not puréed a kind gesture from Thursa, a confirmed vegetarian, he feels guilty putting his elderly housekeeper to all this extra work. Thursa is using her best table manners, Choden Lamas graciously follows Thursa's dining etiquette, mastering the knife and fork quickly. Savouring every mouthful of the unusual taste and textures, chewing multiple times before swallowing, giving his mind time to absorb each individual flavour. The silent one sits to the right of Thursa, unnerving her as he refrains from speech, eyes ever vigilant as he pecks away at his food, taking that long to eat, she's concerned he doesn't like it. Thanking her at the end of the meal for all her hard work. Feeling sated, the group sits around the kitchen table, chattering away freely, the main topic of conversation, the Unity Seminar.

Reluctantly leaving his spiritual family, Father Jimmy closes up the church at nine thirty. He belongs to this parish, more than any other he has led.

Darting through the graveyard, with movement reserved for much smaller creatures, Choden Lamas and his companion catch his eye, disappear by the large oak tree, the big fellow with his back firmly against the tree staring out into the darkness, the monk sits cross-legged at the base. Both dwarfed by the trees stature, peacefully engaging in nature's own soothing music. Peter has joined them, his arrival heard by all, man and beast, leaving Thursa to do the washing up. He intently listens to the monk. A hint of jealousy sneaks into Father Jimmy's heart, a subtle dark attack.

Speaking with his soft gentle voice, bringing a state of ease and calm, Choden Lamas explains the journey that they are on.

"Meditation, like prayer, comes in many forms; it quietens the mind, giving us time to reflect on any careless words, thoughts or deeds that we have encountered through our day and to shake them off, allowing the mind to recover during sleep. We know the brain remains active while sleeping, but the mind and body need to rest, enabling us to think logically and coordinate the following day, without yesterday's dark passengers. I like to meditate surrounded by nature, using the natural environment as a focus for my mind, the changing skyline is my screen, the perfume of a flower my aroma, the bird song my music, a cool breeze my energy and rain droplets on my face, freshening and awakening something inside me, feeling alive accompanied by a sharp intuitive mind, keeping me in a natural rhythm with my creator. I indulge myself with the dreamers, the doers and believers. Confident with their own existence and reliability, with the foresight to trust in something without absolute proof, embracing possibility everywhere. The thinkers do not conform, they transform. Renewing and opening up their minds eager to engage and change.

Life is an adventure, participate in the excitement, run wild with your imagination. Do not wake up with regret, shine through your storms, everything happens for a reason, having its place in our lives, part of its natural rhythm. "

This sweet sounding voice has sent Peter into limbo, realising anything is possible when you remove doubt, which kills more dreams than defeat ever will. Peter visits a region bordering two realms discarding his worries, shame and guilt. Feeling reborn, touched and enriched, he takes time to reflect, feeling a spiritual growth and transformation, removing the decay and rot that had set in, passed down through generations. Peter's fragile body enjoys real freedom in this expanse of endless space; here, anything is possible. All too quickly, the meditation comes to a close.

Choden Lamas touches Peter's hand, sincerity in his eyes. "You need to deal with that wound."

Before Peter can come back with a smart retort, the monk looks into Peter's eyes. "Your parentage. You are Father Jimmy's rock, specially chosen for your gifts. I see a white/silver aura surrounding you, blessing you with the ability to relate to many people, without discrimination. Our forgotten people. A wound as large as you carry, left untreated, will leave you open to attack from the dark one."

That old familiar feeling of self-loathing returns to Peter, Choden Lamas senses it. Reassuringly he places a hand on his shoulder, a firm, strong touch. Moving quickly now he is drawn into Peter's psyche, travelling faster than the speed of light. Each tragic event captured, clicking like a stream of rapid fire images, retaining the events, drugs, homelessness, the army, care system, right back to the womb, a foetus, half loved and yet loathed. Removing his hand, he feels a burning sensation. Peter, unaware of his transparency, permits passage, a clear view of his life's turmoil exposed.

"The temperatures dropping now, Peter."

Appearing from nowhere, feeling protective, Father Jimmy offers a reassuring hand, heaving the large frame up. He too has experienced those visions, feeling them rather than seeing them, during the detox. A thought travels between himself and the Monk.

"Healing of the mind."

Signs of mental instability, impairment and dysfunction, emotions produced from his parentage. Both repeat subconsciously.

"May Peter be renewed in the spirit of his mind, thwarting thine enemy, filling his mind and heart with genuine pure thoughts, honesty and understanding."

Their silhouettes cast shadows on the darkened street as their bodies intercept the light, casting dark images onto the pavement as they walk briskly back to the rectory, huddled together. Shaking off the light spring rain from their clothing. Grumbling, Thursa makes to retrieve her washing left out on the line, Peter beats her to it. The monk smiles, sensing the special bond that is building between the two of them.

"Rain is good, performing its purpose, nourishing the ground, watering the crops, watching them grow, which we in turn eat. Wildlife needs water to survive."

Thursa having heard it all before, wrinkles her nose and mouth, her facial expression showing her irritation. "You would send a glass eye to sleep," she says before looking skyward. "A sermon with everything," she continues.

Choden Lamas smiles, not fully understanding the Scouse humour, but respecting her age, with age comes wisdom, he's preaching to the wrong person. Watching her clutching her clean white tissue as she coughs into it, hastily exiting the room. He sees her yellow aura, a dominant character, known for being workaholics, putting work ahead of personal relationships. Yellow auras are perfectly happy in their own company and don't suffer loneliness. A grey patch just visible in the yellow aura, near her lungs, but the coughing had already given that away. Her heart is content, accepting a special bond between herself and Peter. A gift to her from the creator.

Chapter 10

The much anticipated Spirit of Truth is the centre that Choden Lamas intends to open with his friends. Promoting a safe haven for all, working with Father Jimmy, Peter and Paul, each bringing something different to the table. Addiction a terrible affliction that hits these poorer areas hardest, not only confined to the poor though. The extremely fast pace of life that people live, high powered careers and lifestyle, pressures pushing the middle and upper classes to use social drugs. At first indulging only on a social basis, eventually increasing to cope with daily life and inevitably to warding off withdrawal. Puzzled by that title as he can see nothing social about the devastation and destruction that this is causing the addict or their family. Starting with public awareness, teaching in the parish centre until premises can be found, putting their plan straight into action.

Thursa wakes to shards of bright sunlight filtering through a gap in her floral bedroom curtains, bouncing off her dressing table mirror and giving the impression of a warm day. Morning is always a welcome visitor to the elderly, granted yet another precious day. Thursa sees a yellow tinge to her bedroom ceiling from her crafty fag before bed. Sliding her tiny foot from beneath the bedding, she tests the early morning temperature, swinging her bony arthritic legs over the side of the bed, before contacting with the cold worn lino. She quickly slips them back under the covers. Still a nip in the spring air.

Reluctantly rising, conscious of the tasks ahead of her, she uses the washbasin in the corner of the bedroom, splashing cold water on her aged face, wondering where the years have gone as she looks at her reflection and sees her mother's face staring back at her. Briskly, she completes her strip wash; There are no en suites in the rectory. Making her way slowly down the stairs, restarting her worn out body, wrapped in her woollen skirt and jumper, thick wrinkly tights on her sparrow-like legs, shuffling in her sloppy comfortable slippers, Thursa feels unexpectedly happy belonging to someone or something, a very pleasant feeling. On entering the kitchen she sees a pot of tea and five cups and saucers sitting on the kitchen table. Peter springs to mind, putting an impromptu smile on her face. The kettle begins to whistle on the stove eager to be heard, as a little guilt flashes into her mind, having made contact with his mother. Her intentions are genuine, pushing that self-doubt to the back of her mind. Reducing the heat under the kettle, she leaves it to gently simmer. Throwing on her outdoor coat, she is gasping for a ciggy, needing her nicotine fix. To her surprise and amusement, Father Jimmy, Peter and the Monk are sheltered below the willow tree, at the bottom of a very large garden, a bit overgrown in that area. They remind her of a group of hippies. The strange silent guy watches her, standing some distance away from the others, never verbally engaging. She finds him a bit unnerving as he looks through her, with his all-seeing eyes. Feeling transparent she wraps her outdoor coat tightly around her bony frame, like a protective shield from those prying eyes.

She looks away as she inhales deeply on her cigarette, body relaxing as nicotine, a powerful drug, speeds up the brain and central nervous system, triggers the release of the chemical dopamine in her brain, improving her mood. Leaning against the kitchen door, coughing and spluttering as the chemical hits home and irritates her airways, before that much needed craving has had its fix, a couple more puffs and the cigarette has been devoured. Blinking rapidly as the sharp sunlight hits her sensitive eyes, making them water as she admires the uninterrupted blueness of the sky. Appreciating the bonus of another day, something that she previously took for granted, more aware now of this treasured gift. Slipping back into the kitchen and washing her nicotine-stained fingers before starting the breakfast. The silence in the kitchen that she previously enjoyed, is something she's used to. Then the familiar banging and clattering as Peter enters the kitchen, closely followed by the others, puts a sly grin on her wrinkled face, realising loneliness and isolation are uninvited guests.

Busying herself around the kitchen, she serves up breakfast, pleasure watching Peter devour his as the monk and the silent fellow gracefully peck away at theirs like two little birds. Slowly and methodically, eating the fry-up presented to them. Pushing a piece of black pudding around the plate, causing her more amusement, as they are obviously unsure of its origins. The plan of action is discussed at the breakfast table. No secrets are kept from Thursa; all talking is done openly and her input is always welcomed, for she has found her purpose in life. A far cry from father Mike's visit, all his talking was done behind firmly closed doors, stopping when she entered the room. Making her feel uncomfortable in her own home.

"Once we officially open the Spirit of Truth, we will become prime targets for dark forces, by people who live in malice, envy and hateful ways. Introducing kindness and love, becoming heirs to eternal life, we will teach others to face their enemy, drugs, alcohol, gambling. No point in harbouring bitterness, resentment or anger. By introducing forgiveness, blessing our enemies who curse us, being kind to those who hate us, praying for those who persecute us. Removing all their power, thus conquering evil. Able to walk freely, in the wisdom of forgiveness. Making it difficult to hate the person who shows you love and kindness." The monk finally finishes, breathing heavily.

Thursa stands at the sink, hands submerged in soapy water, fascinated by the amount of transparent bubbles produced; upon closer inspection, the psychedelic patterns that form in soapy water capture her imagination while washing the dishes. Another example of the wonderful images that are all around us, if we only took time to truly look. Faraway eyes now mesmerised, fixed on the steamed up kitchen window, hypnotised by the rhythm of the monk's soothing rhythmic voice, focusing on the sweetness of her spring garden through a porthole in the steam. Peter is alongside her, removing the dishes from the drainer and wiping them dry. Surprised they have any dishes left with the amount he has dropped since joining them. She listens to the monk, realising what he says makes perfect sense. That rugged old heart of hers is softening again, malleable like the bread dough she made yesterday.

"Once our flock increases, evil will come wanting to reclaim its victims, which is when we will come under serious attack."

The kitchen has emptied and quietness descends, Thursa's hardworking hands wrinkling in the lukewarm soapy dish water, her mind deep in thought. Still gazing through the kitchen window, past the pane of glass, her eyes not in focus, vision blurred as her mind wanders, revisiting a painful place, her past. Vanishing down the plughole, following the dishwater, lost in dark thoughts, she is swallowed up, feeling trapped as she revisits her youth.

She was a pretty little thing at nineteen. Petite with shoulder length blonde hair, delicate features and violet-blue eyes, with a hint of red lipstick on her perfectly formed curvy lips, carefree and in love, a gaiety about her, ready to embrace life's journey. Anger clouds her face now, as she recalls the unpleasant events that brought her to Liverpool.

The last to know that her beloved fiancé, William, is seeing another, her identical twin sister, in secret, the excitement of deceit is what motivates him. A double betrayal from those closest to her, still painful. Dwelling on disappointment and heartbreak trapped in someone else's madness. Part of her own DNA, being so callous, Ginny was always dependant on her, the older sister (albeit by a couple of minutes). Now she steals her world, taking what she wants, her fiancé, her life. Filled with anger and resentment, which takes root, like a vine, and wrap tightly around her heart, choking and suffocating it. Then the children arrived. Looking into their perfect precious little faces, she sees what should have been her children, sharing the same DNA as her twin. Her sister twists the knife while callously enjoying her perfect life. So Thursa upped and left, unable to bear the daily pain and humiliation as her sister slipped into her shoes which fitted her so nicely. Her parents forgiving her twin once the grandchildren arrived – the final betrayal. The strong outward character of Thursa smiles silently through her hidden pain but is inconsolable behind closed doors as she fights her daily battle. She has been removed from her own path through lust and secrecy. Getting onto the first train to pull into the station on that wet September morning, the small suitcase carried her few personal belongings, with tears brimming in her torched eyes but her head held high as she started her new life in Liverpool. A city of culture and heritage with a diverse population making disappearing into the community effortless. She cut all ties to her family and friends, in case she weakened. Lugging bitterness with her for many years, which ate away at her daily. Wasting her precious time with isolation and loneliness. Meeting Peter has brought all those old maternal feelings back to life. Not caring enough now to be angry with her old life, which proved that time does heal. Many years have passed since she last saw any of her family. Everyone has a story; as she revisits her path travelled, she learns not to judge herself too harshly. The crash of the front door brings her eyes back into focus, blinking a stray tear away rapidly as it escapes down her face, her wet hands still resting in the empty sink. It's Peter leaving, the thought of his name always brings a smile to her elderly face. She looks out onto the garden, enjoying the spring surprise, unaware the monk is a silent passenger on her journey. He observes her suffering from the hallway. Sorrow, pain and self-doubt; removing those labels, to replace them with love. Encouraging all his team to heal any wounds. He respects this lady, for her courage and for letting go; she is healing herself.

The Spirit of Truth has humble beginnings in the parish centre, a modest banner hangs outside inviting people in. Word of mouth spreads quicker than sound, in this close-knit community. Father Jimmy's flock have gathered, an unassuming bunch of individuals. The reporter is there. She is accompanied by her daughter, who is taller than her mother, with a slender frame, auburn fiery hair, vivid green eyes, quite a looker. A few strangers mingle in as people walk in off the street. The travelling community, not forgetting the homeless group, who are not sure if they're joining in or have just nipped in for a warm cuppa.

Paul has arrived back after visiting his home, accompanied by his mother. There is a subtle change about him, having sedated his emotional pain; an unusual calmness is shining through. Wanting to show his mother the work he is involved in, having retrieved some dignity. Their close bond is plainly visible.

Choden Lamas gives the floor to Father Jimmy as this is his stomping ground.

"I would like to thank you all for coming as we embark on this journey. Instead of filling the time with chatter I would like us all to sit quietly for three minutes, eyes open or closed. Clear your minds, enjoy the here and now."

A few raised eyebrows from older members of the community.

The monk sits in silence, cross legged, at the back of the room, away from the rest of the group. Skilfully observing thoughts as they vaporise, raising from the groups some receptive minds. Some take a while to settle, fidgeting restlessly with an inability to remain calm. Emma's daughter, Ava, releases heartache and sorrow, surrounded by anger that is bordering on sheer rage. Peter is happy and content, having found his path again, and forgiveness is also there. Just a tint shard of greyness is still present. He is trying to bury it rather than deal with it. Many visitors show a degrees of sadness, only a few embrace the gift of real joy.

"What's the first thing we do in the morning?"

The group slowly open their eyes, the bright artificial lighting causing their pupils to constrict as he gains their full attention.

There are a few comical retorts before Father Jimmy continues.

"Most of us moan about the weather, our finances, jobs we hate. Negative energy creeps in as soon as our eyes are open. Envious of our neighbours who only share the highlights of their lives, keeping difficulties hidden and out of sight. Tomorrow when you wake I want you to think for one minute of all the positive things in your life, as the environment we occupy is very important."

"What if you don't have any?" Emma's daughter pipes up, snarling rather than talking, hurt visible in her mischievous eyes.

"You have your health, a family, a home, food on the table, an education, many children in the world don't have these."

Before Father Jimmy can finish, Ava is up and on her feet, stomping out, unable to control her fiery temper, her volatile nature emphasising her irritability. She is closely followed by an apologetic Emma, whose face shows the beginnings of a blush.

"The young lady carries pain in her heart and, as she continues to carry pain, her life will be painful. Tantrums I can deal with," Father Jimmy says, reengaging his followers as he continues with his flow.

"Life is two halves, sometimes happy, sometimes sad. A bridal car travels down a busy road. Passers-by stop to glance, enjoying the traditions, something old, something new, something borrowed and something blue. The bride in her new white dress, only to be worn once, symbolising youth and innocence. Wheat and grains baked in the wedding cake, a symbol of fertility. Confetti and rice thrown to sweeten the union. Ribbons dress the wedding car, the perfume of the bridal bouquet. The bride in her flushing white beauty, anticipation in her heart. Her proud father sits next to her, his precious daughter, ready to givd her away. Confirmation of his blessing is followed by a string of hopes and dreams wafting in the air.

Another family in contrast, mourn the loss of a beloved family member.

Lilies lay erect on a wooden box, guarding this cherished cargo like soldiers on sentry duty. Dark clothing reflects withdrawal from everyday life, during a period of grieving as mourners weep, accompanied by a sombre mood. A strong mistral wind accompanies the final journey as sorrow wraps around them like a tight fitting overcoat as they struggle to let go.

Followed finally by a celebration of the beloved's life and achievement, as family and friends gather, one final toast before releasing this friend into the unknown. We all experience both at some time or other." Finishing, Father Jimmy lets out a long breath.

"What about different religions, Father Jimmy? With this open door policy, all sorts are wandering in to our church."

One of the original clique sits piously with his confrontational character, a big fish in a little pond, always feeling superior. Not keen on change, he prays in full view of his community and he always sits on the front pew at church. Never thinking that someone with poor mobility would benefit from his seat, he shows resentment and anger if anyone tries to sit there. He is always reluctant to engage in practical help or support.

"Our message is simple, we are all united in love, regardless of which religion we worship, He's one and the same. By removing barriers, fear and hatred dies; then communities can merge.

Evil encourages division, separating individuals removing hope. Forgiveness is our key."

"Here, here," Thursa inputs from the back. Although a familiar member of this community, Father Jimmy is surprised by her outburst; she is usually a controlled character in public, exercising restraint.

"This community is flooded with illegal substances, causing untold destruction to families.

Liverpool has a diverse cultural background, The Spirit of Truth is open to all," finishes Father Jimmy.

He calls Paul up to the front, "Paul is our addiction advisor, helping with that side of the community project."

Paul hasn't prepared anything. He hesitantly makes his way to the front and looks at the sea of blank faces staring back at him. A little fear slips into his mind but, once he gets going, the words flow.

"We all know the dealers, drop houses, holders and lookouts in our community. They silence us with fear of repercussions at first. Becoming so used to it now, that it hardly registers anymore. Gamblers betting their last fiver hoping to cover what they have already lost and more. Alcoholics, the socially acceptable intoxicant, they are no longer in control of their daily lives. By helping each other to rethink what they have lost, with a kind word rather than a look of distaste. Working alongside one other, making our lives and our community a better place to live. Encouraging the young into the workplace not gossiping about someone else's misfortune."

There is pride in Moll's eyes as she watches her son fighting for the underdog. She is flushed with a twinkle in her ageing eyes.

"You used to be a dealer, didn't you?" an anonymous voice shouts from the back. Standing tall, Paul inhales deeply puffing out his chest, he invites the mystery heckler forward. No one is forthcoming.

"That is correct, I have been imprisoned twice as well. I have nothing to hide, I am an open book." Paul feels a sense of empowerment filling his body, surreal and dreamlike, when revealing the truth, once it's out there it can no longer hurt you. Feeling the protection of his angel's wings, like a protective shield of steel, deflecting the verbal onslaught. No weapon shall penetrate them.

"That is why I became a qualified drugs councillor."

"Poacher turned game keeper," the coward shouts from the back.

"As some may say. So yes I do know what I'm talking about.

Dealers use fear to paralyse communities, the threat of impending danger spreading like a raging fire until we no longer have control of the epidemic. We are here to put that fire out." He gestures to the whole room. Little Moll starts clapping, her heart brimming with pride and everyone else follows with raucous applause, the feeling in that room is contagious.

The rest of the day is spent forming a committee, organising events, for fundraising. Combining practical support with a wide variety of spiritual techniques. Finishing the day on a high, with a mantra,

"Keep life simple.

Take ownership of your mistakes.

Deal with the consequences of your actions.

Don't judge others or yourself too harshly.

Let go of anguish.

Free will is precious.

Forgiveness is our key."

Enthusiastically, the group disperses, feeling uplifted. Thursa is rushing home to finish off the tea, finding it hard to keep up with Peter's large strides as he carries her heavy shopping bags containing the bits and pieces she has picked up from the outdoor market. Having made a salad, at Father Jimmy's suggestion, she hopes it is also to her guest's pallet.

"What have you got in this bag?" Peter teases. "It weighs a ton." There is laughter on Peter's face that melts her weathered heart.

They bump straight into Jools. "Hello, Thursa."

A simple greeting, followed by an awkward prolonged silence. Thursa's restrained in manner, Peter senses something is wrong. Finally with an uneasiness about her, Thursa returns the greeting. Peter and Jools hold each other's gaze a nano-second too long, unsure of the emotion that travels invisibly between them.

Holding her hand out, Jools introduces herself to Peter, "Jools Brown, pleased to meet you."

A familiar face, thatch of hair poking from beneath her hat, green coat, black patent leather court shoes with a sparkling butterfly brooch on her lapel. Puzzled, Peter takes her hand, shakes it firmly. Small and delicate, there is a familiarity about her, a look, an odour, he's not sure what. An unease fills them both.

"I'm sorry, Jools, I must dash, I have guests and dinner to put on."

Peter is at a loss, as he knows it's salad, but he is sure that Thursa must have her reasons. Briskly they walk off in the opposite direction, leaving Peter baffled.

Emma runs, catching up with Father Jimmy and the monk as they are locking the parish centre up. "I must apologise for my daughter."

"Why?" the monk asks.

"Her behaviour."

Looking awkward, she fiddles with her hair as her cheeks redden somewhat. Not sure if she's embarrassed or red from running. Chaden Lamas takes her hand gently, "Emma my dear, we do not need your apologies for another's actions, we all have flaws."

Eyes penetrating deep inside her, leaving her feeling completely bare, with no hiding place, she can hear her own raspy breath.

"Only by positive response can spiritual progress be made. Engage with goodwill to win over your daughter. Respond to her negativity with positivity, train yourself, when life strikes you, turn the other cheek. Do not give vent to evil words or your mind will be affected by this. Remain full of sympathy, fill your mind with love, not despair. Cease the tit for tat approach.

Happy is the mother who finds wisdom, gaining understanding, thus crushing rebellion."

Emma feels tears building in her eyes. She battles with frustration; being of strong character, she continues to fight them.

"Do not stifle them, let them flow freely, feel the emotional burden release with your tears," Chaden Lamas continues.

The build-up of pressure and anxiety release as her tears reluctantly fall. Reminding Emma of a pressure cooker once the lid is removed.

"Do not retreat into one's self, engage in dialogue, talk things through, self-isolation is a common defence mechanism, tear down those walls."

A downpour of tears floods her pretty face as she feels the burden slowly lifting. Having felt lost and alone, she now feels some comfort.

"Break the rules, strong people weep, a mother's job is not an easy one," the monk encourages.

Choden Lamas senses a smirch on Emma's breast, a tiny dark spot; an illness is coming but he knows that the Supreme Being has a life plan for her. Maybe it's a pit stop, she may need time to take stock, to re-evaluate her lifestyle.

"Walk with me, Emma."

As he guides her over to a large tree, she feels self-conscious. The late afternoon light is fading and the air is turning sharp, soothed and relaxed they loiter under this exquisite creation. Understanding the strength the rough trunk symbolises, decorated with delicate branches fine and far reaching, a great architectural feat. No two species are the same, a bit like the human race. The green of the leaves calm and cool, helping them both to engage with nature. Darkness slowly creeps into the sky, as the sun continues to retreat. The moonlight visits, casting a silvery glint through the open branches. In that moment, time stands still. One hand holds Emma's, the other touches the rugged bark of the sacred tree. Her surroundings blur as Chaden Lamas channels the internal strength of the tree that provides oxygen, cleaning soil, muffling urban noises, fallen trees reducing flash floods, windbreak and shelter. Somewhere to cool off on a hot summer's day, a home to many animals, keeping them safe from predators and a food source to many.

Inhaling deeply and tapping into this wonderful creation, Chaden Lamas gazes at the connection of the roots and the tree, firmly implanted into the earth, immersed deep and spreading wide. While the branches reach to the heavens, connecting him to both replenishing and energising his mortal being. The tree, a conductor, is sacred to life, powerful in stature, ever changing with the seasons, the tree of life, providing him with strength, talking quietly in a dialect she has never heard before, Chaden Lamas requests a suit of armour to protect her from disease. Feeling heady as life swirls around her. Releasing her hand as he finishes with the simple hypnotic melody of his voice.

"Emma, shed negative people who test and use you, draining your energy, wanting to control lives, spreading their discord and misery, filled with envy.

Surround yourself with positivity, friends with integrity, that don't stray from between the lines but bring out the best in you with listening and encouragement, fixing your mistakes rather than judging them. Much like my species of trees, gain peace from them, never underestimate our inner power. They walk together a while, no need for words to be spoken, as peace and serenity surround them until their paths separate.

Turning to look at the eloquent figure, feeling safe in his company, she thanks him, with a simple bow of her head and a large beaming smile.

"Emma, if you feel ill, go seek a doctor."

His English good but not perfect. She is taken aback by this comment.

As Thursa enters the rectory, hand fumbling for the light switch, she scrapes her arthritic fingers along the rough wall and drops the heavy shopping bags down. Removing her outdoor coat, she throws it over the newel post at the foot of the stairs before sighing with relief. Peter is still a little confused by Thursa's abrupt attitude.

"Who was that lady?"

Thursa wants to tell him, it was never her intention to keep secrets. Kicking her shoes off into the cupboard in the hall before replacing them with her sloppy slippers. Feeling pure maternal love for this young man, her heart says one thing but her head another.

"Jools Brown, a volunteer from the hospice."

There is a sharpness to her tone, with her eyes cast down, not meeting his gaze, reminding him of the old Thursa when he first arrived.

"Why the awkwardness?"

Always to the point with Peter, no dressing things up. Slowly she lifts her gaze, to meet his with her violet blue watery eyes.

"My feet are killing me, that corn's playing up again. I just wanted to get home."

Her look conveys that she's only telling half the story.

"I've got four extra for tea, the monk and his silent friend." Rolling her eyes now, "Paul and his mother, plus the three of us. I want to get things ready and she can't half talk."

A plausible explanation but he's not buying it, her body language is all wrong. She's definitely hiding something. Thursa feels really bad, she has never had to lie to Peter before. Well, technically it's not a lie. It's just not the full story. Everything must be right when they discover who they are. The environment is very important, with familiar friends on hand to guide them, surrounding them with positive energy. Giving them the best possible chance of a relationship bur she fears she's risking her own friendship with him. Trust is a very delicate beast, fragile and easy to lose. Once broken, there is no guarantee of getting it back, but it is worth the sacrifice if it brings Peter closure from his old life. She acts like a parent prepared to make the ultimate sacrifice if it helps another.

Moll and Thursa, huddle around the kitchen table deep in conversation, having observed Thursa's obvious distress. Feeling a chill from a cold wind whistling under the kitchen door, wrapping around their legs. This old house is filled with gaps and draughts. Thursa throws a couple more logs on the open fire before returning to the table. A pot of steaming hot tea sits in the middle of the familiar oak table. Cupping their hands around the mugs to generate much needed warmth, which transfers into their bony fingers, they wait patiently for the heat of the logs to take hold as they nibble a freshly baked sandwich cake, after the delicious tea has been polished off. Salad seems to please all her guests bar Peter, who piles his between two slices of thickly sliced bread before devouring it.

The monk and his followers have retired to the garden to meditate under the old tree. Tackling evil head-on, they are engrossed in prayer, surrounded by Mother Nature. Evil is unable to reach them when engaging with the Supreme Being, pleased as these two religions join as one. Choden Lamas visualises the eye of the storm, during their powerful all-consuming prayers. Levitating slightly as he releases worldly ties, these two warriors connect between the two planes. The storm is their shield, protecting them from evil forces. They unite in words of prayer, making them stronger and evil weaker.

"Nothing covered that shall not be revealed, or hidden that will not come to light," the monk roars, completing a ritual, a ritual that prevents curses penetrating them, heightening their ability to sense evil, detecting it before it has time to attack. Half-heartedly, Thursa watches them through the kitchen window.

"What's the story with Peter?" Moll asks, bringing Thursa back from her thoughts.

Thursa trusts this genuine lady, who has waited patiently for her son to return to his rightful path, not wavering from her faith. Moll is a good, strong woman, handsome, never reaching beautiful, her features lined from sheer hard work. A favourable bone structure is hidden behind her translucent skin, chestnut brown hair heavily invaded with grey strands, her eyes are large, warm and brown. They by themselves are truly beautiful and honest. She is small in stature, with a large forgiving spirit, smiling through her pain, working all the hours God sent to rear her family, single handed. Distraught behind closed doors, struggling to keep life and soul together after the disappearance of her husband, left without a goodbye. Sobbing as her first born son was gradually overtaken by drugs, his warm caring character replaced as he turned nasty and aggressive, stealing from her when the demon of addiction ordered. It was not the money that upset her, but the conscious act of betrayal, of loving and yet hating him at the same time. Fighting whatever battles life brought to her door, alone and in silence.

"God had a plan for him, darkness had another," Thursa utters, unaware that Moll is lost in her own painful thoughts.

She thinks how she always showered love on her angry son, making it hard for him to hate the person who supported him with unconditional love. Mourning her special tender relationship shared between a mother and her first born.

Moll believed that Paul was possessed by devils, tightly held in their grip, drugs, sex and rebellion. Heavily carrying sorrow in her heart. Ultimately it was that sighting of his mother that broke through his drug induced blur, registering a vague connection, the invisible unbiblical cord powerful and all consuming. The love that no evil could break, pure love. Moll had tackled evil and won.

"Evil also forced Peter off his path, constantly missing his timing in life. The ripple effects could have affected generations, unbalancing lives. Peter's family tree carries a curse, deep rooted and far reaching, like the old willow outside. Blessings come with forgiveness, understanding is the only way forward. Peter must forgive his father the rapist."

Moll's eyes slowly meet Thursa's gaze, shocked.

"A tremendous sacrifice is needed of him. Then mother and son will find great graces and enlightenment together, breaking the curse once and for all."

"Where do you fit in?" Moll asks her friend, leaning on her elbow, sipping her hot tea from a chunky mug. A story worse than her own.

"I am simply a messenger. Peter is the chosen one. The storm raged around him; he was drowning. Evil pulled him under yet he was chosen for his inner strength. I am happy to bring some sunshine into his life, and he into mine. Now he is being taught wisdom, protection, strength of mind and redemption. Many will follow him, your son was instrumental in breaking the dark hold over Peter. Paul is crucial to the Spirit of Truth and the ongoing war against drugs."

All the pain and sorrow that Paul brought into Moll's life forgotten in an instant, forgiving like only a mother can, a feeling she will celebrate her whole lifetime.

Chapter 11

Adrianna has been closely following the progress of, The Spirit of Truth, its simple approach and transparency, is the secret to its success.

Unlike Adrianna's trickery, lurking in the dark shadows, watching then seizing earthbound spirits. Lost and confused, in unfamiliar surroundings their energy levels zapped. Wandering into the dusky light, hearing whispered sound waves rather than language, making communication challenging, easy pickings for someone with Adrianna's knowledge. A person filled with jealousy, greed and rage, her skills in manipulation are waning, wasted on the monk and the priest as she decreases in strength and prosperity. Her fickle followers' enthusiasm is lessening. They are far too easily swayed, a weak group of individuals, infuriating her. Calling on all her skills in the dark arts, she looks for a person liable to yield. The weak link in the Spirit of Truth. Adrianna applies more pressure to find the fragile spot in their armour. Seeing the hairline crack, Peter is the obvious choice. Knowing his weakness, drugs a side effect of his turbulent parentage. An unpicked scab that she is about to rip off.

Choden Lamas senses a storm coming; glancing through an open window, he feels a cold chill run down his neck, making his body shudder. Watching the paleness of the sky shift and discolour as it descends into darkness, reflecting the heavy menacing mood with unusual manifestations. Dark spirits attack his dreams, tortured earthbound souls controlled by evil forces, haunt his sleeping hours. Visions and sensations throughout the day attack him whilst waking, trying to drain his strength. Demonic spirits play with him, knowing that evil is ready to attack. He would have liked a bit more time but, trusting in the Supreme Being, he gets ready for his first battle.

The Spirit of Truth is up and running, just about to move to new premises after an anonymous donation. Followers are multiplying weekly. There is some resistance from locals at first, but nothing to cause concern.

Paul's addiction programme, weaning users from drugs and alcohol is so successful that he now has a waiting list. Peter works in the community inviting the homeless into the centre, gaining their respect and building trust. Father Jimmy shepherds the flock in his calm unassuming manner. Thursa, Moll and Jools organise the day to day housekeeping side of the centre. While the monk teaches his small group of messengers spiritual warfare to protect them against imminent attack.

Taking Father Jimmy to one side, his messenger with equal spiritual powers, even though he doesn't know it yet, Choden Lamas shares his burden. "We have a responsibility to the others, evil is coming and we need to be ready. I fear they will pick one off at a time to split the group, divide and conquer. Peter's name keeps coming to mind."

"The drugs?" Father Jimmy sighs wearily.

"No, his parentage has not been dealt with."

"I wouldn't know where to find his mother"

Father Jimmy looks worried.

"Really?" The monk replies, eyeing Father Jimmy coolly, pausing, as the priest stares blankly while resting in his favourite old wicker chair, shaking his head and frowning.

"You must have seen the relationship between him and Jools building, I see so much of each of them in the other. Finishing off each other's sentences, mannerisms, the same shape and colour eyes, dimples that appear when they laugh. When have you ever seen Peter so happy?"

Father Jimmy fidgets in his chair as the realisation gradually registers. Obvious in hindsight.

"He is central to our success, but he is weak as he already carries an injury that must be tended to."

Father Jimmy sits up, scratching his forehead, filled with total surprise, unprepared for the monk's disclosure but in retrospect the revelation is obvious

Instinctively on his feet now, Father Jimmy and the monk head to the oak tree in the church grounds, sacred to them both. Bringing Father Jimmy's place of worship together with the monk's love of nature. Forging their friendship through mutual trust, respecting the others' religious background, both seeking assurance. The silent follower, like a shadow, guards, always a few feet away from Choden Lamas, focusing his inner eye, to protect his master. Providing perception beyond normal sight through a state of enlightenment, developing his senses over many years, being more refined and accurate. Understanding that everything is energy, he develops his skills to separate all things into positive or negative energy with relative ease, deducing good from bad. Translating his thoughts into images, some vivid, some blurred, before transmitting them to the monk.

Choden Lamas makes his much needed connection with the oak tree, his hand massaging the familiar rugged bark, sharp and jagged against the softness of his palm, as he engages its natural healing powers. Its roots reach into the soul of the dark, dense earth as they spread uninterrupted, alive with constant new growth. Balancing and energising their minds, he glances upward through a portal in the branches surveying the endless sky seeping through. Calling on the restorative powers of the tree, telepathically Father Jimmy joins him, calling upon a guardian angel who captivates his soul as she rises up next to the tree, huge in stature, expanding her elegant wingspan, her female elements representing nurture. The radiance of her expression is a wondrous sight; her brightness is briefly visible for miles around. She is aware that darkness is trying to penetrate Peter's weakened defences.

The angel enters Peter's bedroom swiftly and with ease, covering him with her unassailable wings, like a mother protecting her new-born child, each feather perfect, glowing brilliant white. Dazzling light surrounds her, painful to the human eye. Her clear soulful eyes warm and inviting, enter Peter's subconscious as he sleeps deeply in his bed. She detects all the hidden pain, anger and resentment of a young lifetime and cleanses his spirit. Under her wings, he takes refuge.

She whispers, "The truth shall be your sword and buckler. No terror will visit you by night, nor arrow through the day, nor pestilence that walks through the darkness, spreading harm and destruction. "

The angel now tends to his physical wound, which has been him since birth, acquired at his conception and in close proximity to his weeping heart.

A shelf cloud, which has been building, quickly rolls in, rumbling overhead announcing the dark one's distaste, a severe instant thunderstorm erupts, exploding onto the skyline, as the monk and priest pray in unison. Accompanied by strong fierce winds, hail and freezing rain, the sky angers, the attack unrelenting. Dark continuous cloud covers the pale blue sky, devouring it with ease. An eerie feeling as the birds take cover in nearby foliage. Fury accompanies the damp cold smell to the air. Father Jimmy and Choden Lamas courageously continue, gripping wildly to the coarse bark of the tree as it provides temporary shelter against the defiant rain, penetrating the branches and making bodies soaked to the skin. Robe and cassock are like paper, no protection at all against this unforgiving onslaught. With faith in the Supreme Being's ability, and guided by their powerful prayer, the wind whips around their feet, knocking them slightly off balance.

Continuing, they visualise, pulling open Peter's wound, the angel supports him as they release the pus festering in the injury, removing the maggots that gnaw away at the unattended wound. A putrid, vile smell rises as the last of the poison is released. Catching the rain water in a leaf, Choden Lamas visualises washing the wound, Father Jimmy removes a vial of holy water from his pocket and pours it onto the gash. Both watch as the wound smoulders, then heals, vanishing before their eyes, Peter's silhouette disappears from their inner sight. Two religions coming together for one purpose; once division is removed, anything is possible. They understand that they are separate chapters from the same book.

Exhausted faces convey their fatigue. As they return to the rectory, the storm surrenders. Their tacky clothing firmly shows the outline of their bodies as they slop watery footprints on to the clean kitchen floor. Thursa's oblivious to their predicament, she is in a flap. Peter has retired to bed without eating his tea. This is virtually unheard of; he is feeling unwell. Having checked on him, she finds him with a raging temperature. Tossing and turning in the bed, screaming a high pitched scream before descending into a deep coma-like sleep.

"He's got a fever," Thursa frets.

Strain shows on her concerned elderly face. Father Jimmy guides her gently to her winged armchair in front of the fire. Perching on the edge of the seat, she is placed with the full view of the kitchen and all of its occupants, watching the flames dance, yellow, gold and orange, with a hint of blue in the middle. The two messengers begin.

"The time has come to introduce Peter to his mother."

Thursa's emotions are confused. She knows the monk is right, she knew this day was coming, but is worried about her own relationship with him.

"Am I a bad person?" she asks, feeling ashamed, head hanging, shoulders slumped, sitting very still. The monk sits down in front of her, resting his hands on her shoulders; he feels a constant stream of heat transfer from his hands to her body. The rest of the kitchen melts away, focusing directly on the monk. The two become one, Surrounded by a soft glow and a feeling of euphoria. He shows her what lies ahead. Transmitting visual information, feelings as well as contents.

"We have a battle coming, Thursa. Evil forces want to discredit us and the work we do. Keeping religions separate weakens them by division, planting fear, encouraging conflict, battles and ultimately war. Peter is paramount to the journey. He has been chosen, having superior power and insight, due to the pain and suffering he has already endured. He moves easily amongst the hardest to engage groups, gaining trust and influence. The physical wound he carried has been healed tonight hence his fever, but not the emotional wound. The healer does not make a prognosis on the physical injury alone, but with Peter's emotional scars, engaging his impenetrable will and mind power needed to conquer through the courage of his spirit. You have made this possible by helping Peter to love himself. Now we must try to bring his parentage to the forefront before evil arrives in the form of a chameleon, with the ability to change, morphing into its surroundings, melting into the background. It is usually hard to detect but, as it has no soul, it carries no shadow. Using any dark warfare available to it. Meditation and prayer transform us into higher energy and focus our minds; it is used at a spiritual level for our own protection. The Supreme Being will not be drawn into dark ways, using only meditation and prayer, alongside Mother Nature, when needed. You have a very powerful mind; use it to forge the energy around you by developing and refining all your senses in conjunction with your mind. Giving you a more powerful sensory organ to determine good from bad, for your protection and that of others."

Releasing his hands, taking with them the feeling of intense wellbeing. Thursa sits, unnerved, absorbing what she has just been told.

The best of her life behind her, she remains here to protect Peter. She keeps watch by his bedside with a cold flannel at hand to mop his burning brow. Brushing his unruly mop of hair from his forehead, she enjoys this maternal love that is far stronger than anything she has ever experienced. A far cry from his first visit to the rectory, when he camped out in the small back bedroom with wildness in those dark, secret eyes. Like a caged animal, he screamed as his body fought the drug detox, sweating, shaking, headaches, irritability and violently sick. Surviving on sips of water and the herbal drink provided by Paul. The clothing he arrived in, with the exception of his outer coat, burned on the open fire, a symbolic cleansing of the existence he left behind. Scouring the local charity shops for clean, fresh clothing. Buying his footwear herself, as nowhere had size eleven shoes. That piece of information Thursa kept to herself. Something about him drew them together; she was not fooled by his fictional hard-man persona, seeing beneath an ease to his manner. His clumsiness annoyed her at first but by now she was used to it.

Fighting the temptation to sleep, heavy eyelids hover over her bloodshot eyes. Slowly the darkness of night retreats as the morning sunlight breaks through a gap in the curtains, always a pleasant visitor as you get older, it reflects off the back wall just as his fever is breaking. Opening his eyes exhaustion in his body, he sees the tired face of Thursa, heavily lined, coughing into another white hankie.

"Have you been here all night?"

He reaches across patting her hand. Bringing a twinkle to her seasoned eyes.

"Where else would I be?" she answers indignantly.

"You've gone all night, without a ciggy?"

Grinning now she cuffs his ear, with her thin bony, arthritic fingers. Life has brought this elderly lady onto his path. Her unwavering faith is making everything possible and her love is unconditional; he has learnt a lot of practical life skills from her. Realising nothing was by chance, all part of life's magnificent tapestry. Letting go of his mistakes has enabled Peter to understand his life and the direction in which he is travelling. A grandmother figure, a true blessing. Peace resides in the room, flowing easily between the two of them. They both wish this moment would last forever.

Emma has a large following on her Unity Seminar blog, which went viral as it is accessed across the world, as she gained unrestricted passage to the monk and his group. Unaware she is an important member of this team of messengers. Hopping into the shower, covering herself in soapy suds, 'Mexican Lime' it says on the bottle, she closes her eyes quickly to reduce a sharp stinging sensation from some wayward bubbles that burn her eyes. Mentally she completes a piece of work in her head setting out the detail, concentrating on that elusive headline. Enjoying the peace and quiet as the water massages her head, filtering through her, hair to ease away the tension from her scalp as she rinses the soapy residue, invigorating her whole body with the sharp scent of fragrant lime. Her thoughts are rudely interrupted by the discovery of a small lump under her skin on her right breast. A sickly feeling runs through her body, accompanied by an adrenalin rush, as she recalls the monk's words.

"Emma, if you feel ill, go seek a doctor."

Unwilling to ignore him a second time, panic strikes. As she tries to calm her erratic breathing, she takes long deep breaths to slow her overworked heart rate. Her grandmother died of cancer, fate springs to mind, that which is inevitable, predetermined, her destiny. Hysteria causes her mind to wander, life has been good. Happiness in some, only realised when it's on the brink of being taken away, health, family life and work. Once it is removed, we crave what we had in the first place, not realising its true value until it is under threat. Thought attacking her mind, constant. Crashing out of the shower cubical, hair dripping wet, staring at her naked reflection in the mirror. Her life has changed in that instant, priorities, goals, everything. She struggles to dress her damp body, hurriedly pulling her clothing over her tacky wet skin, hopping on one foot as she fights with her woollen tights and puts her iPhone on speaker as she cancels all her appointments for the day.

Dave, busy at the breakfast bar, hears the whirlwind rapidly rotating around the house as Emma picks up her bag and flings it over her shoulder. She shoves her iPhone and tablet inside, before dashing out the door, stopping briefly to plant a kiss on Dave's lips.

"Going without breakfast?" he shouts after her, leaving a void in his heart and their home.

Eagerly Adrianna searches for premises to establish The Fountain of Youth, intent upon opening a franchise in the north of the country. Ignoring advice from her business advisor to set up in Manchester, a large city with good rail links to Leeds and Yorkshire, she insists on Liverpool. Finding a large airy warehouse with magnificent, large windows flooding the space with natural light, located on the same road as the Spirit of Truth. Like a game of chess, she plots her next move.

Father Jimmy and the monk, having already viewed the larger property, declining it as it held onto bad energy, feeling sour emotions seeping through the walls, souls ambushed, caught up in someone else's life game. These discarded souls decaying in the deafening silence of abandonment. Forgotten like this ramshackle old building. The monk's third eye senses evil's trap, as destructive energies gather, waiting to sow their evil seed, seeping and slithering through the surfaces, waiting to attack a gullible host body.

"Do not walk in the path of the wicked, nor sit beside it, attracting shameful or scornful ways to leading the righteous off their path."

This message was firmly imprinted in the monk's mind when he viewed this property. Reminding his followers that nothing is stronger than belief. Everyone has their own weaknesses and strengths. Always show your enemy confidence and unity to truly succeed. Daily the monk and priest reinforce their spiritual practices by guided meditation and prayer, thus gaining a deeper understanding of each other's cultures. Honouring the spirit, encouraging harmony and balance amongst themselves and the group. Clearing their minds, leaving behind yesterday's troubles and worries, alert and bright, attracting an uncluttered peaceful mind, ready for the spiritual warfare that sits just beyond the horizon.

Arriving at the rectory before the messengers have had time to finish their spiritual rituals and hammering impatiently on the heavy front door, Emma waits, anxiously shuffling from foot to foot. Dishevelled looking, face blotchy, her eyes glassy from impromptu crying, not advocating the power dressing professional she usually presents. Hair still damp, showing a distinct curl, she carryies fear in her watery eyes.

Rushing up the hall and stubbing her toe on the hall stand, Thursa growls, "Where's the fire?"

Wrenching the front door open, Thursa is presented with this frightened creature. Realising that Emma is fighting a battle from within, Thursa brings her in, quickly applying a sunny smile and a kind word, chattering about nothing of any importance, hoping to bring a bit of light relief into her life, albeit temporarily. Thursa senses a darkness around Emma in tune with her own senses.

"Are they here?"

Eyes searching, flitting swiftly around the room. No need to ask to whom she is referring.

"In the garden, praying, meditating. They like to start the day on a positive. Something like that."

Thursa shakes her head dismissively, ignoring the pain in her little toe, while clearing out the fire grate, her back to Emma, on her knees now.

"Father Jimmy leads them in prayer and the monk embraces nature."

Emma thought she heard a muffled giggle.

Thursa continues talking when silence would have best filled the void. "Still trying to get me head around these new ways."

Rising now, staggering slightly, before washing her hands, she busies herself with the next chore, setting the table, needing a distraction from this awkward prolonged silence.

"Father Jimmy asked me to get all this in for our visitors, have you ever seen the like?"

An array of fresh fruit, muesli and brown bread, is laid out on the table. Thursa grumbles about the smell of the green tea.

"They drink that without milk, you know."

The normality of the domestic situation brings a grin to Emma's face, a moment's respite.

"Who's that for?"

Sizzling on a low heat is a pan of bacon, egg, sausage and tomatoes. The aroma has awakened Emma's taste buds.

With a guilty look, Thursa answers, "Peter."

Perceiving a dilemma as he intercepts a negative energy flow, Choden Lamas quickly wraps the meditation session up. Entering the kitchen, he is hit by the smell of meat cooking in grease, turning his delicate stomach. He is fascinated with the digestive system of the big fellow. Watching Peter devour everything that is put on his plate. The monk is surprised that the plate retains its pattern. Grateful Choden Lamas sees fresh colourful fruit with muesli that has been sweetened, laid out on the oak table, thinking you can't have everything and this elderly lady works like a Trojan. Thankful for the familiar aroma of his soothing green tea, filling his nostrils. Emma shoots him a sidelong glance while hovering uncomfortably in the corner of the kitchen, aware that she is disturbing breakfast, tiredness in her young eyes, the whites slightly discoloured.

"Can I have a word?" Emma says while checking her wrist watch. "I don't like to disturb you, but it's important."

Looking at her aura, he can see the dark specks of fear, filtering into the otherwise bright aura. Subconsciously, she is protecting her breast, with her hand resting over the dark shadow.

"Do you mind?" politely the monk asks Thursa, conscious of the work she puts into every meal.

A quick nod of the head answers his question; she shoves a cup and saucer into his hands as he exits the kitchen. Without a sound, he leads Emma into the parlour.

They are hardly through the door when she begins, rambling at first. "It's a self-fulfilling prophecy, I knew this day would come. Life has been so good to me, us." Inhaling deeply, she continues, "Then Ava, now this. My grandmother died of cancer." She splutters out her words, not making a lot of sense. She stops for a stifled breath and silence falls between them as she waits for his retort.

Surrounded by calmness, taking time to breath, a feeling of peace enters the room, soothing her as he gently guides Emma to the large bay window central to the room. Placing his cup of green tea on the mahogany nest of tables, pulling back the heavy net curtains, light spills through the large Victorian window, to reflect off the walls and spill over the worn furnishings, revealing a bright spring morning sun. She turns her face to enjoy the powerful rays, their warmth magnified by the glass. Rich green grass, hosting crocuses and daffodils, awash with purple and yellow flowers. Pale blue sky, with white fluffy clouds and splinters of sharp bright sunlight breaking through to bounce off the different textures and surfaces, which reminds her of a spot light on stage.

"Only the Supreme Being may foretell or predict what is coming. He may choose to share with his trusted messengers, or He may not. Sometimes a storm crashes around our lives, do not ignore it, for it brings a warning. We can choose our path, but there are consequences that follow. We may need to slow down and take stock. By examining our emotions, we may gain a deeper understanding or maybe there is a role for you to fulfil. The world made beautiful isn't that what most of us desire. These are all things money can't buy, yet that is still the driving force here in the West. Belief will get you through, not money or possessions. When the storm ceases it will take with it the dead wood in your life. Commit yourself to belief. Use your mind power. Do not sit on the fence.

The most powerful drug is the placebo, the power of the mind. Believing you are taking a drug is as powerful as actually taking the drug. Evolution has dulled our inner senses. Embrace how your body works, listen to what is happening on the inside. In the darkest corners there is always hope, all we need to do is trust."

Fear melts from Emma's eyes.

"I want you to take some time off," the monk continues.

Turning her wrist over, he removes her watch, placing it in the palm of her hand.

"We give our life over to time, not enjoying the gift of here and now, our master the clock, tick, tick, tock. Spend the weekend with your family, dreamers, doers and thinkers. Escape into the countryside. Do not take any electronic devices. Enjoy nature go for long walks, talk to each other, eat when you are hungry, drink when thirsty. Your body and the light will tell you when you need sleep. If it asks for a nap in daylight give in to it. You are at a junction on your road, not the end. Come see me when you return."

When his faint, quiet voice finishes, Emma is filled with renewed confidence and a spring in her step, almost dancing down the street. A heavy burden has been lifted from her shoulders after spending only a few minutes in the presence of a positive influence.

Finishing his breakfast bowl of raw fruit, an array of colours, easy to digest, supplying his body with energy a wonderful source of fuel.

Choden Lamas approaches Father Jimmy. "It is time to heal Peter's emotional wound, I wanted to leave it a bit longer, but the enemy is near. We will fetch Jools from the hospice, Thursa has informed me that she will be volunteering there this morning."

Father Jimmy asks Peter to remain with Thursa as she is looking tired, standing leaning against the kitchen sink, hands submerged in dish water, bent slightly with her arthritic back. Peter agrees but is a little put out; he finds purpose by Father Jimmy's side. Looking at Thursa busying herself, guilt pulls at his heartstrings.

The two of them engage on a morning of housework and baking. Thursa is sure none of his cakes will rise, as he has a real heavy-handedness about his baking, but she enjoys this quality time with Peter before the inevitable fallout.

The priest and the monk command a lot of attention as they travel by bus, the eye-catching saffron robe and the priest's cassock. Proud of his religious faith, Father Jimmy chose this outdated long, dark coat with thirty-three buttons running down the front as symbolic of the life of Jesus, unaware of the nudges and giggles. Choden Lamas is happy to provide amusement amongst the commuters, for it is always a positive energy. His travelling companions are fixated on the pair of them.

Alighting from the bus, the two messengers stroll down the country lane that leads to the hospice.

"A magnificent setting," the monk voices enthusiastically, inhaling deeply, filling his chest with country air.

"Not for the people who are here on the brink of death." Father Jimmy says, looking sullen.

"Death is part of the cycle of life, you can't have one without the other. In the same way, we feel ill at ease in a new job. After a couple of hours, we have settled in nicely; it is just the fear of the unknown.

Death is not feared in the East, we're just simply moving from one room into another.

Risk takers and adrenalin junkies enjoy the excitement of the unknown; that is what we should feel about death, starting a new chapter in our own individual story."

Continuing down the lane, admiring the avenue of trees, all the same species to give a uniform appearance. Branches stretch across the road, entwining like praying hands, casting shadows on the grassy verge below. A kaleidoscope of colours creates beautiful patterns due to the reflective rays of the sun breaking through the dense branches. Wildlife moves around freely, spectacular uninterrupted views of nature in its natural habitat, one of our many God-given gifts.

"I can see why the hospice is out here, in this splendid scenery."

Father Jimmy walks silently, apprehensive at what is coming.

"Love is the only emotion needed to improve our lives; with devotion, we can tackle anything. The river of life flows freely, meandering through the ground, never still, gently swept along. Sometimes it flows steadily, occasionally surging over rapids, but it never stops as it adapts and moves on like life. Start each day happy. Let go of any disasters we encountered yesterday; we can't change the past. Cast them into the stream, learn from our actions and accept the consequences. We are rich in life, surrounded by the beauty of nature free to all dwelling in the mist of knowledge. We must never lose hope, or relinquish our freedom to another. That is where negative emotions like anger, stress, depression, anxiety and guilt slip in to take root, spreading like the branches of a tree, far reaching and dense. Each time we help one another the Supreme Being grows strong, reinforcing His decision to give us all free will."

"Why bring us together, we are very different in many ways?" As the question leaves his lips, Father Jimmy grasps the answer to his own question.

"As is the human race. Religion was never about segregation, it was like-minded people enjoying the freedom of life. Learning to live and love one another. Helping and looking out for the less fortunate, the lonely and isolated. Over thousands of years we have tailored religion to suit our own cultures. If we can be brought together, two very different religions and races, then there is hope for the rest of humanity. People still sacrifice their lives to make money, only realising when it is too late that money was a trap. Have you ever visited a person on their death bed, worried about finance?"

"Well, no, they want their family or friends," The priest concedes.

"Having blindly traded their health and happiness in the pursuit of money, they hoped it would increase their enjoyment and standing in life. Greed and a quick profit disturbed their balance and polluted their immediate environment with negativity. Thus begins the root of misery. All it has done is steal their precious sacred time."

Father Jimmy has noticed an increase in the monk's spirituality during his deep connection with nature. While he is amongst a clean positive environment, it impacts greatly on his other layers, bringing him into balance and clearing his connection to himself and others. His fondness for trees helps him tap into a benevolent energy. Looking at each other, a thought springs into Father Jimmy's mind.

"You're learning." The monk grins at him before continuing to explain. "As well as five senses, we have five layers which impact greatly on our lives, each of them affecting the other. The environment we live in, good or bad, affects our Physical Wellbeing. A healthy body is a healthy mind, thus affecting our Mood. A happy mind helps us to progress and makes us able to engage with institutes, groups, religions or governments – any form of establishment. All these connections result in consequences that impact on our Spirit, mediating between body and soul, settling and reconciling the two.

By tapping into nature, that is accessible to us all, we can gain a higher power. By using our intuition and instinctively knowing, without the use of rational processes, we can regain senses lost. Enjoying a connection in the presence of nature deepens our understanding of it and each other.

Greed is disturbing our balance, tugging us in a different direction. Removing some from their path completely, their bodies sick with sin. That is where Karma comes in, the Supreme Being is merciful, showing compassion where He can."

Father Jimmy, relaxed and unhurried, strolls alongside the monk, having mellowed nicely with age, a gentleness about his maturity, brimming with wisdom, giving the monk his full and undivided attention as Choden Lammas relays one of his tales.

"Listening patiently to the greedy, selfish man, whom the Supreme Being gave an abundance of whatever he desired. Glowing with physical and mental health, a family that loved and adored him, for no other reason than he is himself. Never content, always wanting more, a more powerful job, faster car; telling himself it would improve his family's lifestyle considerably. More work meant less family time, putting his life off balance. A large man carrying a small character. Wanting a bigger home, for his small family. Unable to enjoy the present, still he reaches for more. On receipt of everything he had requested, he leaves his family to engage in a lustful relationship with a younger woman. Trying to recapture his waning youth, missing it terribly. Not enjoying the wisdom that comes with age, he ignores his wife and children's plight. The man has vast knowledge but terrible judgment. For seven years he ignores his family's calling, unreachable to all. His wife grows strong in his absence, finding an inner strength, to provide single-handedly, and deposits greatly into her life's account as her husband moves to another country. Then Karma steps in, like the house of cards, the greedy man's life crumbles. He suffers a heart attack, having sacrificed his health in the pursuit of money engaged in a dubious lifestyle. Unable to work, his finances dry up, his younger companion leaves him as he is unable to provide for her financially. On the brink of death, as foolishly he has no health care insurance, one of his sons reaches out the hand of forgiveness, assisting him to return home. To a country that provides unlimited healthcare. He has his operation and is given back time to learn. His family greet him, his wife no longer bitter, befriends him. She receives great graces for this and forgiveness sets her free. He has lost all his possessions, power and standing in his community. Realising now that the most important thing in his life is family. Unable to regain his wife's unconditional love, he gains insight into what he has lost, regrettably settling for her friendship."

"Why give him everything, if you know what is going to happen?" the priest urges.

"So that he and others may learn, no matter how difficult or painful the experience, lessons must be learnt, tolerance can always be found.

The battle we have is great, many live like the greedy man. Our job is to guide them back on their paths, which is why we cannot have any casualties amongst us. A lot is riding on Peter's emotional well-being."

Chapter 12

Music blares out as Emma hastily packs a holdall, grabbing bits and pieces of multi-coloured clothing from her chest of drawers, throwing them into her weekend bag, unlike her usual selection process. Dancing around her bedroom as the music uplifts her mood, releasing serotonin, a hormone that promotes happiness and wellbeing, floods her brain. The window is thrown wide open. She inhales the fresh salt air; her body is warm from movement. Emma loves living close to the sea, watching the spellbinding sunsets, seeing the vibrant colours spread across the rippling water, before disappearing into the unknown. It is the perfect way to relax her mind and body.

Booking time off work, an instruction rather than a request, while she waits for her hospital appointment to come through, knowing she won't be able to concentrate on mundane work. She is busy building happy memories to see her through a difficult time. If it is bad news, she's going to be as physically fit as she can be in order to tackle whatever life throws at her head on. Healthy mind, healthy body.

Destination Cornwall, with its beautiful oak woodlands and peaceful creeks, exploring the secluded beaches of the south west coast, is her chosen destination. Where the villagers live at a slower pace of life, even their language has an easy rhythmic tempo, these friendly Cornish folk.

No phones or tablets to interrupt her precious family time, just the three of them enjoying the simplicity of life. Giving Ava time and space to lick her wounds and time to ready herself for what may lay ahead, Dave, her soul mate, not needing to be in the limelight but choosing to be by her side. Travelling the scenic route misses out the depressing concrete motorway, with lanes full of tense, aggressive drivers dodging in and out of each other's lanes, horns beeping, lights flashing, gesticulating hand signs; Emma removes the negative where possible. Enjoying the slow flow of the B roads, travelling through towns and countryside, the smells and sounds differ greatly, watching the contrast of the two while discovering new destinations. Stopping half-way, the family enjoy a spot of lunch to quieten their grumbling stomachs, talking and listening without any distractions. They stretch their tired limbs and finally take a much needed toilet break.

Arriving late, only the clock in the car is available as all electronic devices have been left behind. Ava refers to her mother as a hippy for removing timepieces from their trip. Not complaining too much now, as she is sure no one would want to contact her anyway. Hiding these insecurities, Ava buries them behind her anger.

"Your father and I never had mobile phones when we were your age."

Ava just rolls her eyes,

"I know, you used a red phone box on the corner of the street in the olden days."

Laughing, Emma realises how funny she must sound. She embraces the quietness and smells of the countryside, even the manure spread on a nearby farmers field. Ava pinches her nose, missing some things from home. A light friendly atmosphere surrounds them as nature just leisurely exists, hiding amongst the black canvas that surrounds them. The hoot of an owl makes them jump as they peer into the pitch of nightfall, using their other sense rather than sight. Hearing the creaking branches of the large trees, the rustling of their leaves and the hedgerows standing to attention, whispering lightly as the birds settle in for the night. These sounds guide them to the entrance of the cottage. Fidgeting with the unfamiliar key in the lock, their eyes start to adjust to the blackness. Finally, they open the stable door. Feeling for the unfamiliar light switch located just inside the door, light floods the wide hallway with artificial light. They are greeted by a solid wooden floor. Removing their outdoor shoes, they rush in from the cold, making their way into an open plan living area. The kitchen houses a range of oak units and a large oak dining table, a basket of goodies in the centre, reading the floral note left perched on top.

"To our guests,

There are some essentials in the fridge and fuel by the wood burner, welcome and enjoy your stay. "

What a kind, thoughtful gesture. Opening the fridge, they discover full fat milk, six freshly laid eggs (the outer shell visibly carrying a bit of debris), and freshly baked bread on the side. A large wood burner draws their attention to the middle of the room. Encased in beautiful stonework, a basket sits next to the fire, stuffed full of wood. Dave sets to, lighting the fire while Emma and Ava prepare some food having brought with them new potatoes, spinach and salmon fillets. Emma is very conscious of her diet, even more so after this health scare. Dave opens a bottle of white wine as they sit and wait for the steamer to cook their food. The pan lid rattles in the background as the steam builds. Huddled together on the couch, wrapped under a fleecy blanket, they wait for the fire to take hold. They are entertained by the flames from the fire which reflect on the walls, dancing; their eyes are automatically drawn to this spectacle. The soft orangey glow, accompanied by a dull table lamp and a few candles dotted sporadically. Laughing till tears roll down their cheeks, free from the constraints of time. With full stomachs, and feeling warm and cosy, they retire to bed; heavy eyes are telling them that it is time to bring this eventful, positive day to a close.

Peter has noticed that Thursa is not herself, dropping things, smoking more than usual – if that's possible. Not sure if she's nervous or agitated, caring Peter asks, "Have I done something to offend you?"

She looks at his handsome, chiselled face, just visible from behind his beard. Even though she is filled with pride, a look of discomfort shows now on Thursa's face.

Peter takes Thursa's hand and looks enquiringly into her worn face. A sharp maternal pain hits her like a sledge hammer as she looks at this young man who freely gives his trust.

"Let's have a cup of tea," he says.

Reluctantly, she sits at the kitchen table, pulling her hand-knitted blue cardigan tightly together. Leaning now across the table as he anticipates some sort of disclosure, he patiently waits. His hands rest in his lap, clasped tightly together, as he apprehensively sits bolt upright, giving his full attention.

Thursa begins. "Peter, we talked about your life before you came here, never really going into detail. The sickness you had last night was the monk and Father Jimmy healing your physical scar."

Passing her hand across her chin now, before settling it back on the table, she shows him that she is unsettled.

Surprisingly, he says, "I know, I thought I was hallucinating. Horrid vile thoughts and images kept popping into my head."

"You said that no one loved you and that no one ever had, because a violent act had produced you."

Thursa gauges his reaction.

The conversation falls still for a moment. Before Peter takes a leap of faith ready to unburden himself.

Self-conscious at first, Peter isunable to meet her gaze. He stares at a painting of a tree, rugged and tall, bending in a fierce wind, leaves ripped from the branches, floating down the canvas, a gift from the monk. It hangs proudly on the kitchen wall just above Thursa's right shoulder. His eyes are transfixed by the painting as his mouth reveals his innermost fears.

"I felt rejected, constantly embarrassed, humiliated, a failure, no one wanting to foster me. This constant rejection led to the transformation of my personality. Giving people what they expected rather than opening up to reveal a frightened young man. The enemy slipped in unnoticed when I was at my lowest ebb. Planting lies like seeds in the ground, spreading and growing, taking hold of my mind. Using devious tactics, evil was free to manipulate me. I didn't want this life brought into being by such an evil act."

Feeling another presence Peter turns quickly, seeing Jools slumped in the hall doorway, wearing her bright red jumper, a dab of matching lipstick on her heart-shaped lips. There is no smile on her usually happy face. Supporting herself on the door frame, tears roll down her cheeks, smudging the foundation on her porcelain-like face.

"What have I done?" she whispers.

Puzzled, Peter silently observes her behaviour.

Choden Lamas appears, bringing Jools to the old kitchen table which has acted as a confessional over the years. This old wooden structure has heard many a secret. Hesitantly, Jools sits.

Thursa exits the room, desperate to leave the wretchedness of the situation and not wanting to see Peter vexed. Clutching her cigarette packet, she decides to pray, seeking answers.

Taking Peter's large hand in his and Jools' in the other, the monk transmits their thoughts and feelings between them. A distinctive strained mood hangs over the kitchen while he channels the other's emotions. Trying role reversal, they each experience the other's hurt, wounds untreated for years. Jools witnesses Peter's early life, his emotional distress and confusion, always waiting to be picked, a couple of weeks here and there fostering, always sent back, his little face drooping with continual rejection. The tears and tantrums of this unwanted young soul, slowly destroy this little boy. His only possession is a knitted blue mouse and he holds onto it. It is his only tangible connection to his mother, having lost its smell over the years to distance them further. His failed attempts at making something of his life, joining the army already carrying a broken mind. The horrors of war too much for him to bear. Returning to the only place he knew, removing all bad memories by self-medicating with drugs.

Jools feels angered by this very personal ambush, having concealed the truth for years. She changes her posture to a harder, defensive stance. Her face and neck redden as her hands shake with anger.

Peter sees into his mother's heart, a happy-go-lucky woman, attractive, witty and smart. Trying to better herself, one of life's dreamers. Confidently applying for a new job, with the courage to succeed, but her youth leaves her at a disadvantage as she is savagely attacked, leaving her broken and vulnerable. Caught in another's evil trap, she is left permanently scarred. The fear and shame she feels when realising she is pregnant, trying to ignore the warning signs, hiding it until it is too late. Avoiding her closest friend, who had advised a termination. Being a courageous young woman, she wanted to give this foetus, conceived out of violence, the chance of life. Disgusted at herself, for not being able to love her child – Peter. Feeling numb when he was born in secret but not wanting to transfer her negative feelings on to him. Giving him a chance, she left him on the church doorstep with the hope of a loving family life for him. Inconsolable thereafter, as fate was not to give her another child. Suffering crushing emotions, nearly going under a few times, even contemplating her own demise, she plunged these feelings deeply into the recesses of her mind. A stalemate falls between then, each recognising the other's plight. They each struggle to move forward as these feelings are still very intense and raw.

Darkness hastily fills the kitchen as the sun withdraws. The positive energy flow retires with the sunshine, to be replaced with a still, awkward hush. It feels very similar to the moment before one plummets from the edge of a cliff into the unknown. Temperatures drop as heavy rain clouds roll in, dark and menacing above the rectory, replicating the mood in the kitchen. Mother Nature warns of her attack as birds flee, taking cover in the surrounding plant life. A cold chill is present in the air as the monk tries unsuccessfully to move this union from the darkness into the light. Thursa and Father Jimmy re-join the group to engage in fervent prayer and strengthen the spiritual warfare. Like warriors, they sense that something or someone is blocking their progress. Driving, heavy rain pummells against the large kitchen window, thrashing wildly, forming instant puddles, constant and unrelenting, filling the occupants of the kitchen with dread.

Undeterred, Choden Lamas rises, showing his courage, to venture into the battered garden, fighting against the vicious storm. Drained of vital energy, accompanied always by his silent follower, both figures stagger against the powerful force of nature. Caught by a blast of wind, they are picked up and swept along like garden debris as trees thrash and bend. Fighting desperately in this labyrinth of darkness, both monks are participants in Jing Chi, an ancient art, which controls the body by celibacy, transforming energy into higher power which can be used at a spiritual level for healing. Needing this higher energy now, they push on. His spirit like a river needs to flow and replenish itself, endlessly recycling and revitalising itself. Challenged by nature to recharge his essential strength and continue sparring against this unforgiving storm. Using all his senses, he hears the tall tree gently calling to him. He reaches the weathered bark of the familiar tree and caresses it with his soft palm, as both monk and follower sit at the bottom of the blackened garden, desperately embracing the tree like an old friend, drawing from its superior strength. An essential part of this ritual, withdrawing from the pith both potency and strength, chanting loudly, his voice just audible over the raging storm. Cautiously waiting to proceed, ready to engage his third eye, he scours for danger. Avoiding evil which, as always, lies in readiness, waiting to attack.

Navigating his path and imploring assistance of the Supreme Being, there is momentary joy as Choden's senses acknowledge His presence, bringing with it unconditional love, watching it multiply and overflow filling the surrounding area with peace and bliss. Vast radiant light wraps itself around nature's precious tree, blinding to human eyes. With depth and feelings visible, it brings together belief, wisdom, healing and trust. Transforming these into mighty energy, using his superior mind to control the powerful wind, blowing the storm clouds that contain evil away. Instantly lifting the darkness, to be flooded with natural sunlight, breaking through. Heightening the presence of the Supreme Being, who alone controls the forces of nature by calming the raging seas; He is creator of all.

Mother Nature, she is His, an all-powerful savage beast with her wild spirit, like a bride on her wedding night, pure of soul, beautiful and daring with her untamed mood.

Enraged by the attack, the Supreme One inhibits the storm, swiftly bringing it to a premature close.

Dominant and in control, the Supreme Being reigns.

Relieved as quietness quickly descends (nature is now silent and wildlife is in hiding), he walks past the garden debris which wraps around his cold feet. Choden Lamas returns to the kitchen, glowing, ready to re-engage. A warmth fills the monk's heart as he sits back at the old familiar kitchen table, host of many a debate. This wooden structure is where he is joined by his spiritual family. Thursa removes herself from the group into the corner, cigarette aglow, balanced effortlessly on her bottom lip, inhaling deeply as the tobacco calms her body.

"For my nerves," she comments.

Letting his eyelids gently dip, unwilling to meet their gaze, the monk recites his master's words.

Mother Nature protects us all,
As we travel through life's unpredictable waters,
They shall not overflow,
When we are surrounded by fire,
No burn or scorch will occur,
Nor shall strong winds unbalance or conquer us,
I alone am permitted to enter the eye of the storm.
Protected by Mother Nature, in the centre of her calm.
No evil shall befall me."

Surprised at this flowing statement, the rest of the group look at the monk bewildered.

"I'm as confused as are you, my mouth opened and out gushed the words," Choden Lamas explains.

Annoyed, Peter makes to leave the table. Bewildering thoughts run wildly around in his head. His mind has been torn wide open during this very personal attack. His masculine palms push heavily on the smooth wooden structure, pressing himself up as fury slips back in, watching from behind his menacing eyes as an uncontrolled volcano bubbles below the surface. Evil moves in with ease, as he is left unguarded.

Peter feels confused and hurt, believing misfortune follows him everywhere. Having buried his parentage deeply for decades, he now feels completely exposed; his soul is bare as all eyes rest on him.

"I never wanted to visit this painful place."

Peter sounds like a man child, throwing an accusing look at Thursa sitting isolated and alone in the corner, his dark, brooding eyes boil with resentment. He might as well have slapped her across the face, the impact would have been the same; she shifts slightly with this unexpected personal attack.

"I was happy," Peter whines, crashing towards the door unable to see through his blind fury. Thursa's arms ache to embrace him burt she quickly controls this powerful maternal urge.

Swiftly Choden Lamas intercepts him with the agility reserved for a man half his age. With a positive touch, gentle, reducing his aggression, he reassures Peter.

"Do not be afraid of uncertainty, embrace it, learn from it, then you can move forward, taking small steps at first."

"What if it's bad?"

"Bad things happen to everyone, it's how you deal with them that counts. We are in charge of our own destiny, do we choose to repeat mistakes or move forward learning from them. Fear only holds us back, stunting our spiritual growth.

Let's look at sociopaths, some are born from a family curse, going untreated or ignored for generations. Smart sociopaths adapt, learning to play the game of life. Outwardly kind and caring, helpful to friends and neighbours, living and working amongst us, they blend in, dressing the same, looking similar, shopping at the supermarket, washing laundry, drawing you in, until one day they have you in their web, trapped. No need for their mask anymore as their true character emerges, dark and dangerous.

That was your father, a clever man, who hatched a wicked plan; he was carrying scars from his childhood, which were untreated, festering, multiplying, and gaining momentum. Without positive reinforcement there was no chance of change for him. Divine Timing is when a window of opportunity appears in our lives, the planets and universe align, with the correct mind-set wondrous things can be achieved. Now is your time, Peter, but first you must find peace within yourself before you can help obtain peace for others. Be a reflection of what you would like to see in others, incorporate positive behaviour. If you are angry, you will absorb anger, if you are forgiving, you will be showered with forgiveness, all you have to do is change your mind-set."

Turning his attention to the seated group, with some of his energy waning already, there is a flatness to his tone as he addresses them.

"We have a lot of work here with the new centre in its infancy, drug treatments, alternative therapies, removing the feeling of worthlessness from the youth, giving families a purpose in life. The enemy fills young parents with addictions, living their lives in a blur, smearing their future, this to be repeated generation after generation. Others working so hard family life is replaced with computers and modern technology. Losing the art of communication and conversation, outdoor pursuits, something that is viewed through a misty window. Things will only change with action."

"Where do I come into all this?" Jools asks, expressing the same sullen look as her son Peter.

"You are a very courageous woman, choosing to keep a child conceived through violence. Many graces will come your way. Your

Peter has been chosen to guide the lost and isolated members of the community. They trust him, he's one of their own, understanding the daily plight of homelessness; trust is a delicate emotion. The good you see in him, comes from within you. He has been cleansed, healing his physical wound was relatively easy. Healing his emotional scar is up to you. His father served various lusts and pleasures; dabbling with the dark arts, he was consumed with malice, envy and rage. Peter has moved past disappointment, fear and worries, shedding sorrow, like a discarded garment of clothing. When things overwhelmed him, he took one step at a time, his burden never heavier than he could carry. Tolerance and patience is the only way, don't judge yourself or others too harshly, leave room for love, through positive thoughts, words and deeds."

It's been an eventful day, Father Jimmy thinks as this powerful group scurries from the kitchen.

"Nothing happens by chance, please visit us again tomorrow."

There is gentleness in the Monks pleading voice as he watches Jools disappear into the hall.

Hastily throwing on her outdoor coat, whilst mentally battered, she looks at Peter sensing a connection of some kind. His features resemble her beloved father, the same large build and square jaw line, soulful dark family eyes. A well-read thoughtful man, her dad always saw the good in people, often advocating a second chance. Without answering, she makes to leave. She is compelled to lightly pat Peter's shoulder, communicating with him through some form of physical contact. She is not sure why; her mind is befuddled. Her touch is like an electric shock, awakening an emotional energy inside him that is unfamiliar, arousing a painful sensation in his heart. Not expecting love from this woman who selflessly cares for others, yet another part of her beautiful nature, he would happily settle for not seeing hatred in her eyes.

Unsettled, Peter heads straight for bed, rushing up the creaking stairs, taking them two at a time, ignoring Thursa's offer of supper. He loves this difficult elderly woman and hates her at the same time as he experiences the highs and lows of today's emotional turmoil. Dragging his heavy velvet curtains across the window, blocking out any specks of light, instantly the room is plummeted into darkness. Throwing his body onto the bed, burying his face in the soft feather pillows. Sinking into the blackness of his room and mood, stifling his sobs as his face rests on the tear stained cotton pillowcases, inhaling the lavender softener used in the last wash. Engaging again on an emotional roller coaster.

Nature in the countryside noisily announces the arrival of the morning. Rising early, excitedly peeping through the curtains to be greeted by the spring sunshine which gives the illusion of a warm morning. Leisurely moving around the heart of the cottage, an unusually bright morning delights Emma's eyes. Having slept soundly, in the silence of the dense countryside, both body and mind feel relaxed. With no idea of the time, her hair is hanging wildly, free to form its own natural curls. Pulling on her padded jacket over her pyjamas and slipping her feet into a pair of oversized willies, she ventures out into the sharp, spring morning air. Cupping her coffee mug in her hands, she inhales the clean fresh country air, feeling the stillness of her soul. Bird song and distant cattle lowing fill the backdrop. Occasionally, the odd vehicle can be heard rumbling past in the distance. While sipping the steaming hot liquid, she watches nature come alive. The red squirrel moves like a ninja between the shrubs, feeding on flower bulbs, rooting them out of the cold, dark earth. He is watching her as she observes him – both of them are keeping their distance from each other, with their territories established. Each respects the other's personal space. She sinks her teeth into the brown toast with lime and mint marmalade, crunching loudly; the sharpness compliments the coffee perfectly. She is appreciating the slowness of life in the countryside, which sets its own pace. Every blade of grass and flower waiting to tell their own individual story, wafting lightly in the spring breeze. Like a piece of priceless artwork, beauty in its entirety. Letting ideas and thoughts flow and develop in these sublime surroundings. Breathing in the garden's unique perfume. Nature so quiet, it's deafening. Emma feels her body unwind, floating, without the pressure of time constraints, free like the birds that glide in the pale blue sky. Appearing in the doorway is her husband, with hair ruffled and sleepy eyes, and he flashes a grin.

"What you doing out here?"

Breaking the hush, he strolls over to her, rubbing his hands up and down his bare arms as he feels the spring nip. The red squirrel sees the large intruder and shoots off to scale a large tree, from where it eyes him with curiosity.

"Enjoying the beauty of life," Emma replies wistfully.

Joining her, he wraps himself around her, inhaling her unique scent and wanting to protect every molecule of her being. Disguising a worried look as it crosses his face, a protective arm around her, he draws her in close, feeling the warmth generated between their two bodies, snuggling in.

"It will be alright," he whispers, planting a reassuring kiss on her forehead. A slight quiver in his voice gives him away.

Their love, stronger than passion, has matured into deeper emotions. Awakening their kindred souls to reach a divine love experienced by few. A magnetic attractive force welding them together, two halves of a whole, completely transcending another level to encompass life itself – this is his soul mate. A burning sensation rises in his throat as he stifles his frightened tears.

"Are we going to tell Ava?"

Emma hears the break in his brave voice and also anger at giving himself away.

"When we get home." She is reassuring him, the strong powerful woman who is the cement that holds this family together. "When I know what I am dealing with. Why worry her? We don't know if it's cancer yet."

That one word stabs him, causing excruciating pain, and he winces. She feels his body briefly tense, feeling like she has told him a lie. In tune with her body, her face is a window to her health. Everything about her feels different as she feels this subtle attack from within.

"Do you know what time it is?" he asks.

"Shush."

Smiling, Emma puts her index finger to his lips, drunk with looking into his loving eyes, enjoying the gift of togetherness, his grip pleasant like protective amour but still able to make her heart race.

"No time constraints, remember?"

Love lights up his watery eyes.

"The smell of toast woke me up," Dave jokes, placing his hand on his tummy.

"That fresh bread smells wonderful toasted."

"You go in. I'll be in, in a minute," Emma instructs.

Reluctantly, he removes his grip, losing their intimate connection. She watches him wander along the winding garden path, shoulders slumped, looking lost on his own, one half of a whole.

Emma experiences a shift within himself, feeling her tiny presence in the vast universe.

Having removed processed foods containing artificial colourants and preservatives rumoured to be linked to certain cancers from their diet after speaking to the monk. Aware that he's an old soul in a younger body, she starts her days as he suggested, with positive, thoughts. Admiring the cottage garden's brilliant display, she introduces alternative therapies, alongside conventional medicine. Meditation and self-belief, increasing her mind power, retaking control, removing self-doubt, with direct prayer. Confident enough to voice her fears.

"Treat the body like a car." the monk said. She recalls his words. "Put the right fuel in and run it daily."

She remembers laughing at this suggestion,

"Even an old banger?"

"Old bangers are reliable and run if you look after them, the more you service them the better they work."

An answer to everything.

"Keep life simple; once you find your own inner peace, understanding will follow and always remember to share a smile."

Retracing her footsteps into the cottage kitchen, watching Ava and Dave setting the table, a wine glass in the middle holds a few wild flowers, picked by Dave. A simple gesture, which holds a much deeper meaning as he wandered over to the far side of the garden.

Priceless is what she has in this room, her own masterpiece, no need for the pursuit of perfection, it doesn't exist. Once we accept that, we can enjoy life.

Adrianna's attack on the monk is relentless; already she has invaded some of his five layers. She has now moved into his environment. Money no object as she pushes on with the Fountain of Youth project, playing on youngsters' vanity as they examine themselves through the microscope of public opinion. Ready to relinquish yet another lost soul of its freedom as she lures it with the promise of perfection. Transferring control from their lives to hers. Disengaging happiness, unable to enjoy the present, no purpose or direction in life, she plants fear to remove all hope. Young impressionable minds remain, unaware that they have surrendered their freedom to another until it is too late.

The monk's amateur set-up angers Adrianna, The Spirit of Truth has gained a lot of public interest across the age ranges. She needs to infiltrate this group and she has chosen Peter as the weakest link. His physical body is open to drugs and his mind will follow as it tortures him with guilt about his parentage, inflicting mental anguish. Then by discrediting the group through the institute, she will be able to break the monk's spirit and his followers will flood to her.

Laughing hysterically to herself, she says, "Addiction – the easiest way to manipulate."

The noiseless kitchen seems empty when Father Jimmy rises; it is like a heart without its beat in Thursa's absence. Table set, with the best bone china cups and saucers, bowls and side plates. With an array of colourful food seen beneath the clear film, the table groans beneath its feast. No sign of Thursa as she left early to attend the hospice, wanting to complete her volunteer hours. Never one to let people down, and probably hoping to avoid Peter and Jools, Thursa, is reliable as ever, fulfilling her commitments. Remembering a conversation with Thursa when he first moved to Liverpool, When Father Jimmy asked her about friends and family, she simply said, "Life is easier without emotional ties; then there is less chance of you getting hurt."

She shut down her feelings years ago. Sighing heavily, Father Jimmy runs his fingers through his thick hair as he worries about this fragile lady whom they all take for granted, for she has gradually grown on them.

Thursa sits quite still at the bedside of Maria Jones, focussing on the crisp white sheets and inhaling the smell of antiseptic. Thursa is adept at concealing her emotions. Not fooling the petite lady lying motionless in the bed, floating blissfully between two worlds. Her beauty radiates outward, still visible at eighty-eight years of age. Warm, tender eyes and a contagious smile, Maria retains a slight Irish accent, even after living on the mainland for seventy of her long years.

Maria's life is no longer a mystery, having travelled a changeable path, sometimes easy, sometimes hard. Life's lessons learned, invited now to return home to family and friends passed. A favourite with the nursing staff, with her positive outlook on life. Waiting patiently on her two beloved daughters arriving, courageous to the end. Maria hovers between the planes.

She acknowledges someone in the far corner of the room, seen only through her eyes. She is comfortable in their presence.

"I'm ready to come home, Mammy," whispers Maria, breathless.

Thursa thinks she hears the whispered voice. She opens her mind as feelings and thoughts rattle around her cluttered head.

"I see the light, just want to say goodnight to my girls," whispers Maria again.

Smiling contentedly in the bed, aglow with happiness, there is no fear present. Thursa gently strokes her hand, a connection to let her know she is not alone. Maria looks at her, love shining in her beautiful blue eyes, seeing Thursa's inner turmoil. Maria is ready to depart, taking with her the guarded secret of life.

"Bless you," she whispers.

Thursa feels a wonderful emotion stirring inside her; she thinks how wonderful life would be if everyone felt like this. In the quietness that surrounds them, God's intentions are heeded. Eyes locked, communicating gratitude no words needed, this second seemingly endless, a eureka moment for Thursa.

Broken only by the whirlwind of the girls rushing through the ward doors, Thursa respectfully retreats as they each take a side of their mother's bed. Like Chinese guardian lions used on pillars at the entrance to a property for protection. Pure, honest, maternal love passing between mother and daughters, adoring this lady, her life path coming to an end. Understanding the treasure of motherly love, her life a success. Silently slipping across the weather bridge from one world, to be greeted in another by passed family who eagerly wait to greet her physical form

Empowered by this spectacle, Thursa struts off to the bus stop, cutting through the spring rain. Not bothering to use her umbrella, her mood deflects the raindrops. Head held high, she decides that she's not going to let Peter slip through her fingers.

Chapter 13

Thursa hammers on Jools' wooden front door with the side of her bony fist, not feeling the pain as her determination takes over. Angrily pulling the door open, Thursa is greeted by an iron face. Undeterred, she marches past Jools, straight and erect, proceeding down the whitewashed hall with her heels click-clacking as they strike the wooden floor and echoing around them. Ignoring the silence, she observes the cleanliness and order, almost sterile.

"Maria Jones passed away this morning; she was asking after you," Thursa barks.

Jools is angry and confused, it's her that should be on the attack, having been hoodwinked by Thursa. Resurfacing hidden historic emotions, picking apart her relationships, Jools finds it difficult to emotionally invest in anyone or anything. She loved the child enough to bring him into the world, desperate to give him a chance at life. Hating the way he was conceived, rage is still buried deep inside her. Then meeting him again, an instant friendship developing, drawn to him, she lets her guard down and her feelings flourish. Only to find out he is the rapist's offspring. She feels betrayed yet again.

Finally, Jools manages to splutter out the words. "I need time."

Thursa wrings her hands together in desperation. "Well, we haven't got that luxury," she snaps, stress showing on her face. Frogmarching Jools into the hall, she retrieves her coat from the hall stand before shoving her through the front door. "The monk needs to see you." It is an order, not a request. She links her arm firmly as she briskly cajoles her down the High Street.

Jools remains stubbornly uncommunicative, so Thursa speaks instead. "This city is full of youngsters with addictions worthlessness about them, no purpose or direction in their miserable little lives, stealing from friends and family. People in dead-end jobs, hating every minute of it. Families ripped apart, children not knowing who their parents are losing all interest in life. Evil is always in readiness to attack when hope disappears. That young man of yours has been to hell and back. We must bring total peace and understanding into his life before he can commit to bringing peace to others, he has been chosen."

Seething, Jools boards the bus, unable to utter a word, her cheeks burn red with anger. She feels like physically striking Thursa in her cuurrent state of agitation. Silently they sit brooding, the environment around them carries tension as they ignore one another. Thursa allows Jools time to ponder as the bus chugs along, giving them both time to cool off.

Choden Lamas engages in his daily guided meditation, preparing for imminent warfare. He feels an attack waiting just beyond the horizon. As he wraps them all in protection, a spiritually exhausting and challenging task, he anticipates what is to come. Father Jimmy and Peter have returned inside as tense unpleasant feelings hang in the air, making meditation difficult. Sitting cross-legged, he rests the backs of his hands on his thighs, Choden Lamas gently releases his eyelids to shut out distractions, slowing and calming his breathing to quietening his mind. He recharges his energy levels, while engaging his third eye. His mind plummets into the vast black mass, making it easier to control his roaming thoughts, light shadows and shade appear, like the smoke from a lit cigarette, small at first, in the centre of the inky blackness, becoming brighter and bigger to form shapes. A chasm of pure brilliant white light in the centre radiates out, forming images, concentrating intently helps him to interpret them. The outside world melts away, noise phases out enabling him to move forward as the monk is at one with these images. Intently watching them he sees a wolf in sheep's clothing form, indicating that evil is near and ready to pounce. Calling on a guide for protection, a large visible cloud forms overhead to morph into an exquisite bird with a huge wing span, soaring freely above them totally weightless. On closer inspection it changes into a guardian angel. The monk bows his head in acknowledgement of Father Jimmy's prayers which he has feverishly commenced in the kitchen. Their power increases when these two messengers work in unison. Like anything in life, when we work together the shared task becomes easier. The commotion from inside the house, brings the meditation session to an abrupt end. Rattled, Choden Lamas enters the kitchen, closely followed by his silent follower.

Thursa is venting her anger at Jools. Surprised to see the two women, the monk acts as referee and gestures for them both to sit.

Thursa looks at Jools inhaling deeply on her cigarette, her body language is agitated, unable to be still, stubbing out her cigarette aggressively before finally sitting. Much to Choden Lama's amusement, Father Jimmy swiftly removes himself from the kitchen as he does not want to be on the receiving end of Thursa's sharp tongue. With his gentle tone, the monk sits between them.

"Ladies, ladies, we're on the same side."

Jools is about to open her mouth, when he continues.

"Jools, we each carry a special gift into this life, doors are opened on their discovery, it's up to the individual if they choose to enter; some find their way others don't. You were entrusted to bring Peter into this world. The supreme Being chose you for your courage and

189

determination as you are not easily swayed by others. You are a strong powerful character."

"He wanted me to be attacked?" Jools shrieks.

This uncontrollable outburst of behaviour, hysteria to her tone, indicates that she does care.

"Of course not, evil roams the earth undeterred, Peter's father was consumed by lust and hate, something that started generations ago. A curse as small as a mustard seed, growing in strength, with each passing generation, undetected, its root system spreading firmly below the earth, similar to the rapid growth of the vine multiplying, contagious like a virus, entwining, suffocating the fragile family tree, picking off the weak. Those who are most liable to yield. They in turn relinquish their free will to the enemy.

"Once we remove forgiveness, we lose all hope and remain trapped in hate. Thursa has a special relationship with Peter, she has risked that to bring you both together, even though she gets the brunt of it from both of you. That is why she is consumed with anger."

"What can I do?" A harsh tartness creeps into Jools's tone as she feels trapped.

"Peter needs cleansing from within and for that you both must participate."

The monk rises, moving away from the ladies, exiting the kitchen, giving them time to reflect.

Jools experiences a shift in her dried up heart, slow at first, tiny droplets of blood attack her guarded heart to seep through the prison bars that surround it. Feeling the maternal love of decades overflowing, saturating, a feeling she never again expected to experience. Her mind pictures the bud of a beautiful flower, gradually opening before displaying all its wonder, accompanied by a delicate fragrant odour filling her from within. She feels ready to burst. Elation absorbs every cell in her mind and body. Jools is unable to move as she undergoes some sort of unexplainable transformation.

Stalemate falls between these two strong women, awkwardly sitting together in the empty kitchen, stifled by their emotions into silence.

Emma has removed structure from the day, ready to enjoy their journey like a leaf in the wind lifted up and carried along with life – she is a free spirit. Eager to listen to earth's native music, her surroundings drawing her in as she adopts the natural pace of life. After breakfast, the three adventurers go for a walk, inspired by a sense of spiritual mystery. Venturing deep into the nearby forest, they are sheltered under large imposing trees with rugged barks and gnarled branches stretching as far as the eye can see. Crisp leaves crunch underfoot as they listen to the whispering universe, bathed in the midday sun as it warms the spring air. Clumps of sodden grass lie drying, after the morning mist, as the three escape into the wilderness. Recharging their energy levels, armed only with an old compass and a backpack containing lunch. Talking and laughing, living life, enjoying the secret treasures of the family unit. The woodland has supplied the magnificent backdrop, plant life appearing through the smallest of cracks in the inky earth, as it battles for sparse sunlight filtering through the dense foliage. With weary legs they stop near a brook, listening to the musical sound of the trickling water. Emma bravely removes her walking boots, wiggling her toes, embracing the balmy breeze before slipping her feet into the ice-cold water. She squeals with delight as her toes squelch in the muddy floor of the stream. Massaged by the steady flow of the spring water, she feels her worries drift away with the hypnotic rhythm of the brook. A subtle spring breeze catches her wispy hair. She realises that she is ready to fight for her life; she is not about to give into this illness as she recognises her inner courage. Stomachs rumbling now, they sit to devour their sandwiches, savouring the fresh flavours, lettuce, tomato and cucumber, sprinkled with black pepper. Tearing the crusts off to feed the fish and breaking the crust into minute pieces, they sprinkle them on top of the moving water, watching the fish bob up to collect the bread as it floats on top of the rippling water.

Leaning up against an oak tree, with its bark imprinted against her slender back, and examining the distant faraway sky, she ponders on life.

Children are a gift, borrowed but for a short period of time. They arrive totally dependent on their parents, turning their lives upside down, these tiny little creatures, gradually learning to walk and talk supported by another. Every action and opinion learnt from within the family unit, whether that be good or bad. The first painful separation at the school gates, another stream of information filters into their lives, before you know it they are ready to stand alone, making judgments of their own. Some head to college or university, some straight into the workplace, wanting their own lives and space, developing into independent beings. Emma realises that Ava is very near this stage in her life, throwing away her L plates, ready to explore. She suffers conflicting emotions – happy to see her child achieve, saddened at her own personal painful loss.

Dave and Ava lay upon the ground looking skyward, huddled together, theirs is a beautiful father and daughter relationship, treasuring these memories that no one can steal.

"Cirrus, cumulus, or stratus?" Dave asks.

"I can only see a horse."

Ava laughs, momentarily forgetting her heartache as she rests awhile, simply enjoying just being part of creation.

After a long break, Emma says, "Come on; time to walk this off."

She wants to lighten the mood before melancholy has time to take root.

Emma is first to spring to her feet ready to embrace life, hiding any mental strain. This is her happy time, no room for regrets, ready to get in the driver's seat. No longer is she a passenger in life.

Father Jimmy and Choden Lamas seek guidance for their dilemma. A dangerous rift is forming between Jools and Thursa, yet another chink appearing in their spiritual armour as a result of the subtle attack.

"The enemy is thwarting our plans. Peter is integral to the journey, knowing he has been chosen he may be evil's next target. We do not have time on our side," the monk says, looking worried.

"What can we do but pray?"

Father Jimmy slips his hand in his cassock pocket, to be reassured by the touch of his worn wooden rosary beads, clutching them between his fingers.

"I will ask for a sign," the monk announces. "I need permission to take Jools and Peter back to the root of the curse, let them feel and experience the enemy that traps each of them."

The monk raises his eyes skyward and waits.

Furrows appear in Father Jimmy's brow, the situation becoming all too real.

"The Supreme Being's mercy is ours," Choden Lamas intones, "The curse of the Evil One lies with the wicked, hastening afar upon many tongues, blessed are the just."

Choden Lamas places a firm hand on Father Jimmy's arm as he speaks, each feeling the others apprehension.

"Do not let thine enemy's spirit of fear enter you, recognise false evidence as it presents itself. The spirit of power and love is with you, thinking purifies the mind, your wisdom will protect you."

It is time to reveal a guarded secret to the priest. The two men enter the small private study at the front of the rectory. The air smells stuffy in the unventilated room, thick wooden blinds block out some of the harsh sunlight. Bookshelves are crammed with religious books, a wooden bureau sits in the bay of the window which is flooded with natural light filtering through the blinds, papers are scattered on the drop leaf desk, and a framed picture of St Jude, the patron saint of lost causes, hangs proudly on the wall, staring down on the desk and its occupant. Talking slowly and quietly the monk begins, perched on a hard backed chair in the corner of the room; yet again, the silent one guards outside the door.

"When the moon orbits the earth, on a certain day in each month the new moon appears nearly in front of the sun. This month the new moon makes a rare appearance twice in the one month, bringing with it changes and a time to wipe the slate clean. On this rare occasion of the second new moon, an opportunity for new beginnings and rebirth occur. Tomorrow this phenomenon presents itself. The sun and moon rise and set about the same time. During sunset, as the moon passes in front of the sun a vortex appears in the earth's crust under the shadow of darkness. A window of opportunity will emerge, this extraordinary event is witnessed only by trusted messengers having been granted permission to observe this transition through time travel. Transporting the chosen one back in time, opening up a channel that only Peter may pass through. Unaccompanied, the chosen one may enter, taking care not to carry a host spirit; presenting himself with evil or hostile energy would be catastrophic.

"Peter must present himself in prayer to purify his soul and clear his mind before we attempt to remove his bloodline curse that may go back centuries, thus outwitting the evil one. Only then can he fully join the path of the wise men. Jools must partake in this ceremony if we are to stand a chance of reuniting them fully. This is the most powerful way to remove a curse, we have a lot to do before tomorrow. That is when the real battle commences."

Automatically, the study door opens. Choden Lamas is greeted by the silent one, who accompanies the monk as the pair briskly depart. There is the customary gracefulness about their movement, but a hastier pace than usual, leaving Father Jimmy scratching his head with a baffled expression.

Taking himself off to his beloved church, feeling the need for some space as his fingers rub his bleary eyes, Father Jimmy asks for cogent guidance; he feels totally bewildered. Opening his mind while praying, sponge-like absorbing any information. He tries to disperse the heavy weight of negativity hanging around his shoulders. Walking to the front of the altar, heavy footed, he wants to increase the intensity of his incisive prayer. His footsteps echo on the familiar wooden floor, highlighting his isolation. Smelling the familiar beeswax on the polished wooden furniture another of Thursa's self-imposed chores. Watching the candles flicker, reflecting colour on the wall, and the dancing shadows as the spring breeze catches the tiny flames filtering through the heavy wooden doors, distracting and entertaining his frightened mind briefly.

He commences in faithful direct prayer, eyes transfixed on the large wooden crucifix suspended in the air dominating the altar. A clever invisible structure supports it. Reminding him of his own trusting faith, belief that is not based on tangible proof. Father Jimmy, the scholar unravelling his personal beliefs, needing to be near his God pursuing his personal growth. Bewildered, he closes his eyes, releasing some of the days tension. As he starts to feel it disperse, he shuts out the visible world, conscious of the positive and negative thought process, and retreats to his special safe place, where he gets to ask all the questions with no correct answers. Visualising a green, grassy verge, exerting himself as he strides up the steep incline, his feet sink into the damp green spongy mass. The scene overlooks a tumbling stream, twisting and turning, which runs through the centre of his image. A welcoming old wooden bench greets him at the top, a resting place for the tired and weary, sheltering under a large creaking tree, with long reaching branches casting a silhouette mirrored on the rippling surface of the water. A slight mist hangs in the air on this warm spring evening. A chorus of birds break the silence, the trees whisper their own language with the rustling of their leaves, moving majestically, as the warm air seeps through the branches, producing a gentle hypnotic sound. Father Jimmy observes himself sitting on the bench, a small dot of positive human energy, encompassed in the vast greatness of nature, he calls his Lord to his side. A powerful contentment fills him entirely, as a presence occupies the seat next to him. Not a human figure but a shining protective energy, filling the space and surrounding them both in a brilliant white light, making him feel comfortable and completely at ease. Father Jimmy engages in mind awareness, accepting experiences as and when they happen; learning from them before moving on, bringing his life into balance.

"Lord. guide me, for I am lost."

He needs to remove the negativity from his life that is trying to dislodge his sacred balance.

There is confusion in his tone as Father Jimmy has witnessed recurring situations, drugs, alcohol, gambling, people gorging themselves, disabling their bodies, shortening their lives considerably. Escapism from the routine and boredom of everyday life, having lost all purpose and reason. Momentarily relieving the pressures of modern-day living, they end up removed completely from their intended paths, blinded to their unique gifts. The ripple effects of their actions are far reaching and multiplying, generations struggling to make sense of life. Rebellious angels roam the earth's planes freely. Curses spreading to individuals, through words or deeds, extending to families, communities and even countries. Continuing from generation to generation, unless a family member of the original blood stock is strong enough to break the curse. Wide-reaching forces work in our lives from previous generations, continuing with these disruptive patterns and behaviours, leaving us unable to accomplish our objectives and goals.

Focusing on curses, transmitted through word, spoken out loud, written down or uttered inwardly to oneself. The tongue a great vehicle to transfer the curse, gossip spreading like a fire, once it gets started, it spreads rapidly taking hold. The more that are involved, the bigger the fire. Until it's completely out of control. The power of suggestion used to manipulate the weak.

Father Jimmy dare not stop for a breath, needing to unload, terrified at the size of the task that lies ahead. Listening to his inner voice, strong and clear.

"Break the curse!"

His body shudders in the presence of the powerful energy.

Hearing a rustling noise, instantly Father Jimmy opens his eyes, sensing he is not alone. Having heightened his remaining senses when his eyes are shut, hearing a muffled breath, his eyes sweep the darkened church, bringing the remaining senses into focus. The beautiful image of the secluded private place disperses instantly, along with the presence of his Lord. Angered a little at the interruption, he turns to see Paul sitting at the back of the church. Rising, Paul makes to leave.

"I'm sorry if I disturbed you," Paul says, a flatness to his tone, standing in the relative darkness of the shadows.

"Is something troubling you, Paul?"

A sincerity to his voice now, unable to avert his gaze, he makes his way towards Paul. Before he can reach him, Paul swiftly exits the building.

He employs slow methodical steps now as he returns to the rectory, a drained expression on Father Jimmy's face. Apprehension surrounds him, the lull before the storm. He wishes to take full advantage of this quiet period. Carefully retracing his footsteps, walked a thousand times before, strolling in the magic of moonlight, alone as the inhabitants of the day are safely indoors. He strains his eyes in the dusk, shades of silver and grey cover the backdrop, wondering is this the view of the colour blind. He is immune to the beauty of this image, too distracted by a strong feeling of foreboding, his thoughts scattered in his troubled mind letting the positivity of his direct prayer slip away. Gazing at the entrance to the rectory, in duskiness, a cold shiver runs down his spine, his multiple layers of clothing can't protect against this unnatural feeling of cold. His good leather brogues squeak in the dead silence of the night, while a sense of doom envelops him. Entering the lifeless hallway, he shivers. Just visible is a spider's web, spun between the legs of the side table, slithers of light coming from behind the kitchen door, left on for him by Thursa. Finding himself at the bottom of the stairs, he rests his weary head on the newel post; his body shudders as he peers at the top disappearing into a black void, and then he makes his way up the creaking stairs. He feels some comfort in joining the others, having taken themselves off to contemplate the events that are imminent.

Refreshed after her short break with the family, Emma visits the rectory full of life and vigour. She settles in the winged armchair next to the hearth, legs crossed and outstretched, a different persona from her last visit. Thursa provides her with a cup of green tea, a disapproving look on her face as she hands Emma the pale green liquid, with a chestnut-like smell. Thursa wrinkles her bony nose.

A telephone conversation between Emma and her oncologist has confirmed breast cancer. Emma, wanting to take control of the situation has accepted a cancellation for the following day. "I am so sorry, I fully intended joining the prayer group at the centre tomorrow evening. I don't want to feel powerless, that is why I have agreed to tomorrow's cancellation. I feel guilty; knowing Thursa, she probably hasn't stopped."

Father Jimmy smiles, reassuring her as he prays over her while she sits, feeling a bit self-conscious at first, her cheeks redden slightly, sitting awkwardly on the edge of her seat.

Emma closes her eyes to relax her body and mind, encouraging positive energy flow, opens her psyche to the possibility. A warm tickly feeling surrounds her head and shoulders, accompanied by a feeling of total calmness and inner peace as the priest continues to pray. Suddenly, she feels a floating sensation, separating mind from body, with a deep sense of contentment. She is above herself now, levitating, experiencing slow calm movements. Feeling light yet giddy, she hears his voice registering at a deeper level. Fascinated with this concept, she is surprised at how comforted she feels.

"I was hoping you might come to the hospital with me in the morning to meet my surgeon."

Needing reassurance she sniffs the light, fresh, soothing fragrance of her tea, distracting her feelings of embarrassment as the priest continues with his prayers.

"Emma, I can't, I have a meeting in the morning with the Bishop and I can't get out of that."

Choden Lamas' face lights up, sitting silently in the corner of the room watching this magnificent process, not unlike Reiki where a practitioner acts as a conductor of energy, flowing through them into the individual.

"I can manage an hour in the morning, if that would be of help."

Father Jimmy looks up, momentarily distracted by the monk's comment. He is worried, fully aware of the mammoth task that they face tomorrow.

Thursa, having made herself scarce, retires upstairs to her floral bedroom which reminds her of home. Pacing restlessly, she busies herself with sorting through a few things, fatigue etched on her elderly face. She rummages through a box of dusty old books that have been dumped on the rectory steps.

"Dumping ground for everything," she hears herself say,

'For use at the Spirit of Truth book exchange.' So says a note which is penned in round, cursive handwriting and shoved on top of the box. Encouraging visitors to read and pass on, one of Thursa's own ideas. Father Jimmy has now retired to his study and is engrossed in working on a scroll, written in hieroglyphics. It appears to be religious literature of some sort, a series of small pictures on delicate worn papyrus paper. Trying to decipher it, he enjoys the distraction. Made from the papyrus plant, it has been passed to him from Thursa. It had turned up in the first delivery of redundant, unwanted books. Interestingly the text is written in gold, sparking his curiosity even further. Painstakingly using a hieroglyphic translator, he confirms it to be some form of ancient prayer. Both are keeping busying themselves before tomorrow, feeling churned up inside, keeping their minds occupied. This is a welcome diversion.

Jools returns home, firmly closing her red front door, having a beautiful house without someone to love in it, it is just an empty shell. She leans her body weight heavily against the wooden structure. Greeted by the sound of the grandfather clock, a dominant structure occupying the hallway, the loud masculine tick dictates time in this house. It rises up from the wooden floorboards and overpowers the hall, a favoured possession of her late husband. She catches her reflection in the gold-rimmed oval mirror. Her own eyes mock her. Suddenly she feels hemmed in as the whitewashed walls close in around her. She is acutely aware of the deadly silence, reaching the high ceilings of the hallway. It spreads throughout the vast void of the neatly furnished house as Jools listens to her own heart beat rapidly pumping in her chest. Surrounded by her many possessions, expensive items and treasured furniture, artwork hanging on the walls, a collection of expensive crystal ornaments, cream leather furniture, loving her possessions that were to be used, ignoring the thing that should have been loved – her son. Children, the most precious gift in life, yet she isolates herself between these stark white walls, closing her front door on the world. Happiness long forgotten, abandoning any emotions, choosing a dispassionate life. Torn as she thinks of Peter, sleeping while tortured and fretful, due to a past mistake that was not of his own making.

Choden Lamas and his silent follower engage in a period of fasting, heightening and empowering their senses, purifying and sharpening the mind and body. The monk motions his follower to sit, while the small stature of the monk stands above the large framed man in saffron robes, directing his plans.

"During this crisis you will remain calm. Standing erect by my side, firm of soul, protecting me with your third eye, we two are one."

Silently his follower listens to understand, not to reply. His eyes rise to meet the potent gaze, no need for a retort from his pencil thin lips. These two in their own transparent bubble, that no one can penetrate or rupture.

The silent one gently tips his head in acknowledgment.

"I accept your precious promise until we reunite with the sacred one."

The monk rests his small palms on the softness of the brightly coloured robe, draped on his companion's large shoulders, an electric current of energy runs between them, a powerful acknowledgment. They continue to communicate in silence, passing each other visual images.

"Tomorrow, during the second new moon, at the darkest time of the month when the moon is closest to the sun, that is when the vortex is visible, under the veil of darkness. Use your third eye to detect any destructive energy that presents itself, during the cover of darkness. We have a long day ahead of us tomorrow, let us both get some rest."

Retiring to his bedroom, the monk throws wide open the heavy velvet curtains, flooding his room with seductive moonlight. His silhouette appears in the open window, admiring the stillness of night, a distant motorcycle screeches past, momentarily breaking the hush. Irritated, he inhales the sharp, fresh evening air. Retiring to his bed and sinking into the comfort of his mattress, he slowly lowers his head, disappearing into the softness of the pillow. Sleep heavily invades his eyelids and he enjoys hours of restful sleep.

At sunrise, his alarm clock comes calling at six eighteen as subtle shards of light break through the darkened sky. Shadows retreat as the room fills with natural sunlight, lifting his watery eyelids; he is greeted with another beautiful day. He thanks the Supreme Being for the gift of another magnificent spring morning.

The aroma of coffee and bacon waft up the stairs to interrupt his thought process. After fasting yesterday, his stomach welcomes these inviting smells; he is secretly gaining a liking for the western diet. Reluctantly he drags his physical body from the comfortable warm bed, having slept so peacefully. Gazing through the open curtains, he pays thanks for the bounty awaiting him on the oak kitchen table. He is conscious that today he must enter into battle; Also mindful of his promise to Emma, he hurriedly cleanses his body. Apprehension tries to slip into his mind but he blocks this persistent emotion with positive thoughts. He floats down the stairs barefoot, his feet feeling the harsh worn carpet underneath; he sees Thursa, who is working like a woman half her age, with speed and dexterity.

Bowing a greeting he makes for the garden, slipping on his tatty leather sandals waiting by the back door. Feasting his eyes on flowers that are just beginning to blossom, their heads curtsy a greeting as he moves among the delicate spring garden.

He starts with a solitary meditation as his silent follower appears from nowhere, always by his side, in statue-like pose. Retreating to a peaceful spot, feeling safe and comfortable, he slips effortlessly into the lotus position. Holding onto the beloved tree, it replicates the strength of the Supreme Being, calling him now with soft, gentle musical tones. His mind recollects their last meeting, filling with joy. Opening his breathing channels helps productive meditation; he rests his eyes slowly now. Withdrawing focus, he drifts into a comfortable haze.

Immediately a wolf in sheep's clothing appears in the pitch darkness of his empty mind, prowling in the vast dark void with menacing eyes and an antagonistic spirit. An individual playing a role contrary to their real character, dangerous and disruptive. This is a very definite warning, filling him with a sombre mood. He controls the dark energy, moulding it in his mind, creating a ball shape, visualising expelling this disruptive dark force far away, replacing the negative with positive.

The rest of the house starts to stir, a lamp left on in Thursa's bedroom casts a comforting, warm orangey glow. Flitting shapes pass to and fro in front of the large window panes, partly obscured by the heavy net curtains. Peter's distinctive large frame fills his window as he draws back the heavy velvet curtains still in one hand; he stretches and yawns laboriously, with his unruly mop of hair flopping to one side. Releasing the curtain now as the smell of food grabs his attention.

Carefully, the monk listens and interprets every sound and sign. This requires extreme concentration; he must pay great attention to every detail. Today, he must be on his guard, having all his senses about him.

The kitchen is abuzz with noise. A blast of heat hits them as the monks enter. Both remove their outdoor sandals and place them neatly by the back door. Steam is rattling out of the kettle before the final click, indicating the water is ready. Dishes and plates clink, toast eagerly pops up out of the toaster. Peter lazily drags back his chair on the tiled floor before flopping into it, brave enough now to enter the kitchen in his housecoat. Like a machine, Thursa churns out the different breakfasts. The monk watches the normality of everyday events. Taking his place at the table, a quick prayer of thanks before the monk savours his breakfast. Carefully tasting the different flavour and texture of his muesli, his stomach rumbles loudly in anticipation. His methodical chewing reminds Thursa of a little bird. Peter's plate is the first to be cleaned with his 'thermal mouth'. Father Jimmy ponders on the early days when this young man couldn't stomach food. All of them are preoccupied with their own private thoughts, apprehensively contemplating what lies ahead.

"I must meet Emma at the hospital this morning. I would like a prayer session when I get back if everyone agrees."

Directed at Thursa, the monk adds, "Will someone fetch Jools?"

Looking up, Thursa says, "Consider it done."

"Blessed is the tongue, like the tree of life, a it brings blessings through positive thought, word and deeds. Use it wisely today. Immerse yourselves in positive energy. There is no Fear in Love, No Hate in Forgiveness and no Deceit in Trust. Remember this today."

Bowing again, Choden Lamas makes to leave, with his robe flowing. As always, he is followed closely by his silent companion, resembling a large dense shadow.

Father Jimmy stops by his church before visiting the Bishop. Summoning up some much needed courage. An uneasy feeling has gripped him. Although he is practising positive thoughts, he can't shake this uneasy sensation, worried what they will discover in the blueprint of Peter's paternal features and traits. Opening his primal wound will be akin to opening Pandora's Box: once opened, there's no going back. Half an hour spent in direct prayer in his special place lifts Father Jimmy's mood; there is a spring to his step as he heads off to see the Bishop.

Greeted warmly by the Bishop, who grasps his hand firmly between his two portly hands, shaking them as they chat about his good work. Tea and biscuits arrive, an unexpected treat, served on his best china. Royal Vale gold chintz, displaying an intricate pattern of golden leaves on a white background finished with a gold trim. Observing three cups and saucers on the tray, Father Jimmy feels suddenly trapped.

"Is someone joining us?" Father Jimmy asks.

Sharp as ever, the Bishop thinks. He ignores that question, continuing with his false flow. Father Jimmy registers the Bishop's ruddy completion creeping up his neck and cheeks, indicating some embarrassment. He is hiding something. Eyes are fixed now on the Bishop's jowls, folds of flesh that wobble as he speaks. He experiences a pressing urge to leave, walk out the front door and return to the rectory, where his presence is truly required.

"I have some funding for your centre, a very generous offer."

A look of surprise crosses Father Jimmy's face. Right on cue, Adrianna enters, having heard the Bishop's poodle yapping, giving her presence away. Outside the old floorboards creak under foot, an indication that she has been loitering. Adrianna approaches the priest, full of confidence, followed by her overpowering perfume. She takes his hand and shakes it. Politely removing it, he returns her greeting.

"Thursa mentioned you were working on a scroll written in hieroglyphics on thin paper-like material."

Direct and to the point. The Bishop is grinning at him. His eyes are riveted on the flesh hanging from his jaw line, his plump fingers wrapped around the handle of his delicate china cup.

Thinking fast, Father Jimmy says, "Oh, that. Yes, I have passed it onto an expert to see if it's genuine."

"Adrianna studied hieroglyphics and was interested in helping you translate the document. As it is the property of the church, I would appreciate it if you could retrieve it from your expert as I have promised Adrianna a look at it."

There is a hint of annoyance in the Bishop's voice. Shoving another biscuit into his greedy mouth, he takes two crunches and it's gone. Turning his back on Father Jimmy, there is an arrogance about his stance. Reaching for a box of cigars, kept on the mantelpiece above the fire, he triumphantly selects a cigar and trims its end before sniffing it and rotating it in his beefy little fingers. Carefully lighting it, he holds it at a ninety degree angle while twisting it above the naked flame, inhaling in short puffs until the end is cherry red. It is almost a ritualistic performance.

"I will talk to him as soon as he returns from his holiday." Father Jimmy tries to hide the snappiness to his tone. "But technically it was given to Thursa, in a box of old books for the centre."

This last comment takes the wind out of the Bishop's sails. The two men lock horns, eyeballing each other. A caustic look covers the Bishop's face. They understand each other perfectly. The Bishop has underestimated Father Jimmy yet again, anger clouds the Bishop's crimson, flabby face.

Suddenly, Father Jimmy recalls that Thursa only received that box a couple of days ago; he's sure she hasn't been in contact with the Bishop in a while. The mood deteriorates considerably in the Bishop's study. An awkward silence is followed by polite conversation, suffering it for as long as he can before making his excuses, Father Jimmy hastily makes to leave.

"Thank you once again for your generous financial support, Adrianna."

There is a hint of sarcasm to Father Jimmy's tone before he sharply exits.

Choden Lamas greets Emma, who is all ready for surgery and wearing a clinical hospital gown. All colour has drained from her porcelain skin; awash with a greyish tinge, she looks frightened and vulnerable.

"Will you pray with me?" she asks sheepishly.

Some fear is detected in her quivering voice. Taking her delicate hands the monk has a refreshing view of a woman, very much in tune with her emotions. Not led by greed or anger, she is encased in confidence, values and self-worth. Freely giving and receiving love.

"Today we will use the tongue to transfer blessings,

When in doubt pray for guidance.

Call on the positive power of prayer.

Live surrounded by people who love you,

Then love will abide in you.

Belief is your key,

Carry the spirit of truth, for he knows you, dwelling within you, like a shield, rejecting evil, as thine enemy confronts you.

Be open and receptive to good energy,

Discard the negative,

Ignore the whispers knocking your confidence in the dark, For that is thine enemy.

Listen to your inner voice, confident and strong,

For he leaves signs for you, wanting to guide your path.

He is your refuge and fortress."

Immersed in a feeling of wellbeing, time doesn't exist when you're deep in prayer .Emma relaxes, resting her head on the soft plump pillow. She feels the negativity release from within her body. The surgeon appears, peeping his head through the flimsy hospital curtains. He is a tall slim man, wearing a set of cotton scrubs, tidy, with neat cropped hair and intense green eyes. He introduces himself, offering a warm steady hand shake to the monk.

Sensing a solid hand, Choden Lamas says, "This man has excellent skills, Emma. He has found his gift in life: saving others. By travelling his chosen path, he will save many lives."

Busy organising the centre, Thursa dashes about with the energy reserved for a woman half her age, wanting the first official prayer meeting at the new centre to go off without a hitch. Involving the local youths, Thursa runs through the practical elements: a supply of coffee and a large tea urn, with toilets cleaned, and soap and paper towels provided. The book exchange is doing very well. Thursa tries to take her mind off tonight's predicament. The squeaky door makes her jump, alerting her to a visitor's attendance. Turning briskly she sees him, heavy footed, and breathless.

"Hello, Bishop." A beaming smile covers her face. "Father Jimmy said he was visiting you this morning."

Curiously, the Bishop looks ill at ease.

"I have seen him, Thursa. I wanted to wish you all well for your first official prayer group at the new centre." An artificial smile rests on his chubby purple lips but does not reach his eyes. "You've all done a wonderful job on this place and we have secured some extra funding."

She is unsure why the Bishop is confiding in her, as she has never been his confidante in the past. Listening as he continues with his idle chit chat, completely out of character for this self-opinionated man.

"I called at the rectory and no one was there, a process of elimination."

He looks slightly awkward, shuffling from foot to foot.

"Is there something I can help you with, bishop? I know how busy you are." A tiny hint of sarcasm to Thursa's tone.

"Father Jimmy promised me a look at the hieroglyphics he's been working on, I was in the area and thought I would call in and see them, if that's not putting you to too much bother."

"I'm heading back to the rectory soon; I will walk with you. Father Jimmy will be back at lunch time. Would you care to join us for a bite to eat, Bishop? I can always fit one more round the table."

Choden Lamas travels back by bus on the uneven road, squashed into the last available seat on the bumpy ride home. His mind elsewhere, deep in thought and contemplation, he feels a powerful force defending him. He must use a variety of spiritual techniques and rituals today calling on all his inner powers. He needs to be more vigilant than ever, at all times.

The monk ponders on reuniting mother and son, one of the strongest bonds there is. By removing all bitterness, anger and malice, they therefore forgive one another. By opening up to compassion and embracing deep sympathy towards one another, despite being stricken by their own misfortune, they alleviate each other's suffering. Not holding a grudge, they must release and forgive, so that mercy may reign. Contentedly resting his palms in his lap, Choden Lamas slowly rests his eyelids.

"Excuse me."

Looking up, a heavily pregnant woman is standing before him with exhaustion on her face. She is a plain looking woman, with dishwater coloured hair, lank and greasy, like a timid little mouse, tilting back slightly off balance with her bulge. No one is willing to give up their seat, the other passengers remain aloof, ignoring the young ladies plight.

"Here, take mine."

He rises quickly, a positive gesture with his outstretched hand. Standing as the bus jolts, braking at the junction in the road, causes him to stumble slightly and his hand contacts her stomach for a brief nanosecond. He pierces her aura, passing through her spiritual skin, sucked into the darkest level. Surrounded by a veil of evil, he realises that she carries no foetus in her extended belly. He witnesses a vast malevolent spirit, carrying a featureless face with dark sunken eye sockets. It is trying to escape the confines of her being. Using astral projection the dark spirit separates from her belly, latching onto the monk. Overpowering and suffocating, it travels rapidly through his hand, along his arm, entwining his entire body. Extremely toxic and damaging with negative energy, it is draining Choden Lamas' unguarded healing aura. It locates his life energy. He raises his hands now to protect his ears, blocking out the high pitched screeching which is multiplied tenfold inside his head. His silent follower reels from this very personal attack, which is visible only on another plane.

Toppling with weakness and exhaustion, the monk briefly looks into her eyes. There is no reflection from this beast; he realises the simplicity of this amateur trap. The silent one catches him as he lurches forward. Half-carrying him, he supportis the small figure beneath his armpits. Oblivious to their plight, the other passengers continue playing with their phones, some with their heads buried in a newspaper. Quickly the pair alight from the bus which has drawn up right outside the church, staggering straight into Father Jimmy's path.

"What has happened?" the priest asks upon seeing the slumped figure, who is supported by the silent follower and is dragging his feet.

Communicating telepathically Choden Lamas says, "A tear in my Aura."

Reaching inside his robe, the silent follower produces a green natural stone. Placing it firmly in Father Jimmy's open palm, he instantly feels an intense heat radiating from it. Instinctively he moves the stone in clockwise movements around the tear. Choden Lamas chants quietly, using the last of his failing strength. The silent one howls, painful and loud as he devours the dark spirit that is being expelled from Choden Lamas' body, ingesting it from the monk's weakened frame. He heals the auric tear.

"In the presence of evil, one's enemy is sometimes the best teacher," the monk mutters.

Suspended between them, the silent one and Father Jimmy get the monk back to the rectory. Unexpectedly heavy for such a small frame, placing his limp body on the bed, laying him on top of the floral feather eiderdown. Walking to the window parting the heavy net curtains, opening the window slightly, a gap for the fresh air to circulate the room, which is warm and mild. Turning the wooden bed frame to face the east, so the monk can absorb the pleasant view, respecting his need to be near nature. Thursa has picked some spring flowers and put them in a vase beside his bed. The silent one staggers slowly before slumping in the corner of his master's room; he manages to cross his legs while wrapping the monk in protective meditative prayer. The silent one indicates to Father Jimmy to leave the room, with a dismissive wave of his hand.

Thursa comes upon Father Jimmy in the hall, concerned by all the commotion.

"Oh, by the way, the Bishop called in."

The strain, which was already showing on Father Jimmy's face, now worsens.

"What for? I was with him this morning."

"He wanted those scrolls you have been working on. I saw him coming out of your bedroom when he went upstairs to use the bathroom."

"That is the second attack we have had today." There is frustration on his normally easy-going face.

Smiling, Thursa produces the scrolls, having hidden them under the duvet on her bed. "I moved them earlier, to flatten them out, placing them under the duvet, so as not to damage them. I placed a box of books on top to weigh them down."

Giving an unusual show of affection, Father Jimmy places a protective arm around her shoulder.

"Get away with you," Thursa says, a tad uncomfortably, but she is smiling.

Chapter 14

Peace resumes briefly as Choden Lamas slowly recovers. Preparing for atonement, he sits alone now, with thoughts whirling constantly around his battered head as he tries to separate and settle them. Cautiously unlocking his old wooden trunk stored beneath his bed, he glances around him, checking he is unseen; a thick layer of dust rests lightly on the lid. Blowing the dust, he watches it disintegrate as tiny particles mix with the air. Opening the creaking lid, the noise reverberates through the silence. Carefully retrieving a smaller hand-carved wooden box, resting it gently on his knees, a highly treasured possession. Opening it with anticipation to reveal a quill pen, housed in a midnight-blue velvet interior, formed from a moulted flight feather of a large golden bird. This tool of choice provides an unmatched sharp writing stroke. Removing the golden quill to handle it tentatively, great sentiment is attached to this ancient writing instrument. Caressing it delicately with fondness, it triggers memories of many a year. He removes three square pieces of parchment, yellowing on the corners, from the trunk.

He writes on one, 'Do not let misfortune find a home'.

Golden ink flows spontaneously from this medieval writing tool, his spiky lettering indicates a scholar who is perceptive and a quick thinker. The words shine back from the dulled paper; he wafts it in the air to dry before folding it into a diamond shape, then carefully places it in his pocket. He makes a mental note to use the other two later.

His silent follower sits alone, separated from his master, completely encompassed within nature, in the hollow of a very large healing tree. Firmly implanted in the dry earth many years ago, its roots push downwards in search of water and nutrients. Branches spread wide, reaching into the sky and beyond. Bright sunlight seeps through the entwined branches, accompanied by a refreshing spring breeze, cooling the fevered follower down. The tree has grown steadily over hundreds of years, silently keeping man's secrets whilst learning to embrace the wind of change. Facing east, it has enjoyed every sunrise. Oak trees are a favoured species as they drive away fear and restore physical and emotional well-being.

The silent one, isolated, has been meditating in this circle of trees for some hours now as evil attacks him from within, so that his physical body experiences excruciating pain. As his mind senses manifestations roaming, circling him, satanic wild creatures, taunting him, discarded earth bound bodies, lost to another gloomy world as evil captures these pathetic souls.

The silent one continues his inner battle, losing some connection with his earthly body. Trying desperately to disengage the dark spirit lodged deep inside his being, as evil tries to abduct another host body. Only himself and Choden Lamas know of this spiritual location.

Sunrise is at 06:14 and sunset is at 18:18. As the sun crosses the celestial equator, from south to north. The earth's axis is tilted 23.5 degrees, in relation to the ecliptic, imaginary plane. Earth's path around the sun. Making equinox day and night nearly the same in length. Balancing the elements of the planets. The March equinox marks the official start of spring, even though most of us class the beginning of March as the start. It brings with it the celebration of rebirth. This equinox occurs the morning after the new moon. It brings all of Mother Nature's positive forces together; alignment is essential to its success. Choden Lamas might not get another opportunity like this for many months, to re-engage Peter and his mother, to reconcile their differences as their paths fuse.

Travel through the vortex is extremely difficult and risky. Safeguarding Peter against evil attachment while entering or exiting the vortex is essential.

Thursa has organised the prayer meeting to coincide with the window in the vortex. She has slipped into the centre, needing some alone time. Cigarette permanently attached to her bottom lip, she shows her unease. Father Jimmy has completed translating the small prayer from the hieroglyphic paperwork, having enjoyed the temporary distraction. He knows that Adrianna was keen to get her hands on the ancient literature. He guesses it must bear some important spiritual contents. Hence the unexpected generous donation, to the centre.

Everyone is aware that they must be in place for 18:00, leaving twenty minutes of prayer and meditation; this is the lead up to Peter moving between the two points in time, known as Time Travel.

Around five o clock, everyone squeezes into the brightly lit centre, a slight hint of cigarette smoke still hangs in the air mixed with a harsh flora air freshener. Thursa runs through health and safety procedures, followed by introductions, then a question and answer session and finally the prayer circle, due to start at six prompt. Surprised at the large turnout, the tea urn hisses and spits in the corner, bubbling coffee pots with an appetising aroma fill the high ceilinged centre. Thursa has even had time to organise a small nibbles table with an assortment of finger food. At five thirty Father Jimmy and Choden Lamas slip out the back way of the centre, joined minutes later by Peter and Jools, hoping their absence goes unnoticed, ready to participate in their own ritual.

Travelling the short distance, the four figures swiftly dart amongst the shadows, wildlife retreats, sensing the supernatural as a dense fog thickens, the low-lying cloud hovers in the air causing havoc as dark forces play tricks with the elements.

Breathless, they reach the circle of trees to draw strength from these magnificent structures with their hard grey bark hosting deep ridges and grooves, a masculine framework producing an inner strength. Choden Lamas has carefully selected this sacred tranquil spot. On the far side of the church grounds a dense, unkempt corner is deserted as night falls. The monk knows the importance of holy ground to Father Jimmy and nature to himself, combining both these elements, considering each other's religious beliefs. Reaching the overgrown abandoned area, the group is instantly immersed in panic as the power of suggestion plays games with their open receptive minds. Huddled at the far side of the cemetery, unlikely to be disturbed, amidst crowded dilapidated head stones which are suffocated by plant life; only a few meagre words are engraved, dictating a person's life.

Large mature trees create shelter and shade for this ritual, a bridge between the two dimensions, shared space and time, protected by the splendour of the circle, surrounded on all sides by an invisible protective force field, subtly separating them from the evil dark arts going on outside. In the centre of the trees there is a clearing in the long grass, the monk makes an inner circle of light, using tea lights. Guiding the spirit of truth amongst them, channelling positive energy, he re-engages the humans' dulled senses. Conducting this ceremony in stages, he begins with their environment and performs a meditative cleansing prayer.

Then he passes the parchment paper to Peter and one to Jools, requesting written heartfelt emotions. This text is a vital part of the ritual. He is carrying a thin wooden box which resembles a book. Hand engraved on the lid is the wise tree. Brushing his fingers over it, he touches it with fondness. Opening the lid carefully he removes the fragile golden quill. Delicately handling it, a wistful smile crosses his face as he passes it first to Peter.

"Open your heart, connect with your spirit; write in your own hand. Keep it clear and simple. Pour out your pain onto this page, then we can move on to sign and date it."

Jools follows the same instructions. Choden Lamas folds Peter's paper into a bird and Jools' into a butterfly. He is obviously a master in origami, with the patience and dexterity to sculpt these intricate shapes, performed with relative ease. He places the three pieces of paper in the centre of the circle of light. Replacing the golden quill gingerly into its wooden housing, he takes it to his silent follower, who is seated some distance away, nestled in the base of a large oak tree, on the perimeter of the copse. Blending into the trunk, with lack of movement and wearing a darkened robe, the silent one hums softly, while moving air in through his nose and chanting, creating sound vibrations.

"OM."

The sound continuously penetrates both body and mind, like a tuning fork, focusing Choden Lamas' psyche.

The meditation and prayers have been performed to protect all who reside within the circle. They sit apprehensively in the still quiet hush before the anticipated raging storm, waiting patiently for the sun and moon to engage the same elliptical longitude, bringing with it a blanket of darkness. Checking and rechecking every element of the ritual, the monk is wearing a white robe, signifying purity and profound insight.

With his sweet musical tone, soothing, resembling a musical instrument, performed effortlessly by the silent follower, helping to remove some of the negative energy. Creating a calmer atmosphere, his posture good, he rests against the coarse tree, dispelling any evil or mischievous spirits, on the edge of wakefulness and sleep, floating between the two.

The silent one's body enters a trance-like state, gradually transcending consciousness and oblivion that come in waves at different frequencies, as his mind cunningly removes his soul carefully from his lifeless body, leaving behind the trapped dark spirit that resides within his physical form. A transparent figure releases itself from the human constraints with jubilation. The silent one observes his motionless shell slumped against the tree as he is free to roam earth's planes, the trusted friend and guardian of Choden Lamas, his protector.

The prayer group is finally seated in a circle, commonly representing unity, wholeness and infinity without a beginning or an end, having removed corners where darkness dwells. Together, they begin with prayers led by Thursa. Some members look a little uncomfortable at first, squirming awkwardly in their hard backed seats. Paul is accompanied by his mother, Molly. He leaves his seat when he sees Thursa struggling. Although difficulty still remains between these two individuals, he maybe sees a bit of himself in this stubborn, elderly housekeeper. Paul plonks himself on the floor in the middle of the prayer circle. He decides to gives a testimony of his troubled life. His path into drugs, dealing and eventually addiction.

His mother battles with a stray tear as memories of his self-destruction remain raw. Empathy attached to her thoughts and feelings. While acknowledging that no one can hurt you like your own child. No wound cuts deeper, verbally berating her as she fought tirelessly to bring this horrible addiction under control. Moll is a mistress at hiding her own feelings; with one quick brush of the hand, she removes the telltale tear. The majority of the group know someone with addiction, so this breaks the ice, as group members discus their heartache with addiction and how it affects the family as a whole. The less formal approach is doing the trick.

"Just before six, I would like to perform a more formal prayer that Father Jimmy has passed to me, if everyone is agreeable."

She is relieved that Paul has taken over, Thursa's not keen on being centre stage. With an awkwardness about her, Thursa thanks Paul for his contribution.

Drastically temperatures plummet as the sun begins to retreat. A cold westerly chill fills the air on the approach to six o'clock, with wild winds whipping through the trees and whistling a menacing song in a relentless savage attack; branches bend, back and forth under the ongoing onslaught. Providing a hostile sound all of its own, the biting blast gathers momentum, leaves ripped effortlessly from the overhanging branches, garden furniture picked up and tossed across the residential areas. Getting louder and louder the evening sky continues to darken as impending greyish clouds loom, filling the vast open space and bringing with it a sense of doom. Tentatively Father Jimmy, Choden Lamas, Peter and Jools enter the inner circle of light prepared for their fate. Drawing their clothing tightly around their shaking bodies as the vicious storm continues its attacks, ripping plant life from the ground with relative ease. Fear escalates quickly. Something in a darkened corner catches Jools' eye, a fleeting misty outline, screaming hysterically as the swaying branches of a tree play tricks on her terrified mind.

With a firm voice, Choden Lamas instils calmness.

"Take up your shield of faith," he booms.

His sitting figure grows in stature and confidence; the four join hands, clutching tightly, forming another circle, as Choden Lamas guides them.

"Repel the fiery darts of the wicked, cover thy soul in prayer," the monk commands, with ferocity in his voice.

The storm rises, causing the candlelight to flicker unsteadily, no match for the raging storm. The silent one's slumped body moans louder, the pitch increases with the velocity radiating from within his physical form.

"Believe in yourself and it will come to pass, cleanse the unity of this mother and son. All that is hidden, bring into the light."

Desperately trying to be heard, Choden Lamas battles against this vicious storm.

"The Spirit of Truth dwells in those whom open their hearts and minds."

The storm erupts, exploding across the pitch of the night sky. Peter is visibly trembling, the candlelight flickers desperately, on the point of extinction, one final blast of wind and the candlelight is extinguished. All that remains is the dancing mist rising from the wick before disappearing completely, plunging them into total darkness. Minus one of their senses now, coinciding with the moon passing in front of the sun. An eerie blackness covers the sky, as the four are rapidly immersed into the void that is darkness. Now that vision has been removed, they must engage their remaining senses while waiting for their eyes to adjust.

"Nothing that is covered, cannot be revealed."

The monk raises his voice to be heard over the battering storm. The group's hearing is acute as sight is temporarily removed.

"Hidden that will not be known,

The wicked will not go unpunished.

For he is our refuge guiding the oppressed in times of trouble.

Peter, call to him and he will answer."

Having faith and confidence in his teacher, Peter reaches a higher level of understanding. Feeling a lifetime of emotions trying to burst through his chest, as an explosion of colour fills his aura. Proudly, the monk witnesses this magnificent epiphany.

"Lord, I am yours."

Simply said, spoken with conviction. Peter calls out into the night.

A thunderous roar fills the blackened air as evil shows its anger, sheet lightning electrifies the sky fleetingly illuminating the backdrop, as a small teardrop shape appears in the earth's magnetic field that shields life on the planet from the sun's high energy radiation as it flows freely. The remaining three transfer their heightened energy into Peter, using a portal in their minds.

Peter separates his mind from his body, to be greeted by a celestial helper as he slips through the temporary chasm. Transporting his mind and core forward across the dimensions, he leaves behind his outer shell, slumped in the circle amongst the clearing. Without words, he communicates on a higher frequency. Peter has successfully entered the vortex. Spontaneously it seals behind him, protection against uninvited guests. Jools gasps, the dark hour is upon her; emotional fear grips her heartstrings. Real understanding of a mother's love flows through her veins, no thoughts of herself as their invisible bloodline bonds mother to son.

She is consumed with adoration for her son, an all-consuming love, as she finally understands the circle of life.

Peter proceeds along the cleansing path at high velocity, feeling intense heat and weightlessness as he enters this magnificent, imperial, pleasing state. There is a carelessness about him as he experiences the energy of just being, reminding him of his first ever drugs trip. That, however, was faux. This is like being a feather caught in a gust of wind, picked up and carried along gracefully, at one with the world and himself. Every experience is, superiorly beautiful, he feels invincible having shed his earthly body, like a snake shedding its outer skin. Heavy human layer, carrying earthly possessions, visible only in the circle of light. An out of body experience as time dilates, he absorbs his heritage, processing it into thoughts.

A small boy stands alone, dread etched permanently on his little face, bedraggled and dirty looking, holes in his clothes, accompanied by an unclean odour.

He feels only sad emotions, frightened and withdrawn. Watching his mother through the crack in her bedroom door entertaining her gentlemen friends. Peter's father invisible, seeking any form of attention, bullied and berated in public by his domineering mother. He grows into an awkward young man, ostracised by his school companions. Fully aware of what goes on between a woman and a man. Filled with lust, wanting a girl of his own to use in the way the men use his mother. Stunted emotionally, caught in an evil trap. Shocked, Peter sees his father for the first time. Looking further and further back into his family tree, Peter sees death and disease seeping into his bloodline, feeding on it, multiplying. He witnesses the destruction that has been passed on. Each new generation hating the last. No room for forgiveness, the same disruptive behaviour repeated over and over again. Sorrow remains prominent in their hearts. Evil using its power, ruling through control, greed, addiction, jealousy and lust. Revenge keeps generations trapped as it captures yet another lost soul.

Engulfed in sorrow as he glimpses his family tree, fully aware that under NO circumstances can history be altered, a truly penitent Peter prays.

"Lord, let the words that pass from my lips and the thoughts that enter my mind be acceptable to you master. As I walk your road, absolve my hands, make me free from guilt, purify my heart, grant me pardon. Remove my ancestors' stains and detach me from the house of the wicked. Fill me with pleasant words and deeds, cleanse my damaged soul. Let not the one who speaks with the sharpened tongue break my spirit or will.

Give me the tongue of the wise, who is just."

Peter awakens images of generations, consumed with rage and anger, freely continuing to carry the family curse. No longer in control of their free will, having handed it over to the evil one.

Peter's spirit is sucked further through an opening into the bright shining lights. He is entering the dazzling core of the vortex. He hears a shrill cry as the grim images are incinerated; he senses the finality.

Instantly, Peter is flooded with euphoria, his brain in a frenzy, trying to absorb life's possibilities, more than a little, intoxicated on life. Hanging onto this blissful, dreamlike state. He feels more powerful than any substance his body has ever succumbed to.

Sensing a feeling of doom hanging heavily above them, three of the four in the darkened circle anticipate her arrival. Calling on their sixth sense, intuition, they use this sacred gift. Increasing their spiritual perception, using the inner eye technique, transmitted to them by the silent one as he scours the perimeters of the trees, for dense energies. The force of evil roams freely, aware the communication channels are open, feeling the pull of the two planes. Anticipating attack, the monk recalls Peter immediately.

Choden Lamas, using his superior mind to project an impenetrable, electromagnetic energy field that emanates from within his body and surrounds them all with an outer circle of blue light. Holding the evil entities at bay, he protects Peter's outer lifeless shell, letting the invisible force invite his soul back into his redundant body. Patiently, he waits for his mind and core to re-enter. Sensing his reluctance as he savours this unique overwhelming sensation.

Time travel is a fiercely guarded secret, evil must never find the entrance to these unexplored regions, exposing it to misuse. Changing the past would imbalance the universe, altering history, impacting significantly on the human race. Choden Lamas painstakingly processes Peter's journey, using himself to conduct thoughts into images, transferring them directly into his mother's mind's eye, giving her an understanding of her attacker. Every vivid image transmitted to Jools fills her with new terror. Sighing at first, then shuddering, before she finally recoils with horror. Father Jimmy caresses his worn wooden rosary beads in his left hand, feverishly praying as he feeds it through his shaking fingers. Jools stares at Peter's slumped, lifeless shell, closing her hand tightly around the monk's like a clamp, he winces with the pain. Peter's body is discarded as his mind transcends time; his mother is worried that she may have lost him for good. Choden Lamas is aware that Peter must return his mind into his body immediately, as this ritual is coming to an end.

Apprehensive of Adrianna's next move, aware that she is near, Choden Lamas senses her coming into the darkness that shrouds her. The monk struggles to maintain his composure.

Her objective is to prevent Peter's reunion of mind and body. Separating him on two planes indefinitely would be disastrous. The most significant danger is evil entering Peter's shell while the channels are open, joining him in the unprotected vortex.

Anxiously the monk waits, ready to call on Mother Nature if needed.

Perceiving imminent danger, interpreting her own thoughts, Thursa has gathered Peter's homeless community, sitting awkwardly amongst the smartly dressed members of the group. They are people who genuinely care for Peter, knowing the true character of the young man hiding behind his brooding eyes. Frantically, they all pray for his safe return.

Through his trials Peter has learned to love his imperfections and his community in turn have learned to accept theirs, turning them into true believers. Increasing the results tenfold, worried in the past that behaviours were passed on through genes, with a clear understanding now that actions can change and that prejudice is ill-informed behaviour.

Rewarded with free will, a very precious gift indeed, given to us all.

Encouraging the rest of the group to be part of the solution and not the problem. Welcoming individuals from all different walks of life, not shunning people because they dare to be different. Thursa proudly wears her Lord's armour, a devout believer for who there is no time for doubt; this can be more damaging than failure itself. Facing her fears, Thursa stands for her audience; the room is awash with pensive faces.

"Do not grow weary, in due course ye shall reap your reward, spread blessings spontaneously, breaking the curses.

Remove the negative saturation of the evil one, discarding his chains. Do not follow him like sheep, stand tall; identify your own strength; use your precious gifts.

Wisdom resides within your soul, let knowledge flood your mind, delivering you from the dark one's grasp.

Take a risk on life and live it."

As Peter takes responsibility for his actions, fully aware they have consequences. Strengthening his spirit and resolve erasing the sorrow that dwells in his young damaged heart. Choosing life for himself and his descendants, he is empowered by his loyal family and friends.

Sitting up stiffly in her bed, Emma's movement is restricted; her body is encased in crisp, white hospital sheets, with the smell of disinfectant saturating the building. Feeling groggy and racked with persistent pain as the anaesthetic wears off, her movements are slow. Emma glances at the inky dark sky, bringing with it a feeling of gloom. She checks her watch: just past six p.m. She should have been at the centre. A sudden shift in mood as thunder rumbles overhead, making her jump slightly, wincing with a sharp pain. Fear embedded within her. Watching the sky fill with anger and rage, like a menacing aura the storm explodes onto the blackness of the sky, reminding her of an artist's blank canvas, using colour for the first time; spreading it wildly. A lightning bolt, jagged, runs across the skyline, appearing briefly with brilliant, fleeting light before disappearing completely, followed by heavy constant rain. Like fingernails tapping loudly on the windowpanes filling her with unease. Trees outside bend, shedding their leaves as high winds surround them gathering momentum.

Given the time and space to reflect her mood, Emma considers what she has been through. Dave and Ava bring her much happiness, not just the highlights, but every second spent on family pursuits.

Her writing is important to her, a way to express her thoughts and feelings. Re-evaluating where she is heading, this is a significant poignant moment. Subtle rather than drastic, she realises that change is needed. Emma has a sense of foreboding. Trusting her instincts, she worries about the monk and Father Jimmy, two new important figures that have strolled onto her busy path. Separated only by space, but not time, she joins then in genuine honest prayer.

Jools feels years of sorrow and shame lifting from her shoulders as she strains to hear.

"Dry your tears, replace it with a mother's intense love, fill your soul full to the brim, pouring over with pure unconditional love."

Acknowledging her inner voice as she witnesses her son's bravery, pride fills her lonely sad eyes.

They were two victims caught up in someone else's madness, removed from their original paths. Through a stranger's lust, the ripple effects far reaching, from her generation into her sons.

Choden Lamas panics, his cool facade slips, everyone has their limits.

Peter delays reengaging with his body, drunk on the exposure to astral projection, not just the experience of freedom from the physical body, but released from heavy emotional bondage, while peeping at the unknown world beyond. His rash behaviour risks evil entities getting through the open channel.

Peter's emotional scar has now been healed and time is of the essence, he must re-enter his physical body without delay, if not the results could be catastrophic. Feeling a bad omen concealed in the thick murky fog hovering beyond the trees, the three huddle together filled with anxiety, silence reigns momentarily, instantly hushing nature's beast. Eyes zoom into focus, catching the outer blue protective circle shattering, breaking into thousands of tiny pieces, exploding into the air, resembling broken glass. Shards flying everywhere, barely missing Jools' head. Gulping for air, their faces drain of colour. Frozen to the spot, accompanied by a high pitched screech which lingers in the air, they cover their painful ears. Trepidation forces the monk to re-think, as terror surrounds them.

Evil entities, like birds of prey, stand perfectly still on the tree branches, camouflaged by the darkened night, suddenly dive, circling above, gliding effortlessly, swooping with a superior night vision, ready to seize their prey, champions in their own hunting ground. These drastic changes compel Choden Lamas to scheme quickly as hideous vile translucent creatures attack. Disfigured creations bearing tortured souls attached to their outer shapes, their hunting trophies draped from them with pride, their evil acts on display for all to see, Adrianna's reluctant warriors.

The silent one's lifeless body, propped up against the tree, grows in stature as he re-enters his physical being, shuddering violently at the fierce speed of re-entry. His skin rapidly regains its colour as he uses every last ounce of strength, inhaling one long continuous deep breath, sucking in these vile creatures. They howl as he devours these evil entities, blood-curdling screams as they realise defeat, his body recoiling under maximum strain. Then he slumps silently back against the tree. Momentarily, the messengers enjoy the silence, looking from one to the other.

Abruptly the earth below them shudders violently with the release of pressure from earth's crust, shaking and vibrating intensely due to movements of the earth's plates, as the surface of the ground parts. A vast gaping horizontal void appears and they misplace their balance. A blast of wind howls as, rearing up from the dense void, a large grotesque apparition appears, vile and menacing in nature. Adrianna is draped with the many tortured souls, having previously devoured their free will. Boasting supernatural powers, using the black arts to enter the weak, stealing lives, thus many lost souls remain trapped within her. Too omnipotent for the silent one, fixing her hardened gaze on Choden Lamas. Evil has many faces, sometimes impossible to detect. Throwing her head back, there is bitterness to her wicked cackle.

Hurriedly Choden Lamas fumbles as he relights the candles, fear gripping his actions. The trio drag Peter's barren shell, minus his spirit, into the middle of the circle of light. Jools, Father Jimmy and the monk hold hands tightly, creating a human outer circle around Peter to prevent evil penetrating the ring. Surrounded by a mother's all-encompassing love and blending two religions to join as one, desperate to protect the chosen one. Their faith multiplies with positive affirmations, believing nothing is impossible.

Focused on the candle light, a violet blue flame represents the bringing together, green in the flame is for healing, orangey red is protection and a vivid pink flame to seal the mother's love. The energy shifts as the trio call on their helpers.

A magnificent guardian angel appears in the sky, his light filling the dark intimidating space, his colossal wing span – when expanded fully – covers them all, a stunningly beautiful, superior creation. He blocks the evil entities as they continue to attack, repelling them with his wings, a brilliant reflective light illuminates the dismal sky. Jools gasps at the splendour, her heart races, filled with a mother's unwavering love, ready to exchange places with HER son, trade her life for his, the ultimate sacrifice, pure honest love. The monk calls for infinite powers, loaned from the Supreme Being. He feels it quickly enter his crown chakra and seizes the heightened energy, unlimited in its flow. It resides in his third eye, the knowledge area, before spreading through his entire body. He grows in stature, guided by the Almighty's presence, ready to snare. The energy travels forcefully through to his root chakra, before finally entering the compact damp earth below him where it is swiftly transported along the tree's root systems, hidden tentacles that are three times the height of the oak tree. Unstoppable magnificent energy is hidden beneath the cold dark earth, waiting to catch evil off guard.

The Supreme Being is now alert, calling Mother Nature to his side. The faithful break their ties with evil, invisible chains broken as graces are showered upon the believers.

Clouded with anger and rage, Adrianna approaches the monk, her eyes, red like fiery rubies, sit amongst her macabre features as she calls upon the storm. Heavy unforgiving rain beats down on them, accompanied by fierce powerful winds causing an uncontrollable fire to rage, spreading from the circle of light. Laughter leaves her twisted lips, her haggard face revealing a woman centuries old. She is ready to take the last few steps, break through the centre of light and enter Peter's redundant shell. Then the balance of control will be hers forever.

Quickly setting the parchments alight and tossing them towards the inner circle in the final part of the ritual, Choden Lamas recites his final prayer.

"Mother Nature, maternal, creative and caring,
I call upon your splendour and power
Mystify as storm clouds roll in,
Beating rain and hail,
Refreshing cool winds,
Hear the angry thunder clouds roar,
Witness the piercing electricity burst across the barren sky,
Nature is the ultimate gift bestowed upon mankind.
Supreme Being come amongst us,
Intervene with the selfish and greedy, who trash your existence

Forgive the wicked who hurt the earth, watching her cry."

Fury covers Adrianna's distorted face thinking Mother Nature is hers to control, but Mother Nature has never been controlled. The Supreme Being brought her to the earth to water our crops, quench the thirsty. Sunshine to grow food, winds to cool us down on a hot summer's days. The untameable weather howls on, guided only by her creator.

"Say what is in your heart," the inner voice commands the monk.

Now realising where the real power lies, he says, "I forgive you, I forgive you, I forgive you, over and over again."

These positive affirmations are repeated by the monk, who is joined then by Father Jimmy and Jools, as well as Thursa's group. They recite these three powerful words, words which enter Emma's head, uniting her with the other warriors. Faith is their armour, belief their sword, and forgiveness their shield. Making them stronger together, the power of unity. Karma balances positively in their favour. Peter realises nothing is impossible with a positive mind-set, all you need to do is truly believe.

Adrianna is weakening, like a wave on the sea fiercely picking up speed before being tossed by the wind, losing its strength as it crashes against the solid wall. With one last defiant attempt to provoke a reaction, Adrianna catches the flames, morphing them into a spear and thrusting it in the direction of Choden Lamas, her nemesis. However, it is intercepted swiftly as he guides a gust of wind, turning it back towards her, raging as it engulfs her hideous form. A shriek pierces the night sky, a signal that evil's reign here has come to an abrupt end, before finally being extinguished by the intense rain her shrivelled, charred organism, lies motionless on the cold dark earth. Beaten by a truly superior adversary.

Calm fills the air as Peter clumsily re-enters his greyish body, slowly beginning to regain its colour as life flows freely once again, bringing with him a chance of new beginnings.

The silent one, released from evil's grip, opens his mouth as the dark entities expel from his earthly form to descend deep into the darkened earth, following their mistress.

Optimistically, the silent one recalls the mustard seed and the mountain: the smallest grain of faith can achieve great things. Wearily, he re-joins the group. A communication from him to the monk indicates that the golden quill is buried at the base of the large commanding oak tree. Hidden in full view. In a state of spiritual enlightenment and mirthfulness the group are ready to move forward. A fresh chapter has been written in life's colourful book.

It takes two to have an argument. Forgiveness sets you free.